Eddie ii
(Becoming a diamond)

By
Hery Acosta

Copyright © 2024 Hery Acosta
All rights reserved.
No portion of this book may be reproduced in any form without written permission from the publisher or author except as permitted by U.S. copyright law.

TRIGGER WARNING

Note that this book contains instances of childhood physical/sexual abuse, as well as substance use/abuse.

SPECIAL THANKS

The names are Billie Woodall Robinson and Julie Bonn Blank.
Special Thanks
Billie Woodall Robinson, Thank you for helping me make my dream come true.
Julie Bonn Blank, Thank you for all of your help on this project.

Contents

Chapter 1 (Mostly) Before Me 1

Chapter 2 Tony 10

Chapter 3 Foster Home 22

Chapter 4 Dad 31

Chapter 5 New Home 41

Chapter 6 Trouble Begins 45

Chapter 7 Train Trouble 55

Chapter 8 Moving Around 62

Chapter 9 Auntie Kai and Uncle Ryan 67

Chapter 10 New Beginnings 76

Chapter 11 The Mercy Rule 87

Chapter 12 Javel Loses Out 94

Chapter 13 Trouble in the White House 99

Chapter 14 Girls & Gangs 110

Chapter 15 The Refugees 123

Chapter 16 Kent 130

Chapter 17 Gangsters Disciples 145

Chapter 18 Sheltering 153

Chapter 19 The Motel 171

Chapter 20 Florida 180

Chapter 21 Jasmine 207

Chapter 22 Independence 212

Chapter 23 Friends 238

Chapter 24 Business 255

Chapter 25 Home 268

CHAPTER 1

(MOSTLY) BEFORE ME

In 1980, during the Mariel Boatlift, 125,000 Spanish refugees entered the United States looking for a better life. Among those refugees, the Acosta family—a dad, a mom,, and their two-year-old son, Hector—crossed on a little boat named Landy Dandy. Hector was my older brother.

On the first day of their journey, Mom (Estrella) sat in the sun with Hector in her arms when severe weather hit. As the boat rocked vigorously, she pushed little Hector into Dad's arms and ran over to the side of the boat, where she threw up. Later that day, without notice, she fainted.

"Help!" My dad, Roman, shouted in Spanish as he shook her shoulder. "Wake up, woman!" He pushed her arm roughly. Fortunately, a nurse came to her aid and later determined that Mom was a few months pregnant.

On the second day, the heat and the boredom became more challenging. They were all on deck, Hector crawling around in front of them, and the baby crawled over to a hole in the boat and tilted his head. Out of nowhere, a huge wave cleared the side of the boat and hit Hector, shoving him into the hole. Hector screamed, and Mom went right along with him. A bystander ran over and caught Hector by one ankle before he was washed completely into the hole.

Upon arrival in Key West, the processing started. The US government only wanted to house non-criminals, of course. When they had completed the long process, Mom and Dad landed at the Orange Bowl stadium in Florida, where they lived in big tents with a lot of other families. "I cannot stand this for very long." Mom fanned herself with a piece of paper while chasing Hector, who seemed to be finding places to explore despite the hot and crowded conditions. This was the only option for refugees until a sponsor volunteered to take them in. After a week of living in the tents, Dad took charge.

"I will call Olga. She is in Miami."

Mom rolled her eyes. Olga was her husband's old girlfriend. But what else were they to do? Dad gave her a stern look, and she relented.

Olga grudgingly agreed to sponsor them, so they packed up and left.

Although happy to have left the Orange Bowl, Mom felt uncomfortable staying at Olga's house. "It feels so tense. Every single room. Roman, we must talk. Enough of this, I say!"

"Aren't you ungrateful?" Dad sneered. "Isn't it better than a tent with 20 others?"

Olga overheard the conversation and added her piece. "I cannot live like this either, even though it has been only two days. You go."

The following day, a church contacted them with a possible sponsor in Portland, Oregon. Father Pac, a pastor who helped the refugees, told them about a wealthy man looking for a family to sponsor. He chose them.

Father Pac and the family boarded a plane to Portland. In nine hours, they arrived there. When they got off the plane, Father Pac led them to the receiving area, where the sponsor waited.

"All will be well." Pastor Pac patted Hector gently on the back.

The sponsor, a young, wealthy, good-looking man, stood waiting. José owned two houses, two duplexes, and a 16-unit apartment complex. He took the family to his own house. "Do whatever you want. The shower is in the hall, and the kitchen over there has food."

Mom sat sideways on the couch talking to José when she caught a glimpse of an older woman walking down the stairs behind them. "Here comes your mom . . ."

"Not my mom. Wife." José laughed.

She shifted nervously. "I'm sorry. I didn't mean anything by it." She smiled at the older Spanish lady who'd just entered her full view around the front of the couch. "I just didn't realize . . . you look, uh, so young."

Alicia sniffed and turned to walk into the kitchen. "Well, he *is* my husband."

After their first meeting, Alicia didn't care for Mom very much.

The Acosta family lived with José and Alicia for about two months. At the end of the two months, Mom heard Alicia tell José she was done. José owned a duplex right across the street with a vacant, lower unit. He moved them there, free of charge.

***

After more than two months of not talking to Mom, Alicia invited her out for a few drinks.

"I'll go out," she agreed. Dad could watch Hector.

Later that evening at the bar, Mom was enjoying a drink when Alicia appeared after being gone a bit. "I'm going to the ladies' room with some friends. Back soon." But half an hour passed with no sign of her so Mom decided to check on them. While Mom headed to the bathroom, she saw Alicia walk out of a nearby bar.

"What?" Alicia put her hands on her hips. "We were in the parking lot." She pushed on the outside door and disappeared. Mom later walked out and saw Alicia and her friends steaming up car windows. Alicia cracked the window, and Mom realized the extent of what was really going on.

Alicia stuck her head out the window. "Come on, *una amiga*. There's one for you."

Mom wanted to throw up. "No thanks." She stomped back into the bar.

Eventually, Alicia returned and pulled Mom aside. "If you say anything to José about what you saw here tonight, I will beat the crap out of you."

Mom stepped back, leveling her gaze at Alicia's face. "Just because you threatened me, I am now going to tell José everything."

One of Alicia's friends stepped closer. "My son works for immigration. You should keep your mouth shut, or I will call my son."

Alicia's other friends started threatening Mom with bodily harm.

Mom sneered. "I'm not only going to tell José, I'm also going to take your man because I like him, and you're too old for him." She floated off, her chin held high.

The next morning, Mom woke up early and waited in the window to watch José leave for work. As soon as she heard his Mustang start up, she took off outside, calling him. José exited his car and asked her if she needed anything.

"I do not need anything. I just wanted to talk to you."

"What's the matter?"

Without a pause, Mom told José all the events of the previous night.

José shook his head, thanked her for telling him, got into his car, and drove to work. A few weeks later, while José visited, Mom confided in him, telling him how abusive Dad was. "He threatens to kill me or slash me if I ever leave." She cried, and the baby inside kicked her hard.

"Here in America, there are different laws." José hugged her. "He can't hurt you anymore here."

But the abuse continued. José stopped by the duplex often to bring them whatever they wanted or needed. If it was food, he brought it in bulk. If it was diapers, he brought the biggest box he could find.

A rich man indeed. Only later would we understand why.

"Whatever you need, my dear," José, the savior, often told Mom.

Mom fell hard for José. They started an affair shortly after she confided in him.

On the fifteenth day of October 1980, Mom gave birth to my next brother, Javel. José and Alicia agreed to be Javel's godparents.

Shortly after Mom had Javel, she became pregnant again. She birthed another son on November 30, 1981.

This was me, Hery (aka Eddie).

There was a huge deal over who fathered me. If I was José's child, then I would be an heir to José's fortune.

Jesus (ChuCho) Pena, José's father, came to visit after I appeared. "He looks just like my son, who passed away years ago in the Dominican Republic." This made Alicia furious. Not only were José and Mom having a long-term affair, but they also now might have a child together.

José and Estrella continued to see each other, and she again became pregnant. She gave birth to another boy on the tenth day of July 1983. She named him Leonel. Right after "Lorenzo" was born, Mom got preggo again. On the eleventh day of September 1984, Mom had a daughter, and I finally had a sister. Mom named her Jannet.

We now lived in the Columbia Villas projects. One day, Mom was washing dishes and cooking in the kitchen when she looked out the window and realized I was missing from the backyard where the rest of the kids played. "*¡Maldita sea!* One is missing! Hery is gone!" She threw her towel down and frantically called the police.

"Check around the house, ma'am. He's three? He couldn't have gone far."

They sent patrol officers and searched for an hour. The police finally put out a statewide search.

Hours later, they found me on the state line between Oregon and California. Omar, Alicia's brother, told the police that Mom had given him permission to take me for a drive.

"I did no such thing!" Estrella announced firmly.

Omar was arrested.

***

About two years later, when I was five, ChuCho, José's father, approached Mom. "Hery needs to go to the Dominican Republic. Meet his family."

Mom thought it was a good idea and agreed. She got me a passport and visited immigration to sign some paper saying that I was only going over to visit for a month.

I remember the plane ride with ChuCho well.

Mom continued her relationship with José and again became pregnant with her sixth child. But something had changed inside her. Fed up with Dad's threats, abuse, and harassment, she left him. Choosing the farthest state away, she picked Miami, Florida, and moved there. We lived with José's sister, Samantha. She then gave birth to her sixth baby, Jesse. This time, she gave him her father's last name instead of Acosta. This baby was a Bellmas instead.

***

After a month and a half of being in the Dominican Republic and still no word about me coming home, Mom called José. "José, what the heck is going on? Where is Hery?"

"I've been trying to get a hold of them there. No luck yet."

Mom screamed at José, telling him to get her son back. She later contacted immigration only to get a bunch of questions. Why was I over there in the first place? Was I an American or Cuban?

"He's an American! He just went for a visit." She answered all their questions, but they told her that they couldn't just go and get me. The US did not have any authority in the Dominican Republic. The only thing they could do was have the Dominican government fine the family $300.00 a week while I was there.

ChuCho called José. "I need money, son. Money for food."

José knew they lived on a completely food-filled farm but sent money anyway.

Another month passed, and I still resided in the Dominican Republic.

Mom called José again, threatening this time. "Get my son back to me, José. Now!"

ChuCho called José again, asking for money, and José bit back his irritation. "You need to get Hery on a plane and back home, Papa."

"It's too late for that."

José's fists clenched, and he pounded the table in front of him. "What do you mean?"

"Your sister Rosa. She cannot have children. She is in the process of adopting Hery. Estrella gave Hery to me, you see. He looks so much like the son I lost . . . the one trampled by cows . . ." His voice drifted off.

José swore. "You're wrong. She would never allow that. And Hery is not yours. I'm not sending money for that fine. You cannot afford Hery now. Bring him home."

***

When I finally returned home, I arrived with José's parents. We drove to Samantha's house, where Mom lived.

ChuCho headed straight to Mom. "You gave Hery to me."

"I gave you permission to have him visit only." She glared at him. "For one month. That is why I signed the papers at the immigration office!"

Samantha then introduced Mom to her mother. José's mother held Jannet and cooed over her. But she quickly looked up with hate in her eyes. "I don't care about the mother—I just care about the babies."

Mom marched over and grabbed Jannet from José's mother. "I made these babies!"

"Whoa, now, don't disrespect my mother!" Samantha stepped closer.

Still holding Jannet, Mom stormed out of the house. ChuCho later asked Mom to forgive his wife—she didn't mean what she had said. Later that night, he left and found Mom an apartment in Miami Beach. We soon moved out of Samantha's house into new digs.

A few months after we moved, Dad showed up in Miami looking for Mom. He'd searched all over Miami. He often parked his car in front of her apartment complex once he found it. When the apartment managers complained, Dad claimed he lived there. Mom, fed up with his continued harassment, decided to leave again. She packed up our things, and we took off to Portland, Oregon.

There, she met Tony. Eventually, Dad followed us there. My life veered into a deep, downhill slide.

CHAPTER 2

TONY

A couple of weeks after Mom met Tony at a mutual friend's house, they moved in together. We lived in northeast Portland in a white house with purple trim, a small front yard, and a decent backyard with a few trees. A little concrete walkway led to the steps of the front porch. I later heard they rented the house from a friend of Mom. I also heard José owned the house but lost it, and we were squatting.

I was five. Javel was six, Lorenzo four, my sister Jannet was three, and my youngest brother Jesse was only two. My eldest brother, Hector, lived elsewhere. Mom's boyfriend, Tony, a short, dark-haired, cocky, Puerto Rican man, claimed a couple of kids, but they mostly lived somewhere else too, at least in the beginning.

At first, things were good. We made friends quickly. We spent our days playing tag and Hide-and-Go-Seek and running around the neighborhood.

One day, while playing tag with friends, I felt someone push my back hard, and I fell, hitting my head on a concrete walkway. I instantly developed a goose egg and started crying. A neighbor lady ran to the rescue. "We better get some ice on that." She helped me up.

"I'm so tired," I moaned.

"Shake it off. If you go to sleep, you might not wake up."

I became very scared of falling asleep after hearing that.

Our block mimicked a little village. We kids played at each other's houses most of the time. If not playing, we hit the corner store that blasted music we could hear from down the street. I heard the song *Lean on Me*, written by Bill Withers, for the first time blaring out of that place. I enjoyed the music, but what really caught my attention was watching people play the arcade game Punch Out, a boxing game where a player needed a win to move on to the next fighter. The place had a few other games, but Punch Out was the newest and most popular. The second most popular game? Pac-Man. All the older kids and even some adults crowded around the game box, waiting their turn. I didn't have any money to play. The older kids wouldn't have let me anyway. I became content to just watch.

Across the street from us lived two middle-aged white men with an awesome yard growing many kinds of pretty flowers. Shortly after meeting them, they offered me the job of pulling weeds in their garden.

"We'll give you a couple of dollars for wedding."

"Yes!" I'd now have money to play Punch Out around the corner.

We walked around to their garden in the backyard. I learned what a weed looked like and the proper way to pull one. When I finished, they told Mom how well I worked, and one of them gave me a few dollars. Mom snatched it out of my hand and claimed to hold onto it for me. I never saw it again. I went over there about twice a week.

One day, instead of going to the backyard, they showed me their almost empty basement. All it held was a queen-sized bed against a wall and a projector like the ones schools used for health films. Across from the bed on the opposite wall, a white bed sheet lined the wall. One of the guys told me to hop up on the bed, so I did, while the other dude messed with the projector. A light popped on, and a film showed up on the sheet. The reel rotated around.

I realized quickly that the film showed a naked woman running around in a cellar. A man caught her and pushed her onto the bed. He climbed on top of her.

One of the two men started touching me—molesting me. I lay there in shock.

When finished, they sent me back home with a few dollars in my pocket. A couple of days later, I attempted to tell Mom, but she didn't believe me. "They touched my privates and put their mouths on me."

"Go inside, son." She gave me a funny look.

I never mentioned it again, and neither did she. Why didn't she believe me? My stomach rolled, and my head ached when I saw the house across the street. Why wasn't Mom doing something? I sometimes had weird dreams.

I also told Javel about it. And I never understood why I was the only one molested out of all my siblings.

***

One evening, the boys got in big trouble, and Tony decided to whoop us. He took his belt, and one by one, he whipped us and sent us to our room. In the bedroom, we stewed.

"We should leave. Climb out the window." Javel nodded as he spoke and looked outside. I agreed.

We climbed out the window and looked down the street. We ran for about a block or two, always looking back over our shoulders. After we were safely away, we spent some time trying to figure out our next move. We wandered around for about an hour.

"Javel!" Someone called my brother's name from a car. "Hey! Javel!"

Turned out it was Dad who happened to drive by. He still spoke Spanish, having refused to learn English. He rolled down the window. "What the heck do you think you're doing? It's getting dark!"

"Tony whooped us." Javel looked at the ground. "We weren't stayin' there."

"Go home." Dad frowned deeply. "Now. But I'll meet you on your way to school tomorrow."

As we climbed back through the bedroom window, a sudden light blinded me. Tony and Mom stood in the doorway. Tony, his face scrunched up in a mean-looking mask, charged across the room. We instantly dropped into the corner of the room beneath the window, balled up while he rained down punches on us, yelling. He tore off his belt and added lashings to the assault.

I curled up in a tight ball against the wall with Lorenzo, flexing every muscle in my body to ease the pain from the blows, crying hysterically. Tony beat us until we spent. After he was done, he left the room and came back with a hammer and a handful of nails.

He nailed the window closed.

Later, Javel cried and started examining the nail job on the window. He finagled opened the window, and we left again. This time, we just ran around for a couple of hours until we calmed down. We decided to return and leave again in time for school the next day.

We got caught climbing back into the window again. Tony attacked us. This time, the beating was not as severe, but when he was done, he threw us in the bedroom closet. He nailed the closet doors closed on one side and made a lock on the other that only he could open and close.

We weren't allowed to go to school until the bruises either healed or lightened. It took a few days, and we spent that time locked in the closet. Eventually, the bruises faded, and we returned. In pre-kindergarten, I attended school for the first half of each day. Javel also attended the same school, but he was older, so he attended all day.

When it was time, I happily attended school, thrilled to finally be out of that closet. I grew upset when school released that day because I knew what that meant. When I returned home, Tony indeed plopped me right back into the closet. All of us. We waited in there for Javel to come home.

But hours passed and still no Javel arrived. Mom came into the room and called through the closet door. "Hery, do you know where Javel is?"

"I have no idea," I yelled through the crack in the closet, just in case she couldn't hear me. Eventually, we discovered that Dad had picked Javel up on his way home from school; with Javel gone, that left Lorenzo, Jesse, and me in the closet. Jannet and Mom were with Tony, and Javel and Hector were now with Dad.

Javel came back and forth. After he left each time, our activity was again restricted, even school. We spent our days in the closet, wearing only pants and a T-shirt. The closet measured about eight feet wide and two and a half feet deep. We saw only a little bit of light that shined through the crack.

We got out for bathroom breaks, but only a couple of times a day when Tony said so. If it became an emergency, we knocked on the wall to let Tony know. He let us use the bathroom and pushed us right back into the closet.

The only person who entered the bedroom at all, except that one time when Mom came, was Tony. He only had a few reasons to appear—to feed us, beat us, or escort us to the bathroom. He fed us once or twice a day. He brought plain bread and water—or sometimes leftovers, and other times, rotten food he found in the fridge.

While in the closet, we grew bored and invented little games. We used the bar in the closet for hangers as something to play on. We swung and hung onto the bar for sheer entertainment. With no toys, we played with our hands, acting like our fingers were fighting action figures.

One time, while playing, we thought we heard the bedroom door open but continued playing. The closet door crashed open and there stood Tony, with an outraged look on his face.

"What are you doing?" He started frantically punching and slapping the three of us for about four or five minutes. Just as suddenly, he stopped, and stomped out of the room.

Once, we huddled in the corner of the closet crying and we heard noise. As I peeked out, I saw Tony walking toward the closet with a big pot in his hands. He opened the closet door and dumped a pot filled with cold water on top of us.

"Ah! Tony!" It was like jumping into a northwest lake for the first time. When the water hit, I arched my back and gasped for air. Tony turned around and left the bedroom, leaving Lorenzo, Jesse, and me sitting cold, wet, scared, and worried about what might happen next. Soaked and shivering in a puddle of water, we gathered close. I decided to move to the other side of the closet where it was dry. "Come over here. Well, stay warmer." After all, as the oldest at five, I took my responsibilities seriously. We huddled together.

We heard Tony in the kitchen filling the pot again. He opened the bedroom door about ten minutes later as we still shivered. He flung the closet door open and seemed surprised to find us on the other side. His surprise turned to rage. He leaned into the closet. "Well, this will warm you up." He dumped the pot of now very hot water over us.

We jumped when the water hit us. "Ouch! Stop!" Lorenzo cried. "Mama!"

Tony slammed the closet door shut and left. He returned about five minutes later with another pot full. He opened the closet a third time and dumped another torrent of cold water over us. I started feeling numb, trying to tune out. Where was Mom anyway?

We sat quietly huddled together for the next few hours, not knowing if Tony would return with a beating in mind or more water torture. Eventually, I decided to climb up to the shelf part of the closet to get out of the puddle of water that expanded whenever we sat on the carpet. We all slept on the shelf that night, but we climbed down and sat back in the puddle of water before Tony came in.

We learned to listen for and dread the sound of footsteps. Whenever we heard them, we froze. If the door did open, a terrifying feeling squeezed me, making it hard to breathe. What was next? And why was Tony doing this?

"You're bad kids," he claimed. But it didn't make any sense to me because we were always in the closet. When did we even have a chance to be bad? I again wondered why Mom didn't rescue us. I heard her talking near the door sometimes, and each time, butterflies circled my stomach. Was she finally going to come let us out? But she always walked by.

"Eddie in the Rough, Forming a Diamond Book 1" by Eddie Acosta.

My fear turned to anger, and one of the biggest things that made me mad was the fact that it remained only the boys who received this torture and not Jannet. Why hadn't I been born a girl? It would have changed a lot of things so far in my life.

One day, we all fell asleep on the dry shelf after getting soaked. We woke up to Tony entering the bedroom, and it was too late to climb down. He opened the closet door and his monster face contorted. He reached up, grabbed me by the arm, and yanked me onto the closet floor.

"Ouch!" The tears started again. My two brothers followed me down just as harshly.

"Shut up and stop crying!" Tony seethed and then seemed lost in thought for a moment. He then took us to the basement. We'd been in the closet for what seemed a lifetime. In reality, it was a few months. It was a scrawny and mellowed group of boys led to their next station. I wondered if anyone at school noticed we were missing.

The basement, small and unfinished, had a little window on the wall opposite the door. There was no light—only what shone in from the window. On one side of the basement, piles of old, dirty clothes reeked. The other side of the basement held a pile of old furniture. We huddled up together on the floor in the little bit of light available to stay warm and in fear of all the dark nooks and corners.

The beatings continued but not as frequently as in the closet, and the pots of water stopped. Tony seemed to forget about us instead. I didn't mind when he forgot about us—except for not feeding us. Someone's stomach was always growling.

There was a time when Tony did bring food—rotten food. Jesse ate and started throwing up. I headed up the stairs and knocked on the door to let Tony know. When Tony came to the door, he raged. "What the f- are you doing?"

"Sorry. Jesse is throwing up." I cringed at the look on Tony's face.

Tony pushed me aside, rushed down the stairs, and saw the mess. He snatched Jesse off his feet, turned him upside down, and used Jesse's head as a mop to clean it up.

I'm not sure how long we stayed in the basement, but I was pretty sure it was another lifetime. Tony decided on some new punishments at some point—including forcing us to kneel on raw rice and bottle caps.

Shortly after the throw-up incident, we moved across town to another house. At the new house, Tony chose a room in the back of the house and installed a lock on the door. He nailed the windows shut and created a makeshift lock on the closet. Lorenzo, Jesse, and I entered our new world. Tony continued surprise beatings, added the water attacks back in, and withheld food. But there were some differences this time.

At the new house, Tony brought his own kids to live full time—two boys, one a year older than me and the other one about Jesse's age. But Tony's boys enjoyed being allowed to do whatever they wanted. Jannet was treated similarly—allowed to roam the house freely, eat whatever they wanted, whenever they wanted, and play outside.

Locked in our small room, we struggled to understand. Sometimes, I felt my heart grow dark and angry. Sometimes, it felt like fiery darts poked my insides.

"Why do they hate us?" I cried until numbness settled once again.

Every now and again, Tony used Jannet and his kids to help. After some of our beatings, Tony brought his boys and our sister into the room. "Laugh. Mock them," Tony demanded as we cried.

They brought in food. The "three good kids" ate in front of us while we salivated, stomachs growling. "That's right. Tell 'em how good it tastes." Jannet tended to stand off to the side next to the bedroom door and cry while Tony and his kids tried to entice her to join.

That usually was the stopping point. Jannet cried and wanted to help us, but Tony always stopped and walked her out. "They're bad, bad kids." He put his arm around her as they exited the room each time. "They don't deserve this food, and they need to be locked up."

His kids willingly joined in on the torture.

Some freedom arrived when attending a new school. I was six years old and in kindergarten, and Lorenzo, four, attended pre-kindergarten. I left early after each school day to pick Lorenzo up from his school and walk him home.

With my whole being, I loathed leaving my safe classroom. But one good thing about it was that when I picked Lorenzo up, he shared his snack as we walked. One little half snack and stretching our legs became a highlight of the day.

On one of these early walks home, Lorenzo and I started playing in one of the many open fields we passed each weekday. We arrived at the house about an hour late. When we walked into the house, Tony beat the heck out of me. "It's your responsibility to get your brother home right after school, not to be roaming the streets!" He punched me again, sending me reeling against the wall, where I crumpled into a corner. From then on, I ensured that we never strayed from the route and arrived home on time.

At times in that house, freedom reigned. But only for a couple of reasons. The first was school. The second reason was when Tony, Mom, and the good kids left the house. Then Tony let us out, and we scored by having the house to ourselves.

My job became watching the younger kids and keeping us out of trouble. "Remember, don't open the door to anyone except Mom and Tony," I reminded them constantly. "Let's find some food and watch TV." A brand-new TV show called "Duck Tales" premiered. It became my favorite.

One day, while home alone, a knock sounded. I cautiously peeked out the window. Javel and Dad stood there. My heart started pounding against my chest. I ran over to the door and opened it. They entered the house, and I gave Javel a big hug.

Dad became agitated when he saw us alone and starving. "Gosh darn it!" he yelled, and tears tinged his voice.

After a moment, I realized that if Tony and Mom came home, I'd get beat for sure. I quickly called Javel into the kitchen. "You gotta go now." Tears poured down my cheeks. "Please. I'm gonna get in big trouble." After Javel finally got it, we both went to plead with Dad for a few minutes until they finally left.

Shortly afterward, I felt warmth and looked up from the TV, startled. "The curtains are on fire!" I shot to my feet, rushing everyone outside to the front yard. The police and a firetruck came.

Mom showed up right after the police did. I stood off to the right as I saw the police officer walk over to her and talk. He placed her in the back of the police car. Mom motioned for me to come over, so I did. "Open the door for me, Hery."

I reached out my hand, but the police officer grabbed it in midair. "Don't do that, ma'am." He reprimanded her, then walked me over to another car and put me in the back.

I held my head, terrified.

Chapter 3

Foster Home

I eventually looked out the car window and watched other adults arrive at the scene of the fire. I learned later that they helped children in bad homes. They paired us up in twos and placed us in separate cars. Jesse and Lorenzo were together, and Jannet and I waited in another vehicle. At least I was out of the police car. No jail for me, apparently. Even though I was in charge when the fire happened.

We drove for quite a while as I tried to reassure my sister. As it started getting dark outside, we pulled into the driveway of a big brown house. We parked, and the caseworker told us to step out. The front porch light lit up, the door opened, and a man and a woman stepped out on the porch. "Hello, everyone. Welcome."

We shuffled into the house.

"Are you hungry?" The lady wore a concerned look. "What do you like to eat?"

The lady who drove us there and the husband walked into the kitchen to talk. About five minutes later, she left.

Jannet and I sat in the living room, not knowing what to expect.

"Let's find you two something to eat." The woman motioned us to the kitchen, and we sat at the table. Despite our fear, these people seemed kind—and we always needed food.

The woman made each of us a sandwich. She prattled on about things I don't even remember. The man poured us glasses of milk.

Jannet ate her sandwich primly. I scarfed mine.

"You'll take a bath before you go to bed, please." The man nodded his head.

"OK."

The couple seemed to really like Jannet. "You're so beautiful," they mused as they played with her hair. "You would be a good fit for us." I watched them gawk at her.

Then came bathtime. Jannet and I took one together, and the lady guided us to beds.

The next day, I woke up and walked into the kitchen to see the couple and Jannet eating breakfast.

"Would you like some cereal?" The woman opened the cupboard.

"Yes, please."

When I was eating, the man smiled at me. "You'll be leaving later this morning."

While I waited for our ride, I realized that Jannet wasn't going. The couple kept telling her about exciting plans for the rest of the day.

Why was I leaving alone? What would happen to Jannet? My stomach rolled with fear. I didn't move from the couch. When the social worker came to pick me up, he reached his hand down, and I grabbed it. I shuffled to the door in tears. I didn't understand why I was moving by myself.

On the drive to my new home, Mr. Finnigan became chatty. "You're going to stay with the Bennets family. They are very nice and are looking forward to meeting you."

But what about Jannet? And what about my other siblings? Were they at least together? I lay on the back seat, trying not to puke.

After a long time, we turned into a gravel driveway. A big house and a swing hanging from a tree greeted me. After parking, Mr. Finnigan motioned for me to get out. "Everything's going to be OK, Hery."

I opened the door hesitantly and stepped out. Gravel crunched under my feet. I looked up into the tree with its swaying, colored leaves. "Hery, come on." Mr. Finnigan gently touched my shoulder. After obediently closing the car door, we walked along what seemed like a long sidewalk to a front door. He knocked and stepped back.

I heard footsteps. Dread worked into my heart. What awaited me here? And would my siblings be OK without me?

A heavyset white woman, who I later found out was Rose, opened the door, her face wreathed in smiles. "Hi there. Welcome to my home. Please come in. Are you Hery?"

"No." Hery had gone away after doing the worst things ever—abandoning his little siblings.

Mr. Finnigan grimaced, then walked in, motioning for me to follow. I tiptoed. With wide eyes, I absorbed big, tall ceilings and a clean floor.

The lady who answered the door, Rose, didn't live alone. Her husband, Victor, boasted a big belly and a full beard. The Bennets' four children, Kira, Darcy, Mason, and Earl, soon appeared.

When Mr. Finnigan left, I shuffled my feet, an uncomfortable knot wedging in my stomach. I wanted to cry.

Rose looked at my clothes and hair. "We need to get him out of those clothes and into a shower." She called for her sons to check for a pair of pajamas that might fit me.

Numb, I obediently took a shower and, when done, climbed into the pajamas, which were a tight fit. I exited the bathroom and found Kira. "Can I get my clothes back? These don't fit."

"Oh, I'm sorry. Mom told me to throw them out, and she'll get you some new ones tomorrow." She offered to comb my hair. After a couple of minutes into this project, she stopped and called Rose. "Look, Mom. What is this? It's moving!"

Rose peered closer and tugged her daughter out of the room. I looked in the mirror and frowned. What was wrong with me now? I stuck my tongue out at the mirror.

Victor accompanied them back into the bathroom. He leaned over to get a better look at my head. "Yeah, you're going to have to shave his head completely."

What?

"Hey, why don't you come with me?" Kira cheerfully tapped me on the shoulder. I followed her as she grabbed the clippers and headed out to the back porch. She sat me in a chair. The little machine with a handle buzzed against my head, and I jumped. "I'm sorry, Hery." She wrinkled her forehead and patted me on the shoulder.

I slumped in the chair. I really must have done something wrong. I watched pieces of my hair fall on the cement. Would Jannet get shaved tonight, too?

Kira turned off the noisy little machine. "Now, I need you to take another shower. Wash all the hair off."

After my second shower, someone led me to a bedroom on the top level of the house with bunk beds. Learning which one was mine, I curled up and slept. I hoped when I woke up, I'd be home.

The next day, I awoke, not at home, to the sound of hustle, bustle, and clanking downstairs. Rubbing the sleep from my eyes, I plopped down from my upper bunk, hitting the carpet with a not-so-soft whomp. I walked out and found my way down to the kitchen. I hovered at the entryway.

"Good morning! How did you sleep?" Rose motioned for me to come into the kitchen.

"Fine." I walked into the kitchen and sat on a stool on the island. I started swiveling around. No one corrected me, so I kept going. This could be fun.

"What kind of cereal do you like?" Kira passed me a bowl.

I stopped swiveling and looked at the selection lined up on the table. "Grape Nuts, please." I poured myself a big bowl and added milk.

"You like that kind of cereal?" Victor straightened in his chair. "I figured you would go for the sweet stuff."

"Oh yeah, I like these." Truth was, I had never eaten Grape Nuts, but I'd seen the commercials. I ate about seven or eight very crunchy bites, and I was full. The bowl of cereal remained full as well.

"Are you really done?" Rose frowned just a bit.

I nodded, staring at the bowl. I started lightly kicking the counter wall in front of my feet.

"Please don't kick. Next time, only pour what you're going to eat. Okay?"

"OK."

After breakfast, the other kids headed to school, and Victor went to work. "Off I go! See you later!"

"OK."

Rose and I drove to the store for clothes. She bought me a couple of pairs of pants and a few shirts, making me try everything on first. A pack of underwear and a pack of socks later, we headed back to their van. I felt good having new clothes. I remember happiness welling up. I started chatting as Rose drove to a school. I stood on tiptoe to try to see over the counter as she filled out paperwork.

The office lady with blond hair smiled at me. "Now you'll be able to come to school, Hery."

Hery, Hery, Hery. Maybe I could change my name. Hery had brothers and sisters and Mom. I had no one—not anymore.

Mr. Williams, a tall, skinny brown-haired white man with a full beard, taught my class. I started enjoying school because he created fun projects. One project I remember was creating Class of 2000 glasses. They consisted of a big yellow cutout of the number two thousand, using the two middle zeroes as eye holes. That left a 2 on one side of my eyes and a 0 on the other side of my eyes.

When I came home from school, I ran into the house and up the stairs to the living room. I plopped my butt down on the living room floor and watched what became my favorite movie, *The Land Before Time*. Shortly after starting, I munched on the sandwich Rose always made and brought me.

A few days into my stay with the Bennets, I hurt Mason. We shared a room, and one night, I kept making noises.

"Trying to sleep." Mason's bed squealed as he flopped over and sighed.

Of course, I just made more noise.

"I'm gonna tell on you!" Mason lifted his head off his pillow.

"I'm gonna hurt you if you do!"

When he flipped back his covers to come after me, I picked up a toy and threw it at him as hard as I could. It hit him solid, and he started bawling.

Victor and Rose ran into the room. "What's going on? Why is Mason crying?"

I remained silent.

"He-he threw a toy! At my head!" Mason hiccupped between sobs.

Victor and Rose sent me out to the living room while they talked. Good, now they'd send me away, and I could go home.

They soon cleaned out a little storage area on the main floor and converted it into my bedroom. It fits a twin-sized bed and a dresser with minimal walking room. Awesome! It was the first bedroom I'd had all to myself. But when bedtime came, I started sweating. The bed, placed under a long window the same length as the bed, gave me a huge view of the yard. I stayed up very late, watching the shadows of the branches swaying in the wind. "Creepy fingers want to get me." I shuddered and hid my face under my covers until I fell asleep.

Kira's room was also on the main floor. I often walked over to her doorway and stood until invited in. We listened to Bon Jovi. She was a huge fan and had a poster of him on her wall. I must be growing up.

One day, in Kira's room, she told me I was her boyfriend. After all, I was a boy and her friend. I didn't know all the details, but I knew what a boyfriend was for the most part. Happiness bubbled up in my stomach and enveloped me. I started telling people I'd gained a girlfriend. People always smiled at me then. I wasn't sure why.

One day, a teenage boy visited. Who was this? Both cool and funny, for sure. He hung out for an hour or two, visiting with the family until Kira wandered away. "I gotta get going. I'll go say bye to Kira." He ran downstairs toward her room. I followed him, and as I turned the corner, my heart dropped. They were kissing!

I pounded down the stairs, a physical pain piercing my heart. I hid in the corner of the room as tears rolled down my cheeks.

"What's wrong?" family members asked. I couldn't stop crying long enough to explain. But after I calmed down a little, I told Rose I saw the guy kissing Kira.

Rose and Victor called a family meeting at the dinner table. "Hery got his feelings hurt." Rose drummed her fingers on the table.

Victor chuckled, in a kind way, once I explained more. "Kira didn't really mean she's your girlfriend. That guy is her boyfriend, Hery." He turned to Rose and kissed her gently on the lips. "And this, kids, is what an appropriate kiss looks like."

Of course, we all started making kissing noises and running around the table, teasing them. Rose later explained to me that what

I was feeling was called a crush. "It happens to people all the time, and it's okay."

***

Sometimes, I met with counselors and people from the state.

"I have news, Hery." A new worker folded her hands in front of her on the table. "We'd like you to start having supervised visitations with your parents."

I felt instantly happy and didn't understand why my heart suddenly started pounding hard. Then, I no longer felt happy; I felt nauseated. I recognized the familiar feeling of fear.

Chapter 4

Dad

I'd lived with Rose and Victor for a few months. I'd also visited with my parents a couple of times and enjoyed seeing my siblings.

But after a few visits, Mom stopped showing up.

One evening, Rose and Victor sat me down in the living room. "Hery, you're moving. You're going to live with your dad and siblings."

Yes! I shot out of my seat and flew down the stairs and into my room to pack my few outfits. When all packed, I threw myself into Rose and Victor's arms.

"We wish you well, Hery." They hugged me tightly as a wave of sadness slugged me. Tears rolled down my face.

"It will be OK." Rose walked me to the caseworker's car, squeezing my shoulder.

Tears ran down my cheeks all the way to the services office. Once I arrived and saw my brothers and sisters, the sadness melted away. I ran and threw myself into their arms. While we reunited, Dad and our caseworker finished up the paperwork. We finally finished, and it was time to go home.

Dad lived in the same apartment complex we'd lived in when Mom and Dad were still together. A big yellow complex on the corner of two streets. We lived on the top level in the upper right-hand apartment. We shared three bedrooms. The bigger kids, Hector, Javel, and I, shared one room. The younger kids, Lorenzo,

Jannet, and Jesse, shared the second bedroom. Dad occupied the master bedroom at the end of the hall.

When we first arrived, we ran up and down the hallway with sheer joy. Inside our new home, we literally climbed the walls with one hand and one foot against each side of the wall—all the way to the ceiling.

"This is my room!" Jesse ran into one.

"No, I like this one!" Lorenzo followed behind him and pushed him aside.

But the fun didn't last forever. Javel started teasing me, "You have a different dad than me. Your dad's name is José Pena."

José Pena, the man who sponsored my family to get us to Oregon. I sneered at Javel, then felt puzzled.

"Not Pena. Pinga!" Javel laughed. Pinga is Spanish slang for a man's private area. He started to chant, "José Pinga, José Pinga" over and over again throughout the apartment.

"Stop, Javel!" I stomped my foot.

Dad burst into the room. "What is going on? Why are you yelling?"

"Javel needs to shut up! He says my dad is José Pinga!"

Dad turned and slapped Javel across the face. "That man's not your father, Hery. I am." He glared at Javel. "If I ever hear you say that again, I will beat your ass. He stormed off, muttering. "That jerk-wad never even claimed any of the kids."

That was the first time I remember seeing him get really angry. But it would not be the last.

***

Kim Ford, Dad's friend, lived a couple of streets over. Her eldest child, a girl named Amir, was about ten. Next in line was Dana, who was around seven. Iris followed, about four. Kim's last child was named Jay, but everyone called him June Bug and he was around two.

Kim and Dad hung out and talked. She helped Dad get welfare. She encouraged him to fill out all the applications and assisted him with the whole process. "And they have to be in school." She helped Dad enroll us all. We spent a lot of time with the Fords. We were either at their apartment, or they visited ours.

***

About a month after we moved, Javel and I made top ramen noodles for lunch. We stood side by side in front of the stove, each cooking our own packet. Javel stirred his noodles and pulled his spoon out of the pot. He touched the spoon to the burner for a couple of seconds. He turned quickly and touched the back of my hand with the spoon. "Does this hurt?"

I screamed and ran around the kitchen crying. I started yelling and felt an ugly wave of tension well up in my heart. What had I done to deserve that?

Hector ran into the kitchen. Meanwhile, Javel frantically tried to calm me down so he wouldn't get in trouble.

"What's going on in here?" Hector didn't look too concerned.

"Nothing. He just got burnt." Javel crossed his arms.

"What happened?"

"Javel put his spoon on the burner and burned my hand." Fat tears still rolled down my cheeks.

Hector snatched the fork I was using out of my hand and put it on the burner for a little while longer than Javel had with the spoon. Hector yanked Javel's hand forward and touched the hot fork to the back of Javel's hand.

Javel started jumping up and down, screaming and crying while holding his hand.

"Now you know how it feels." Hector strolled out of the kitchen.

I wiped my tears, and Javel and I continued making our noodles in silence. I glanced at the back of my hand and saw a red welt forming. I glanced over at the back of Javel's hand to see that it seemed far worse than mine. His hand was redder, with four white blisters.

I felt bad for Javel. I shouldn't have cried so loudly.

***

One day, I played with Dana and some others behind her cousin's house on the next street. We used a few discarded mattresses by the dumpster for an obstacle course. We ran, jumped on the mattresses, then over a chair.

Three older kids walked around the building, all smoking cigarettes. "You kids need to get the heck out of here!"

"No!" Dana sneered back.

"What!" The older kids advanced. We took off running, but before I could get away, one of them grabbed the back of my shirt.

He spun me around. "The next time I tell you something, you do it."

I squirmed, trying to break his grip. "Stop! Stop!"

He didn't, of course.

"If you don't stop, I'm going to tell on you guys." I tried to puff up, even though he held fast to me.

"Hold him down." One of the boys, who I'd heard called Tuck, demanded. The two held me on the ground. Turk took four big pulls off his cigarette and touched me on the forehead with it. I kicked and screamed as loud as I could. They finally let me go, and I took off running toward home, bawling.

When I reached the house, Dad appeared. "What's going on? Why are you crying?" As I was trying to explain, I saw Turk approaching with his grandmother.

"I'm sorry." Turk shuffled his feet and looked at the ground as his grandmother firmly turned him and marched away.

***

Dad smoked crack cocaine and liked to go for long walks when he was high. For some reason, he didn't like shoes and walked barefoot. Another thing he liked to do while high was chase women. Dad, being a white Spanish man in his mid-forties who didn't speak any English, found it difficult to convince women to hang out. But he knew women who used crack only cared about crack. So, he easily acquired them by providing them. One of these ladies, Faye, became his girlfriend.

One afternoon, Javel and I started fighting.

"Take that!" Javel pummeled me, but I managed to get free. I ran as fast as I could to tell on him. Javel grabbed me just as I reached for the doorknob of Dad's room. In the ensuing scuffle, the door opened.

We froze. Dad had Faye bent over the bed, and they were naked.

"Leo! The kids!" Faye closed her eyes and turned her head away. Dad often went by his middle name, Leo.

Dad turned around, saw us, and started laughing.

We turned around, pushing each other and stumbling in our haste to leave. As we closed the door behind us, we gave each other a crazy look and ran off to tell the others what we had seen.

***

Hector, the eldest, took charge of the rest of us when Dad went out. And he was out a lot because of his addiction. When Hector was in charge, my brother oozed creativity. We served as his personal stewards and obeyed whatever he said. He often put orders in for water, juice, food, or whatever else he could think of. To refuse meant physical harm—usually, he'd beat us up.

One time, Hector's friend visited, and Dad decided to leave. Hector and his friend made fun of us, and one of us told them to shut up. They charged and started whacking us on the heads. Hector's friend kneed me in the leg, and I dropped to the floor, crying. When I started crying, they halted. They seemed out of breath and sat as my little brother and I walked out.

"Hery, get us water."

I shrugged and walked to the kitchen. I filled two glasses with water and brought them back.

"You better not have done anything to it." Hector's friend grabbed a glass out of my hand.

"Like what?" This puzzled me.

"Like pee in it or something."

"It would be yellow." Hector laughed. "But we will beat your ass if you do anything to it."

"I didn't." I shuffled my feet and pushed my hands into my pockets.

They smelled their cups, looked at me, and then took little sips. When done, they demanded more water.

But they'd implanted an idea that wouldn't leave my head. I decided to pee in Hector's friend's new cup of water as payback for kneeing me in the leg. I quickly filled both glasses with water, then added a couple of urine drops to his glass. I mixed it up with my finger. I held Hector's cup in my right hand and his friend's in my left so I wouldn't mix them up.

Back in the bedroom, I gave Hector his first, and he drank it quickly. I then handed Hector's friend his glass. He took a sip.

I don't know if he smelled it, tasted it, or both, but he spit it out. "He pissed in my water!" He flew out of his seat, and before I could turn around, he landed on top of me, punching me.

"For real?" Hector stepped over, joining his friend. "I told you that if you pissed in our water that we were going to beat your ass."

***

Dad had a friend named Mathew—a black guy with dreads. He loved anything Jamaican, including the music and the culture. We called him "Junkie Man"—I think because he was a pack rat. He threw nothing away. Several sheds on his property stayed jam-packed with miscellaneous stuff. He lived only a few blocks away.

My siblings and I loved going over to his house because he gave each of us a whole candy bar. The only other time we got a whole candy bar was when we were out alone with an adult, and they felt generous. Other than that, we always split the candy bars in threes, because there were so many of us.

Mathew wasn't just Dad's friend—he was also Dad's weed dealer. Weed was still illegal back then. Dad visited, bought pot, then hung out in Mathew's front yard under a tree, sipping Night Train wine. He hung out for hours talking to all the people who also bought from Mathew or walked by. Dad spent a lot of his time there.

***

Dad enjoyed fixing bikes. He built them from parts gathered from all over the neighborhood. Some of the neighborhood kids asked him to fix their bikes as well. He sometimes built bikes for the kids who didn't have one.

The bike he made for me had no brakes. I pressed my heel against the back tire for it to stop. A couple of days after receiving it, I rode through the alley that ran behind our apartment. One end of the alley let out to the street. On the other side of the alley, a steep hill connected to the road. As I cruised through the alley, I realized that the hill grew quickly in front of me, so I shoved my heel against the back tire to stop myself.

As soon as my shoe touched the top of the back tire, it stuck in the tire. "Oh no!" I hit the ground with my foot still entrapped. I landed on my chin in the alley. I stood, crying and bleeding from my chin. I ran to the house, and Dad drove me to the hospital.

I received about six to eight stitches in my chin. Lucky me.

***

One day, Javel and I were playing outside our apartment when we noticed that the house across the street was vacated.

"I'm goin' in." Javel headed over, and I followed. We jumped over the chain-link fence and landed in the backyard. We searched for a way to get in, and Javel found a cracked open window. He climbed up, slid it open all the way, and crawled through. Then he went to the back door and unlocked it for me.

"Someone's fixing it up. The kitchen is new." The smell of fresh paint tickled my nose. "That's probably why the window was open a bit."

We searched the house, looking for things to steal. We didn't find anything—the house was empty.

"Wait, here's a closet." Javel saw it as we were leaving. Inside, he found a half full can of gasoline. He poured a little on the kitchen floor, and a lot came out. Now, a big puddle of gas rested in the middle of the kitchen floor.

"Dare me to light it up?" Javel pulled a lighter out of his pocket.

"You won't do it." No way would my brother do that.

But Javel flicked the lighter and slowly moved closer and closer to the puddle, with it flaring. He looked at me to say something and closed his mouth when the floor erupted in flames. We jumped back, frantically looked at each other, and took off out the back door, running.

We ran behind our apartment into the alley. We hid in someone's yard and watched. About five minutes later, tons of smoke poured from the house.

"I called the fire department," We heard a neighbor call out. About fifteen minutes after we ran out of the house, the fire truck showed up, hoses came out, and the firefighters put out the flames. We watched from our hiding spot in the alley from across the street, not daring to move.

"I hope no one saw us." I'm quite sure my brown face was a usual shade of lighter tan. I jammed my hands into my armpits and hopped around.

"Shut your trap." My brother flicked his hand at me.

Chapter 5

New Home

One day after school, everybody seemed happy. We'd been accepted for Section 8 housing. That meant public assistance would pay rent at a new place. We were headed toward a four-bedroom apartment in what was commonly known as "The Villas."

When the time came, we packed up Dad's blue Ford station wagon with our belongings. While we were making multiple trips to the new apartment, our friends stopped by to say goodbye. It wrenched my heart.

Dad's friend, Kim, stopped packing boxes for a moment when she saw my regret. "You'll make all kinds of new friends." She smiled at me and patted my hair.

We moved into a townhouse, which was a lot bigger than our old apartment. Besides the four bedrooms, the apartment included a little fenced-in backyard and linoleum floors both upstairs and down. We enjoyed three bedrooms upstairs and one downstairs next to the bathroom.

Within a few days, Dad left. "Take care of the kids," he told Hector in Spanish.

As soon as Dad stepped out, Hector also took off to a friend's house, leaving us five kids alone. Soon, Javel, Lorenzo, and I watched TV in the living room. Then we heard Jannet and Jesse screaming upstairs.

"What the heck?" We sprinted to the staircase and headed up.

"There's a mouse in the closet!" Jannet shuddered and hid in the hallway, peering into the room.

"Someone get me a shoe or something!" Javel took charge.

I grabbed a shoe. He cornered the mouse, whacking it while it withered in the closet. It squeaked, and a couple of twitches later, it lay still. Javel scooped it up with a piece of cardboard and slowly started to carry it out of the room and downstairs. We followed closely and cautiously.

My brother opened the front door and walked out to the sidewalk. He placed the mouse on the ground underneath the lit streetlight.

"Gross." Jannet had followed us out, the most cautious of all. We formed a circle around the mouse, peering at the lifeless form. Javel poked at it a few times.

"Nasty." I took my turn to poke at it, too, and then it quickly became a game. We started pushing the mouse around, trying to scare one another.

Spooked, Jannet ran back to the front door of the apartment. But when she tried to turn the knob, it didn't move. "Guys, the door is locked!"

Javel jogged over. He checked the window—also locked. We ran around to the back of the apartment, and Javel jumped the fence to check the back door. Locked, as well! I shook my head. Javel sent me to the neighbor's house to see if Hector was there, but he wasn't. After a few more attempts to get in, we finally gave up.

"I'm cold." Jannet shivered in her t-shirt. I had to agree. We started searching for a warmer perch.

At first, we all stayed together while we searched. But the longer we searched, the more the cold seeped in through our clothes. We'd better split up.

I searched for about fifteen minutes when I saw Javel trying to get my attention.

"What did you find?" I ran over. "Oh hey. An unlocked car!"

Javel, Lorenzo, Jesse, and I all piled into the back seat of the car and huddled together.

"But where's Jannet?" Lorenzo looked at each one of us, his forehead scrunched up.

"Stay in the car," Javel ordered Lorenzo and Jesse. "Come on, Hery." We walked around the apartments, searching for and calling Jannet's name.

A big black guy walked down the walkway. He stared at us, then walked in and out of an apartment a couple of times. He finally headed over to Javel. "What you all looking for?"

"Our sister."

"Whoa, OK. I saw this little girl walking around cold and alone, so I took her inside my apartment. What are you kids doing out alone, anyway?"

Javel rolled his eyes. "We got locked out of our apartment and can't find our dad or our oldest brother."

The man nodded. "Where do you live?"

I just listened as Javel told a stranger all about where we lived. The man followed us home and tried the door with the same result as Jannet. Then he walked to the living room window and, after some juggling, slid it open. "Here ya go."

Javel jumped in through the window and opened the front door. The man left to get Jannet.

She ran to us, sobbing. I was looking for you guys, and I couldn't find anyone."

"Shhhh, it's OK." I calmed her down while Javel went back to the car for Lorenzo and Jesse.

The warmth of the apartment felt like heaven. Exhausted after running around cold for six hours, we curled up under our blankets and fell fast asleep. Javel and I slept on the couch in the front room.

Javel and I awoke to Dad hitting us with a plastic Little Tike's car, the ride-around one with the red bottom and yellow top. I hissed in pain and curled up into a ball. After hitting us four or five times, he stormed off toward the kitchen, cursing. Obviously, he'd found out about the incident the night before.

Chapter 6

Trouble Begins

A week after we moved into the Villas, Lorenzo, Jannet, Jesse, and I decided to explore. Who lived where? There seemed to be sections. Each section had two to three buildings with two duplexes per building and a parking lot and was separated by a fence. Some included play equipment. We walked until we noted buildings without sections. We later found out that the Villas included a police station and a health clinic.

After exploring, we returned to our section. As we played, we saw a door open and a few kids run out of an apartment. What seemed to be the oldest girl asked to play.

"Sure. What's your name?" I grinned.

"Francis." She pointed toward the kids with her. "This is Rachel and Brad. We live in there with our mom." Francis inclined her head at a nearby building.

At the young age of six or so, I was instantly crushed by the beautiful and confident Francis. Surely, she liked me, too. We kept pretty consistent eye contact. That is until Javel wandered over, and Francis noticed. They were closer to the same age. Suddenly, she seemed to like him more.

But this didn't stop me. From then on, I spent as much time with them as possible. I was always at Francis' house, watching TV or just hanging out.

One afternoon, her mom, Samantha, invited us for a sleepover and to watch a scary movie. Javel, Lorenzo, Jannet, Jesse, and I gladly accepted. Hector decided not to go. Once we got to

Samantha's, we laughed uproariously while making a huge bed in the middle of the living room.

With our "bed" completed, Samantha set snacks out. "Who's ready for the movie?"

"Me!" Several of us chimed in.

"What is it?" Rachel tilted her head while Lorenzo grabbed a pillow from the couch.

"Pet Sematary." Samantha grinned.

We watched as a new, small-town doctor grew obsessed with bringing back loved ones from the dead. Terrifying! I tried to keep my hand from shaking when I reached for the snacks and also to hide that my eyes kept closing when it got especially bad.

That night, I struggled to sleep. This lasted for nights and nights. But the thing that scared me the most about the movie wasn't the people coming back from the dead. It was the mom's disabled sister.

***

Dad left again, leaving Hector in charge. Hector, not wanting to babysit, took off afterward, putting Javel in charge. Jesse played upstairs in Dad's room by himself. Sure enough, he found a lighter and caught the wall on fire. "Help!" We heard Jesse screaming on his way down the stairs.

What was it with us and fires?

Javel and I raced upstairs. Javel quickly put the fire out, but the whole corner of the room now blistered a black color.

"Oh man, now what?" Lorenzo sat by the door, looking defeated.

We were all in deep dirt, and we knew it. And there was no way to hide it.

Hector came home and frowned as we announced the damage. He ran straight upstairs to Dad's room. We followed.

Hector exploded. He spun around and slapped Javel hard in the face. "Why in the heck weren't you watching him?" He walked over to Jesse and slapped him soundly. "Never play with lighters again, you dumb ass." He grabbed Jesse by the wrist and dragged him down to the kitchen. Hector held Jesse's wrist tightly while he turned on the burner. He pulled butter out of the fridge and put some on Jesse's palm. "You want to burn stuff?" Hector touched Jess's hand to the burner. Jesse's scream filled my ears—one I will never forget. He fell to the floor, crying.

One of my dad's friends must have been walking by the apartment when Jesse screamed because she appeared like a ghost. "What happened? What's going on? Oh my gosh."

"Jesse was playing with a lighter. Set Dad's bedroom wall on fire."

"But what happened to Jesse?" She knelt to him, gently turned his hand over, and gasped.

"I burned him to show he can't play with lighters." Hector shrugged and hopped up onto the kitchen counter, legs dangling.

"Dang, you!" She rose from the floor, suddenly seeming six feet tall. She marched over to Hector and firmly slapped him across the face.

"Ouch, you bitch!"

She stepped back and shook a finger at his face. "I'll be talking to your dad." She turned back to Jesse and tenderly cared for his hand the best she could.

We stared open-mouthed as she stormed out of the kitchen.

***

While I lived in the Villas, I attended John Ball Elementary. I didn't like school too much due to a lack of friends. But this all changed when I met Roy. Roy also lived in the Villas, a couple of sections from the health clinic. We walked home from school together, and I stopped to play at his house for a while before heading home. Roy's family moved out of the Villas a few weeks after we became friends. After Roy moved, I returned to not having friends and greatly disliking school.

This is when I started getting into trouble.

Our class featured Show-and-Tell once a week. Students brought something from home to school, showed their classmates up front, and told everyone a little something about it. One time, a classmate brought in his penny collection.

"I have about fourteen bucks and some change," he bragged.

It seemed like a lot. I could really use that money.

I watched him after Show-and-Tell. He put the penny collection into his backpack before going out to recess. When the bell rang for lunch, and everybody lined up at the door, I waited behind. Once the coast was clear, I quickly ran over and pulled the pennies out of his backpack, and I hid them behind a bookshelf near my desk. I hurried and caught up with my class.

After recess, we returned to the classroom. Soon, my classmate realized the problem. "Hey! My pennies are gone."

"Everyone, let's look around." The teacher sighed.

I pretended to look, but I just stood next to the loot. In all the searching, another classmate also hovered near the hiding spot.

I had to relocate it now. As I tried to move the penny collection to a better hiding place, the bag shifted, shuffling the pennies. Loudly. The owner of the pennies perked up and headed toward me. He looked around for a minute as I pushed the bag slightly with my foot.

Looking down, he frowned. He met my eyes with a glare. I stared back—a challenge. He grabbed the bag of pennies from my hiding place and held them up. "Hery took 'em!"

The kids stopped searching and stared. I, of course, was escorted first to the hallway to be talked to and then sent to the principal's office.

The principal looked at me over his glasses. I never did understand that. Why wear glasses if they were so low on your nose that you couldn't actually see through them? "Young man, it's very important not to steal. That was wrong."

My face warmed, and I scuffed my feet. "OK, sir."

I really didn't want to go to school anymore after that. I had stolen—and everyone knew.

***

Every now and again, Hector, Javel, and I skipped school. We either hung out in the neighborhood or in town. One time, we decided to chill in our own neighborhood. We left home as if we were going to school, but instead, we headed into the woods behind our house. We bonked each other with sticks as we walked through the woods.

On the other side of the woods, there was an opening in the trees, and through the opening, there were train tracks.

"Hey, remember that bridge we saw last time?" Javel forged ahead.

"Oh yeah. That was cool." Hector followed. "That golf course on the other side."

Their pace quickened, and my shorter legs struggled to keep up. What was so cool about a golf course?

They crossed the train tracks across the bridge, which was made only for trains. I stared at the large gaps between the large wooden beams. They were wide—at least as wide as my steps. I was going to fall right through!

My brothers tore ahead as I hesitated with each one. And what if a train showed up? My hand started shaking as my heart raced. I hurried across as fast as I could—I didn't want my brothers to know how freaked out I was.

We finally all made it. My knees shook for several minutes afterward.

We found the grass golf lot, getting the craziest looks from golfers. But one golfer appreciated us. He hit one of his balls into the tall grass and started cursing. He turned to Hector. "Hey, kid, I'll give you a dollar if you get that ball for me."

"Help me look." My brother elbowed Javel. I helped, but Javel actually found the ball.

Hector gave the golfer the ball and received his dollar.

The man grinned. "Hey, if you find any of these balls with this little red symbol, I'll give you a dollar for three of them."

We ran back into the tall grass to search for the balls with the little red symbols on them. We found eight. The man gave Hector $2.50. He took the balls to a machine, and we watched as a machine cleaned them up.

"You know, there are other guys who would buy them from you, too. They'll pay more if they're clean." He winked at us.

After Hector realized he could make a lot of money selling balls at the golf course, he convinced Javel and me to keep skipping school in favor of our new business venture.

"I'll split the money with you," he promised. "We'll find more with all of us looking."

Yes, I made it back and forth on those train tracks several more times.

We often waded through tall grass in search of the treasured balls. Hector cleaned them in the machine. Then it was time to sell. "Want some balls?" he asked one golfer.

"No." Several answered.

"How much?" One paused and shifted his hat.

"Three for a buck."

If they asked too many questions, Hector walked away, but most of the players would at least take a look at either Javel's shirt full of balls or mine.

We made around five dollars a day selling balls there, and Hector tried to keep all he could. He developed reasons why we didn't get the amount of money he'd promised. Javel and I began hesitating to help, but Hector threatened to beat our butts if we didn't go.

Things just started getting worse after that.

One time, we sat in the shade of a tree near a pond, watching the golfers. I jumped as a ball flew into the pond near the shore, splashing.

"Gosh darn it!" The golfer flushed bright red. Swear words flew out of his mouth.

"I'll get it for a buck." Hector stood up.

The dude agreed. Hector sat and sent Javel and me to get the golf ball. We slowly inched our way into the cold, nasty, algae-covered pond. My feet sank lower and lower. Gross. But eventually, we started feeling balls under our feet.

"Here's one!" I held up one triumphantly and tossed it at Hector.

"Got another!" Javel threw one at him, too.

We never found the guy's ball, but we did find one he liked more.

After the disgusting water incident, Hector worked harder to convince us to return. Once, security chased us off. After that, we all stayed away. But this didn't mean a return to school.

Hector found a few prized hangouts we used to replace the school hours. Other than going to his friend's house, he enjoyed stealing at the local shopping center. We'd act like we were going to school and then catch the city bus out to Jantzen Beach.

On the morning of my eighth birthday, we headed to school, but then Hector decided he didn't want to go. "Store." He grinned.

"It's my birthday." My voice hitched up a notch. "It's fun at school on my birthday."

Hector sneered. "Don't be a baby."

As usual, I ended up following along—even though I didn't want to.

As soon as we walked into the store, we split up. I went straight for the toy section. It was my birthday, after all—I deserved this. I grabbed the toy I wanted, steadily flipping my head back and forth to watch for any lookers. I shoved the toy down the front of my jeans.

But where were my brothers? I checked each aisle again with no luck. I'd better wait outside the store.

Near the exit, a security officer grabbed my arm. "Come with me." He pulled me to a little room in the back of the store. I stopped when I saw Hector and Javel handcuffed to chairs. The officer urged me along, cuffed me to a handrail, and told me to sit on the step.

I started shaking inside—just a little bit. Javel looked a little panicked. Hector just sneered and shrugged his shoulders.

"Where do you live? Where are your parents?" There was more than one officer now, and they started tossing questions. The only one we answered was which school we attended.

One officer tried to call Dad for an hour. He finally slammed down the phone, grunting. They decided to take us to school. The police officer drove us and dropped me off in the main office. I received another chat about stealing—this time from the principal.

"It's my birthday." I looked at the floor. "I just wanted a toy."

The principal sighed deeply. He stood and left his office.

"Eddie in the Rough, Forming a Diamond Book 1" by Eddie Acosta.

I must be in big trouble now. I shifted restlessly as my stomach burbled. I felt my throat thicken, and my eyes wanted to cry. But then the receptionist walked into the office carrying a pastry with a candle.

"Happy birthday!" She sang me the whole song and gave me the pastry, which I wolfed down.

Chapter 7

Train Trouble

Lorenzo and I headed home from a friend's house who lived a few blocks away. I walked alongside my bike while we chatted.

Screech! I froze. A yellow VW Rabbit pulled up and stopped in the middle of the street ahead of us. A guy climbed out and walked over to a group of known Columbia Villas Crips (CVCs) hanging out on the curb.

I kept an eye on them as we started to pass. Then, out of nowhere, the guy talking to the CVCs grabbed something from another dude, turned around, and started shooting at the car.

Pop! Pop! The people in the car shot back. More of them pulled out guns and joined in.

Lorenzo and I stood frozen in fear.

We should run. The thought circled my head, but my body wouldn't move. Gunshots continued, and bullets whizzed by our heads like we were in a war movie.

It ended quickly, and the Rabbit sped off. The Crips took off running.

I shook my head fast, then grabbed Lorenzo's arm. His eyes were wide, staring at the now-empty street. We walked home quickly.

That was a close call, but then again, there were a lot of close calls when we lived in the Villas.

***

I wandered around on a Saturday morning, trying to find something to do. Past a fence, I spotted a friend named Jamal. He wasn't a friend you hung out with every day, but a once-in-awhile-friend. I jaunted over. "What the heck are you up to, Jamal?"

"Oh yeah, I have this." He reached into his pocket and pulled out a three-inch long pocketknife with folding lock blades.

"Oh yeah? I'll kick your butt and take the knife." I puffed up.

Jamal sneered. "Yeah, you just try it."

I flicked my arm toward him. He startled. When his arm shot out, I felt a sharp pain drag across the left side of my face. He took off, running.

"You—ouch! Dang you!" I grabbed the side of my face and ran after him. Now, he really deserved a beating.

Jamal ran across the foggy street, up a hill, and through a game of football that was in progress. As I chased, I saw a piece of white curtain rod on the ground and snapped it up. I chased him right through the football game, and before I pooped out, I threw the piece of curtain rod at the back of his head. "Take that, jerk-head!"

I stormed home, knowing I hadn't hurt him enough. I remembered Dad's mallet hanging over the shoulder of the couch. Once home, I found it in its usual place. Dad snored on the couch.

But there was a quandary. To get the mallet, the couch needed to move. I grunted as I slowly tried to scoot the couch forward without waking Dad. It moved an inch.

"What the heck are you doing?" His head popped up.

I jumped. "What?"

He sat. "What—are—you—doing?"

I crossed my arms over my chest. "Nothing." I stomped out of the house.

About a week later, I finally saw Jamal walking down the street. The mostly healed cut on my face looked OK, and I'd calmed down a little. "Hey. Why'd you threaten me?"

"Man, I thought you were seriously going to kick my ass. I got scared. Sorry. Hey, you got my ear with that curtain rod. Idiot."

I peered at his ear, trying not to throw up. Nasty, red, with all kinds of lint and crap stuck to it. Disgusting.

I walked off with my head held high. At least I got him back.

***

Hector, Javel, and I spent a lot of time on the train tracks. Hours, really. We placed pennies on the tracks and waited for a train—it flattened the coins paper thin. When a train passed, we attempted to hit and break the little red light at the end of the caboose with a handful of rocks. "If you hit it hard enough, the train stops instantly." Hector insisted. We managed several hits, but it was not hard enough to break the cover.

But flattening pennies and trying to stop the train only entertained us for a short while.

We discovered train hopping. Train hopping was jumping on the trains as they chugged along. To get on it, we ran alongside, next to a little ladder mounted on each car. We held the ladder with one hand until we gathered the guts to jump onto it and pull ourselves up. We held on for a while. Then came the scariest part of the hopping trains—getting off. To jump off, we first looked ahead for a soft-landing spot. Once we committed to one, we gathered a big ball of courage. Sometimes, it took a long time to build up that nerve. The days it took so long to get courage became the worst because we had to walk that much farther to get home.

On one of these occasions, while Hector, Javel, and I were playing on the train tracks, a railroad worker showed up out of nowhere. He saw us trying to hop on the train. "Knock that off! Boys!" He pulled us to a safer spot. "Don't you know how dangerous that is?"

He walked us to his truck, which was parked nearby. He reached into the passenger side and pulled out a gallon of water. He handed it to Hector. "Give some to them, too." He nodded at us. He started rifling through his truck, and his hand appeared with a few Union Pacific hats. "Here. And if you're going to play around trains, you need to know a few things. If you ever get caught in a train tunnel, make your bodies as small as possible and stay close to the bottom of the tunnel. That's so you don't get sucked into the tracks. Did you know you can feel if a train is coming by feeling the tracks? They vibrate."

We grinned as we put on our hats and tipped the gallon jug into our mouths one more time. He'd just given us a brand-new adventure to attempt.

As we were leaving, he called a final warning. "Stay off the tracks. It's private property anyway and dangerous!"

We waved goodbye. It was time to step things up.

Hector brought it up first a few days later. "I'm goin' through the tunnel behind our house." He recruited one of his friends to come along. Hector, his friend, and I headed out. We took the bus to the store to get some flashlights first.

I wanted a big, manly flashlight with a far-reaching beam. But the bigger the flashlight, the harder it was to steal. I made do with a small black one that I slid down in my pants. I headed to the exit to see that Hector and his friend were already waiting for me outside. We ran for the bus back to the Villas.

On our return, we hiked through the woods back to the train tracks.

Hector flashed his light inside the tunnel while we stood, shuffling our feet and daring each other with our eyes to step in first. We tested all our lights. Although they all worked, it took us thirty minutes to venture inside.

In the tunnel, the light far ahead on the other side became basketball-sized. I tried to keep my knees from shaking.

Every few feet, Hector or his friend stopped, knelt down, and grabbed the rail to feel for vibrations. Guess we'd learned something from the railroad guy. We also kept a good eye on the entrance to make sure a train wasn't coming from behind us.

The closer we got to the other side, the chattier and louder we got.

"What if a train comes from the side we're walking toward?" Hector's friend kicked the track.

"Man, why in the heck would you say that?" Hector whipped around and shone his light in our eyes. The sudden quiet could have bounced off the tunnel walls. We started jogging toward the end of the tunnel. My stomach knotted up, and my feet urged me to move faster like they had their own brain—and knew something my other brain didn't.

A good hundred feet away from the exit, we heard a train whistle. We jumped and turned to see a train heading toward the tunnel entrance behind us. We ran hard out the other end of the tunnel and climbed a steep embankment. Eventually, we found our way home.

***

Most of the time, Dad was absent, but not always. Sometimes, we found him hanging out in front of our apartment. One time, while we threw rocks at the bats flying around the light poles, Dad ambled over. "If you throw balls of foil up there, they'll try to catch them." We ran into the apartment and grabbed foil, balling it up as we headed back to Dad. "We can catch them too," Dad claimed. "One of you, go get a white bedsheet." I brought one, and he tied the corners into a knot, throwing the sheet into the air. The sheet landed on the ground.

"It's moving!" I ran to the sheet. Dad got ahead of me and pinned the bat under the sheet, then flipped it over. In his hand lay a little bat. It fluttered away, dazed when Dad let it go.

A few weeks later, Dad headed outside our house again, drinking his favorite drink, Night Train. A group of CVCs loitered not too far away. Known by all the CVCs as Crazy Leo, Dad had earned that nickname by getting into an argument with a local gang member and flipping out on him. From that day forward, Crazy Leo stuck.

"Hey, Leo. Come over." One of the gang members waved his hand as the others started teasing Dad about his accent. "Leo, tonight's what we call the Fourth of July. It's an American holiday, and everyone shoots their guns into the air at midnight."

"I got my 22," Dad bragged.

At 11:59, everyone watched Dad. Sure enough, he pulled out his 22 pistol and fired two rounds into the air. The gang members erupted in laughter after all the spectators got their laughs without Dad even understanding why; they quickly left.

About half an hour later, a loud knock sounded on our door. Lorenzo opened it to the police. "We're looking for Roberto."

They stepped in, and Dad appeared at the top of the stairs.

"Sir, come downstairs, please." One of them rested his hand on his gun.

Dad started arguing. We watched nervously as he pulled out a bayonet and waved it around from the top of the stairs.

The police hustled us out of the house and placed us in the back of a police car. "Where are we going?" Jesse protested as the door closed almost in his face. The rest of us just sighed.

It was an unwelcome return to the foster care system.

CHAPTER

8 MOVING AROUND

After the caseworker picked us up from the police station, he herded Javel, Jesse, and me to his car. Jannet didn't come. He drove us to a big house. We walked on another long sidewalk. The wind blew, and I shuddered. "Come on." He sighed and rang the doorbell. Jesse blinked when the porch light snapped on.

I watched through the glass as a white lady drifted toward the door and opened it with a slightly guarded look on her face. "Hello." She bent down to Jesse's level. "Come in. Please sit down."

A quiet bunch, we shuffled to the couch and sat.

"Are you hungry? Thirsty?" She trilled with a sing-song voice.

Of course, we were never ones to turn down food. "Yes." We grinned.

While she was in what I assumed was the kitchen, the caseworker walked toward the front door. "You'll spend the night here." He closed the door behind him as we stared at it.

The lady soon returned with sandwiches and three glasses of milk, which we scarfed down like starving lions at the zoo.

She smiled. "Are you finished? Let me show you your room." She gathered up our glasses, took them to the kitchen, and motioned us over. We climbed the stairs. The room had both regular beds and bunk beds.

"I want the top." I climbed up and plopped on the mattress. I tucked my arms behind my head and checked out the ceiling.

"Goodnight." The lady left after we settled but kept the door open a crack.

I thought about all the events of the night. "Javel?"

No answer.

"Jesse?"

No answer.

Were they asleep already? They must be.

About twenty-five minutes later, the lady returned to check on us and then entered a little room at the far end of the bedroom. I peeked over the blanket out of sheer curiosity. No way! Mario Bros on Nintendo zipped around the screen. I sat, watching her play. She kept dying at the same spot in the game, and I laughed.

"Go back to sleep." She turned around and pointed at me.

She continued to play and die, and I continued laughing. She finally got upset, set the remote down hard, and hurried out of the room. She hovered close to the bed. "If you keep it up, I'll call the social worker, and they'll come pick you up." She returned to the little room and continued playing.

Now, that wasn't fair. I decided to call her bluff. I started to make annoying noises and laughed at her again. I watched her slam the controller down and turn off the TV. She stormed out of the little room and then out of the bedroom. She returned about ten minutes later. "Come down to the living room. You're going to another home instead."

When I arrived at the next foster home, the clock there chimed ten times. Exhausted, I fell asleep quickly. The next morning, when I woke up, I lay in bed thinking about what it might take to get back home. If I misbehaved, the foster parents obviously would call the social worker, and I'd get to leave. I thought about it for a while. If I got kicked out of all the foster homes, eventually, I'd be sent home.

My mission was clear: I started cursing out the foster parents at every chance I got. I yelled at them, threw things, broke things, kicked the family dog, and did anything and everything I could think of to send them over the edge. They often stomped to their phones as I grinned in delight.

After about a week of being moved every single day, I grew weary of behaving badly. I didn't feel like myself at all. Couldn't a kid just go home? Confusion rose, causing my head to ache.

Next, I moved out of the country with a very old couple. As soon as I entered the large house, I noticed huge bookshelves full of VHS movies across the living room. Oh yeah. "Can I see what movies you have?"

"Sure." The old guy shuffled over to supervise my efforts. A few minutes later, I overheard the social worker saying goodbye. I picked a movie to watch and sat down while the old man popped the movie into the VCR. About halfway through the movie, the old lady brought me a sandwich and a glass of milk. The standard fare of foster homes.

After I finished my movie, they showed me the house. My room contained a twin bed, dresser, and closet. After I saw the house, they introduced me to the horse they had out back. They let me feed it hay through the fence. The old man gave me a couple of carrots to feed him, too. I jumped when the horse reached out with its nose and started trying to eat my hair. I ran away from the gate.

The old man started laughing. "It's OK, son. He means well."

Later, they showed me the barn where they kept the hay. It was filled to the top with bales. I remember climbing up to the top of the stacks to play. With the movies, the horse, and the stacks of hay piled up to the ceiling, I decided I could stay.

The next day, after breakfast, the couple hosted some friends. When one of them met me, he shook my hand and then felt my hair. "It feels like wool."

I ran back to the barn to play, leaving the adults to talk. I played until lunch. After lunch, I wanted to watch another movie, but the old lady told me no.

"Please? I want a movie." I asked her again and again.

"Not right now, Hery."

I decided to grab the movie by myself. I started to climb the bookshelf when she left the room. I was halfway up when I started to feel like I was gliding in the air. I hit the ground at the same time as about a hundred VHS tapes. The old lady ran into the living room to find me underneath her massive movie collection. "Go to your room!"

I stormed off. In my room, I paced, wondering how I could leave. I noticed a cracked window. Good, I'd run away. I pulled the window up, climbed outside, and took off. I arrived at the corner, noting it was a four-way stop. I looked around. All I saw was the woods. Man, I was out in the country. There were no lights or even sidewalks. I turned around, ran back to the house, and climbed back in through the window. About an hour later, the couple packed up my belongings, and I got in the car with the old man to return to the CSD office.

On the drive, I noticed a feather hanging from the car's rearview mirror. "What's the feather for?"

He launched into his story. "My wife and I picked up a hitchhiker. We never do that, but it was raining. The guy was Native American. Know what that means?"

I shook my head. He met my eyes in the mirror. "Indian. After a few miles of driving in silence, the guy pulls out a knife and starts to clean his nails. I got scared, so I told him it was the end of the line and pulled over. When he reached into his bag, I about had a heart attack. But then I saw it was only a feather in his hand. He was trying to pay for the ride. So, I took it. Least I could do."

After hearing the story, I felt bad about running away from the old couple, but I knew it was too late. I had messed up again and was already on my way elsewhere.

CHAPTER 9

AUNTIE KAI AND UNCLE RYAN

We sat at the now-familiar office. "You're going to another home now with your brothers," someone said way too cheerfully as I said goodbye to the old man. About half an hour later, we headed out. The foster parents had agreed to take in Hector, Javel, Lorenzo, Jesse, and now me. When I saw them, I figured that this was as close as I was going to get to home, living with my brothers. I'd better be good.

We lived in a two-story house with a basement. The foster mom was a short, bowlegged Korean woman with really long black hair. We called her Auntie Kai. Uncle Ryan, a black man, wore a baseball cap and glasses—and looked about ten feet tall. Three nieces also lived there due to their mom having some personal issues. Layla was, first, an older teenager. Then, Maya, who was in middle school aged. Last was Diana, in elementary school. Because they called them "Auntie and Uncle," it was easy to pick up. It stuck.

Uncle Ryan worked long hours as an electrician. We didn't see him very often. When he wasn't working, he loved movies. He drove to Blockbuster every Friday, where he rented a movie for the kids and a few for the adults and teenagers. They weren't the type of parents who banned movies because of adult content; they'd just have us turn our heads during love scenes, killing scenes, or when people used drugs. During those forbidden scenes, we figured out a trick. The thick glasses Auntie Kai wore gave us a great reflection of the TV screen. We saw everything clearly.

"Why are you guys staring at me?" She asked us now and again.

We lied. "We're just waiting for you to tell us when we can watch again."

The boys shared one big room on the top floor. Although they had a bathroom at the bottom of the stairs that led to our room, they told us to only use the bathroom in the basement. We hated using the basement bathroom at night.

During the day, it was alright, but nighttime bathroom runs became terrifying. We'd first head downstairs, then through the little hallway that led to the kitchen. We'd tiptoe through the kitchen and slink down the basement stairs. The stairs to the basement had a few steps, then turned left, and five more steps appeared. The light from the kitchen no longer illuminated our path after the first turn, and the light switch for the basement was mounted on the far wall of the basement. To get to the light switch, we ran from the stairs across the open space of darkness to the wall and groped, trying to hit the switch.

After we finished using the bathroom, we had to turn out the light before returning to bed. We'd build up our nerve, hit the switch as we were running, and then scoot up the stairs without looking back.

Javel returned from the bathroom one night, frantic. "I saw red eyes glowing in the corner. They came toward me as I ran upstairs." He seemed out of breath.

The rest of us shuddered, and after that, I started looking for the red eyes each time I ran up those stairs.

Layla didn't have a lot of time to deal with us. She spent most of her time with one of her best friends who lived a block away. She'd often arrive home for a little while, then leave again. She later had a boyfriend named Bruno, who hung out with us. He also cut our hair. He was a kind dude, and he also knew how to cut all kinds of designs in our hair (which was the style back then). Bruno cut the Nike swoosh in our hair, and all the kids at school were jealous.

Maya yelled at Javel or Lorenzo for the littlest things. She shamed my brothers every chance she got. I avoided her. One day, I saw her get in Lorenzo's face. "You're so stupid! So dumb! You're a freak!"

I ran over. "Hey, leave him alone!"

She turned and started screaming at me, and from then forward, she treated me meanly, just like she treated them.

Diana, too young to pick on any of us, tattled every chance she got—about everything. "Auntie! Jesse did this, Auntie! Javel said this, Auntie! Auntie!" Times grew tough with Maya and Diana. Apparently, actual blood families assumed more rights than foster kids.

With Uncle Ryan mostly at work, we spent most of our time with Auntie Kai. She taught us a lot about her Korean culture. She introduced us to kimchee and some dried squid that we ate like jerky. I ate the dried squid, but I couldn't do the kimchee. Auntie Kai told us stories about Korea. She even taught us how to play her favorite card game, Gin Rummy, on the dining room table. Auntie had a certain way she liked it played. For example, in the game, we were allowed to make a spread in two different ways. First, there must be at least three of the same type of cards, such as diamonds.

Once, I made a spread of three kings. That was a mistake

"Bad move! Selfish!" She slapped the table in her angst. Yes, when it came to playing Rummy with Auntie Kai, unspoken standards also ruled.

Auntie Kai could cook just about anything. She cooked her Korean food, and we didn't always like it. She also made American food. She even made soul food as if she were from the South. She made gumbo, greens, and sweet potato pie. We ate well there.

Auntie Kai was very strict about chores. She also had "The Check" in place. She'd walk into the kitchen while you were doing the dishes, grab a dish out of the strainer, and run her finger across it.

"What are you doing?" Hector asked the first time.

"Listening for a squeak, boy. If it doesn't squeak, it ain't clean. This one needs to be done again." She entered the kitchen each night to pour about a cup of bleach into the dishwater.

We ran errands. Her relatives owned the corner store. She wrote lists in Korean, and we took them, walking the six blocks to the store. Once there, we handed the clerk the list, and they filled the order. It always included cigarettes. Only once in a while did it include cooking ingredients.

***

A couple of months after I moved to Auntie Kai and Uncle Ryan's, Dad showed up as we played in the front yard.

"Dad's here! Dad's here!" Lorenzo called out as he ran. We all jogged over.

Auntie Kai walked out onto the porch. "Who is it?"

"Our dad." Hector smiled, his teeth flashing at her from across the yard.

Dad waved at her. "Hector, translate. Ask her if I can bring you gifts."

"I suppose." She agreed once Hector translated.

"What do you want?" he asked us.

"Nintendo!" Hector yelled.

"OK, I'll get you that." Dad slid back behind his steering wheel and waved as he drove away. He didn't come back for a few weeks, but when he did, he brought a Nintendo system. During this visit, Dad had Hector ask Auntie Kai if he could stop by from time to time and visit.

"Oh, alright." She agreed, even though it was against the rules to allow parents to have contact with their children once in State custody.

So, Dad started stopping by every couple of weeks with little candies or toys.

***

I started attending Martin Luther King Elementary School at the end of my second-grade year. Javel, Lorenzo, and I walked the seven blocks back and forth from Auntie Kai's house.

On my first day, we lined up to go to recess when a black dude cut me in line.

"What the heck?" I glared at his back.

He turned around. "Shut up before I jump you."

I grinned. "What, by yourself?"

The teacher saw what happened and told him to go to the end of the line. He left me alone after that first incident. Obviously, I had no fear of him.

In my third-grade year, I made a couple of friends but only saw them at school. We loved to play on the pullup bar. We did cherry drops, where you hang upside down on the bar from your knees, swing back and forth, and push off the bar, landing on your feet. We also hung upside down on the pullup bar by one leg, holding on with both hands. We swung back and forth until we gained enough momentum to sail over the bar repeatedly. We had competitions on the playground, and when it came to the swings and tire swings, distance became the name of the game. We'd sit on the swings side by side and wait to see who could launch off and land the farthest. We did the same with the tire swing.

The school year was uneventful except for two incidents. The first one was Sarah, a light-skinned gal that I crushed on right away. Sarah sat in the aisle to the right, about two seats behind me. I developed every excuse to turn and look back at her. One day, I developed a new idea. I'd make a little book of our lives together. On the first page of my book, I started with a picture of Sarah and me holding hands. At the bottom of the picture, I wrote, "Sarah and I are holding hands." Page two was a picture of us kissing, and under the picture, I wrote, "Sarah and I kissing." On the third page, I drew a bed with both of us on it, and underneath I wrote. "Sarah and me making love." I started to draw a house around us.

"Hery. Hery, did you hear me?" I focused my eyes on the teacher to see her almost to my desk. I quickly tried to stash my book, but the teacher was faster. She snatched it out of my hand. "Class, should I read you the book?"

"Yes! Yes!" The room erupted in glee.

My face grew hot, and I bit my lip.

The teacher flipped through a page or two, then she stopped, looked me in the eye, and put it in her pocket. "Pay attention now." She returned to her desk.

A couple of days passed, and I completely forgot about the little book. The teacher started us on a group project. Before I could get started, she called me out into the hall. "I want to talk to you, Hery."

Being a foster child, it wasn't out of the ordinary to have to talk to some counselor, teacher, or shrink while at school. We walked out into the hall, which housed a little working table. We sat. She pulled out the book and put it on the table in front of me.

My heart dropped out of my chest and onto the floor.

"Please explain the drawings, Hery." But she skipped the first two pictures and pointed at the third. "Is that a bed?"

"Yes," I mumbled.

"And what are you doing on the bed?"

"Playing."

She started to point out the writing on the page when the teacher's assistant called her into the class to ask a question. She stood and walked into the classroom, leaving the book on the table in front of me. As soon as she left, I ripped out page three. I crumbled it up and threw it under the table in the hall.

She returned. "Okay, now about the bed?" She opened the book. "Where's the page?"

"I don't know." I shuffled my feet back and forth.

She frowned. "We both know that there was another page here, but now it isn't."

Ring! Ring! I literally got saved by the school bell. She gave me a stern look. "We will finish this conversation later."

The third page was the only part I figured I'd get in trouble for, and it was now gone. If she ever brought it up again, I'd play dumb.

The second memorable incident happened at recess. I recently received a talking-to for not letting staff know when I had a problem with someone and using violence to solve my issues. I made an agreement with the school counselor that if I had issues, I'd tell a teacher.

Well, I argued with a classmate on the playground. When I felt like hitting the kid, I decided instead to honor that agreement. I walked over to the teacher on recess duty. "That kid's messing with me."

"It's okay, just don't pay him any mind."

My blood boiled. Here, I was doing the right thing instead of handling it myself, and she blew me off. I couldn't believe it. I decided this was BS and walked off the school grounds. I headed to the corner store that Auntie Kai's family owned. Then it hit me. Where in the heck was I going? I couldn't go home—I'd get in trouble for leaving school. I decided to keep walking. I started to think about my sister Jannet. I got a little farther when I recognized the route to the CSD office. Our caseworker took us to the CSD office on the same route every time we went.

"I'm going to go in and demand to see Jannet," I decided. I started wondering how it was best to present that as a tall, skinny fourth grader. They weren't going to listen to me. I hatched a different plan. "I know! I'll ask for our caseworker, William." When Will came out, I could threaten him. My heart started beating a little harder, and adrenaline built up in my body. I grabbed a long, skinny piece of metal with a point at one end from the ground. I slid it up my sleeve to conceal it. Holding the sharp end to Will's neck would force them to bring me Jannet. I started trying to build up some courage. By the time I got to the parking lot of the building, I felt completely pumped. Nothing could have stopped me. I stormed past a guy walking out of the building.

Once inside, I scanned the lobby, looking for the receptionist's desk, and stomped across the room. As I approached, I noticed a tall, slender black man next to the desk looking at a piece of paper. He looked up from his paper, and I realized it was William, standing right where I was headed. All the courage I built up escaped, like a two-year-old Houdini escaping his crib.

"Hey, Hery, come on over. What are you doing? What's going on? Is someone with you?"

I froze. Then, I took a deep breath. "I want to see my sister."

"Come with me, kiddo." We walked to his office, where he called Auntie Kai. He hung up. "I'm going to take you home, Hery. Everyone was worried about you. Your school is called Kai."

"I just want to see Jannet," I mumbled.

As we neared Auntie Kai's house, I remembered the weapon still hidden in my sleeve. I slowly slid it out and placed it on the floor of the car near the door.

Once back at Auntie Kai's house, Will talked with her. Later that night, she sternly reprimanded me for almost getting her in trouble with Will.

Back at school, they sent me to the principal's office. After I explained what I did and why, the principal frowned. "If this happens again, go tell another teacher or go to the main office. You are not allowed to leave campus for any reason."

"OK," I agreed.

Chapter 10

New Beginnings

My brothers and I saw a counselor regularly, as required by the State. While living at Auntie Kai's house, Godwin drew our names. A stocky, black man with a strong West Indian accent, he always dressed well. He wore suits every time I saw him—even in the middle of summer. He also drove a small, red sports car. He asked all the usual questions: how do you feel about your parents? Are you happy where you're living, and do you feel safe?

Each time after returning from one of our sessions, Auntie Kai grilled us. "How did you answer that question?" She wanted to know repeatedly.

On one occasion, Godwin asked if we ever were hungry.

"No," everyone else replied.

Except for me.

When we got home, Auntie Kai asked her usual questions.

"Eddie told Godwin he was hungry sometimes." Hector laughed.

I turned to Auntie Kai, my face warming. Shoot.

Kai glared at me. "You said what to the counselor? We feed you! Why are you making people think we're mistreating you? Remember the last time Will came? We even had pizza. He mentioned how much you eat, Eddie."

Yes, sometime in recent months, I'd started calling myself Eddie, as well as writing it on my papers. The rest of the family quickly followed—all of us felt like we had finally gained a fresh start after all. But from that day forth, I tried to make sure I answered all questions with Auntie Kai in mind.

As we left one visit with Godwin, he stopped me in the hall. "Hery, uh, Eddie, tell me about the little book you made in class."

My heart started pounding loudly. Well, so much for a fresh start! I turned to Hector. Had my brother heard about the book?

"Your teacher said she tried to talk to you about it."

I remembered I'd determined to play dumb if ever asked. "What book?" My voice shook a bit.

Godwin gave me a weird look. "Well. We'll talk about it on the next visit." I nodded as I hurried out the door to the parking lot.

Godwin never brought the book up again. Thankfully, that was the last time I heard about that book.

I found quite a bit of trouble in the next few months until, one day, I decided to do everything I knew that would make Auntie Kai happy. It was time to straighten up and stop finding mischief. I started studying her. I started playing Gin Rummy with her rules in mind. If I heard her mumble, "I wish these kids would clean up after themselves," I'd start cleaning. Auntie Kai hated two things: a mess and kids who were in grownups' business. I volunteered to clean and stopped asking questions about adult conversations.

Auntie Kai started treating me much better than my siblings. I received a nickname of "the good one." My life grew much easier when my parents liked me, and that became my goal.

***

Growing up in any hood in the country, you see crackheads. And this was the case in Portland, too. Still is. These addicted people stole anything you desired and sold it to you for a discount. They literally took orders. Many people utilized them to get what they couldn't afford. Auntie Kai used the system, too. Every couple of weeks, a couple of crackheads stopped by with clothes. They knew our sizes and brought only the styles she'd bought in the past.

Auntie Kai loved white gold, and whenever any of them acquired some, they quickly found Auntie Kai. On one occasion, one guy brought her a gold ring with diamonds and a couple of rubies. After she talked him down to about forty bucks, Auntie Kai ducked inside and got the money from Uncle Ryan. She never turned down a good gold deal. Auntie Kai also bought food stamps from the crackheads.

Perhaps due to all the good food, I had a huge growth spurt. I grew so much in a year that I caught up with Javel, who was 13 months older than me. For a while, people thought Javel and I were twins. Constantly hungry, I couldn't get enough to eat. Every night at the kitchen table, I announced that I would take anything someone didn't want. They started calling me "the human garbage can." I wouldn't let anyone throw away their leftovers.

One time, Diana refused to give me her leftover chicken when I asked. She smiled and quickly threw it in the trash. I stood over the trash can, and I realized it hadn't touched anything but a paper plate. "It'll be fine." I reached in and grabbed it, bringing it quickly to my mouth.

"What the heck; you're eating out of the garbage now?" Auntie Kai put her hands on her hips, her voice raised

Of course, I never lived that down.

***

One evening, Auntie Kai talked with one of her neighbors, who invited us to church. She started to take us to a black church a couple of blocks away from the house. In the little white building on the corner of two busy downtown streets, the congregation, mostly black, sang vivacious gospel music. It was so lively, and it made me want to dance sometimes. The sermons were very boring, and I couldn't wait for them to finish.

I hated church despite the music. Going to church meant we missed all the Sunday morning cartoons. We started attending only on Sundays, but it soon became Wednesdays too.

Tedious. Both times.

One day after church, Auntie Kai called us all into her bedroom, where we often hung out. "Who has been baptized?" She smiled and nodded, encouraging us to talk.

"Me. I was a baby in Cuba," Hector announced.

"Good then. All of you are getting dunked."

Dunked? Didn't she mean to get water sprinkled on our heads? I was many things, but dumb was not one.

I went along with it to make everybody happy. Javel and I were baptized two weeks later. They gave us white gowns. I remember freezing while I waited to be called. Finally, the pastor called us forward. Javel and I walked up on stage and watched the people ahead of us.

They weren't getting sprinkled.

The pastor pulled a heavyset black woman out of the water, water pouring from her.

Javel elbowed me, whispering loudly, "Look!"

I glanced over. We could see right through her shirt! The woman hadn't worn a bra. With hot faces, we tried not to snicker as we were called forward to walk past her.

The pastor called me up and read some scripture. "Eddie, is it your desire to be baptized today?" I nodded, my eyes riveted on my brother. He dunked me backward in the tank, and then I watched him do the same with Javel.

We stood on stage soaking wet and freezing until the last person was baptized.

***

One afternoon, Auntie Kai called us boys into the house. "I got a call from Jannet's foster parents. Your sister is on the phone."

I grabbed the receiver. "Hi, Jannet! Where are you?"

She giggled. "I'm with a white family in somewhere called St. Helens. They're alright."

I loved hearing from my sister. After we all had a turn, with me trying to listen in on each one, Auntie Kai and Jannet's foster mom talked for a while.

Auntie Kai hung up the phone, smiling. "Jannet will come for the weekend."

We whooped and hollered. I never slept that night.

Finally, the day came. I waited outside until I saw a van pull up in front of the house. Jannet popped out with a huge smile on her face. We ran to her—talking over each other, fighting for her attention.

But when it was time for bed, Jannet started crying.

"What's the matter, sis?" Jesse hugged her. I came alongside and patted her on the shoulder.

She sniffed. "I miss Amy. My—my foster mom." She cried harder.

I frowned. "What? You'd rather be with her?" My heart hurt bad.

Auntie Kai called Jannet's foster mom to come and pick her up after eleven o'clock. Jannet cried when she arrived. From then on, Auntie Kai said no to visits. It was Jannet's first and last trip to Auntie Kai's house.

***

The summer before fourth grade, Uncle Ryan called us all into the living room. "We're going on vacation. To Marysville for a week to see my folks."

This caused a bit of bedlam amongst us. A happy lump welled up in my throat. I'd never been on vacation before. I stayed awake the whole night, waiting for the trip to begin. The next morning, Uncle Ryan rented a van, and we all piled in. I beamed as we loaded up, but the actual drive was so boring I started to question my initial elation. We finally drove into a beautiful neighborhood, and Uncle Ryan pulled into the driveway of a very nice little house.

"Better be on your best behavior," he informed us as we clamored out of the van.

An older black couple greeted us. "Glad to meet all of you." We grabbed our bags and followed Uncle Ryan. Uncle Ryan's dad walked us to the garage, which he'd fixed up for sleeping quarters. While we settled in, Uncle Ryan's mom popped in. "I've got a good movie for us to watch."

Sure enough, she did. We sat in the living room, and she started *Paint Your Wagon*. The movie starts out with a picture of a covered wagon on a dirt road. But soon, we grew restless.

"Is there any action in this movie?" Hector shifted on the couch for the umpteenth time.

"Yeah. Where's the killing?" Javel complained.

Uncle Ryan's mom sniffed. "Stop. No cursing or violence in this movie. That's why I picked it. This is a movie that is appropriate for kids. You kids shouldn't be watching movies like that anyway."

"This is boring!" Lorenzo announced. I had to agree. We complained so much that Uncle Ryan finally left to rent us some real movies.

"Yeah! *Rocky V*!" I pumped my fist into the air when he returned and handed it to me.

A few minutes later, Lorenzo, Jesse, and I started messing around on the living room floor, and I pinched Lorenzo really good under his arm.

"Ow, Eddie!" Lorenzo screamed.

Uncle Ryan marched over. "What now?"

"Eddie pinched me!" Lorenzo even worked up a tear.

Uncle Ryan pulled me up from the floor. "Eddie, goodnight."

"What? No. I was just playing! I'm sorry, Lorenzo. Can I get another chance, please? I really want to watch this. I'll sit quietly."

"Goodnight." Uncle Ryan repeated and crossed his arms. I looked at the floor and made my way to the garage room to pout and go to sleep. I didn't get a chance to see *Rocky V* for another five years.

Extreme heat soured the next five days. One hundred and fifteen degrees—the hottest days I'd experienced. Ryan drove us around, looking for a swimming hole, but each one we found had a sign: "No swimming." We continued searching for a watering hole. We finally drove by a spot where we saw people swimming.

"Stop, Uncle Ryan!" We kept screeching until he braked, and we flew out and into the water.

Ten minutes later, a police cruiser pulled up. A cop rolled down his window. "This water is off limits."

"Oh great," I complained when Uncle Ryan called us out. I suspected within minutes that our clothes would dry and we'd start sweating again.

Once again, Uncle Ryan placed his hands on the steering wheel of the van. "How about a movie? It's air-conditioned in the theaters." We couldn't agree more. And, of course, I loved movies. We watched *Stone Cold*, and we didn't even wrestle. It featured a cop who went undercover in a motorcycle gang.

Going to the movies remained the highlight of my trip to Marysville, California.

***

One day, in mid-fall, Hector and Uncle Ryan started yelling. I'm not sure what started it. "You need to leave my house." Uncle Ryan sounded firm, his voice on edge.

Wow. This must be bad.

"Fine. I'll leave." Hector stomped across the room. "But I'm taking the Nintendo Dad brought."

Uncle Ryan stepped in front of Hector. "No. You're leaving only with the clothes on your back." Auntie Kai sniffed. Little wrinkles appeared in between her eyes. She touched Uncle Ryan's arm, and he shook her off.

Hector tried to squeeze past Uncle Ryan, who was now in the doorway to the kitchen. Uncle Ryan pushed Hector back. "Go out the other way."

Hector tried again and managed to squirm by him. Uncle Ryan grabbed Hector by the back of his shirt and yanked him back into the living room. Hector flew back into the door frame. He hit the floor.

Hector pushed himself up, now crying and holding his back. "I-I need that Nintendo."

"You're not getting it!"

My brother turned and walked out of the house crying, still holding his back. I stood rooted to the floor while Auntie Kai ran to the window to watch him leave.

Later, when asked by our social worker what had happened, we knew better than to tell the truth and displease Auntie Kai. We did exactly that—despite knowing that CSD wouldn't believe Hector's version of the story because of our lies.

***

Shortly after the incident with Hector, news came about Jannet leaving foster care and moving back with Mom. Around this same time, I also heard whispers of us boys receiving a new foster home placement. It was a crazy time. We'd just lost one of our siblings, and another was heading home to Mom. And now, a new home for the rest of us.

The phone rang, and Uncle Ryan grabbed it. He talked a bit and then hung up. "That was my folks. I need to head back to Marysville."

We started jumping up and down. "When? When?"

"Not so fast. I can only take one of you."

The clamor stopped. Instant competition.

"Eddie. I'm taking Eddie."

"Me?" I paused. Had I heard right?

"Yes, go and pack your backpack for the weekend."

I jumped up and ran upstairs. All the kids were mad and jealous—and I loved it. I strutted about proudly for the entire evening.

The next afternoon, Uncle Ryan and I hopped in his little red truck and headed off to California. We arrived at Uncle Ryan's parents' house after dark. The next morning, Uncle Ryan pulled me aside. "We'll be heading back to Portland shortly."

"What?" A mixture of emotions filtered through my brain. I'm sure he saw them all on my face. "I thought we were coming for the weekend."

On the drive back to Portland, Uncle Ryan sighed. "Your brothers already went to another home. When we get back, CSD will pick you up."

I almost reached for the truck door handle. Tears blurred my eyes. I blinked hard as I stared out the window. At the same time, I reasoned, there were a lot of things at Uncle Ryan's and Auntie Kai's that I didn't like. "At least I won't have to deal with you anymore," I mumbled while watching the passing landscape.

The rest of the way back to Portland, silence reigned. You could have heard a mouse peeing on cotton. We finally turned on Ninth Street, and I saw Auntie Kai on the porch, smoking a cigarette. We pulled into the driveway and got out of the truck. I took a second look at Auntie Kai. Her eyes were swollen from crying. I shuffled up the stairs and onto the porch. A black garbage bag rested there. All my stuff, apparently.

Auntie Kai rubbed my hair for a quick second. "They should be here any minute." And then, the best news I'd heard all day. "Jannet's current foster parents decided to accept you all. You won't have to be split up again."

Hearing the sadness in Auntie Kai's voice opened a cage of butterflies in my stomach. "I want to stay." I rubbed my toe against the porch boards. "But I want to be with them." Confusion whirled in my heart. I decided to run away and took off down Ninth Street for three blocks, then turned left.

"Eddie!" I turned around. The social worker drove up to me and I took off again—this time toward the house. He drove past me, pulled over, and stepped out in front of me on the street. I decided to give up. About ten minutes of running surely would convince Uncle Ryan and Auntie Kai that I really wanted to stay. That should help her feel better.

Back at Auntie Kai's, I grabbed my belongings and gave Uncle Ryan and Auntie Kai hugs before hopping in the car and heading off. On the way to St. Helens, joy welled up in my stomach, all the way to my chest and then my head. I would be with my brothers and with Jannet—the way it should have always been.

"Eddie in the Rough, Forming a Diamond Book 1" by Eddie Acosta.

Chapter 11

The Mercy Rule

I arrived at the Eatons' house about sunset. I burst through the door, excited to see my brothers and Jannet.

"Hey, Eddie. 'Bout time." Javel punched me on the shoulder.

But Jannet wasn't there. She'd been returned to Mom. I slumped as I toured the house and received introductions to the rest of the family. Sophia, the foster mom, had shoulder-length brown hair. Scarlet, the eldest sister, apparently received her height from her dad's side, but her hair looked just like her mom's. "I'm heading for the military pretty soon." She flipped her hair over her shoulder. Indeed, she left about a week after I arrived. Next, I met Sam. Sam, the eldest brother, was a very fit junior or senior in high school. Then came Spenser, the middle-schooler. Later, I met Sage, a year younger than me. The Eatons had two more kids. Sarah, about 3, and baby Steve. Yes, everyone's name started with an "S," which I found humorous. It didn't take me long to start smiling again.

After meeting everybody, they took me to my room. I shared a bedroom with Javel, Lorenzo, and Jesse. It had two bunk beds in it and was located conveniently next to the kitchen. Everybody else slept upstairs. After unpacking my belongings, we ate dinner.

"Time for a shower," Sophia announced. I was used to the routine now. Introductions, tour, food, and shower. Although occasionally, showering placed higher on the list. Maybe it was the foster parents' idea of a fresh start. Or maybe we stank. I grabbed my clothes and ran upstairs. Their shower had a sliding door on the edge of the tub instead of a shower curtain. When finished, I opened the door, grabbed my towel, stepped out, closed the shower door, and started to dry off.

The bathroom door flew open. A man charged in and grabbed me by the throat. "Stop slamming the shower door!" Just as fast, he turned and left, slamming the door behind him. I held my throat, my heart pounding the hardest it had beat in a long time. My chest ached, and now my neck hurt too. Who was that? Why had he choked me? Shaking, I quickly got dressed and hurried downstairs to my room. I crawled into bed and went straight to sleep, still shaking.

The next day, at breakfast, I met Simon, the foster father, and the shower choker.

***

I started the second half of my fourth-grade year at McBride Elementary. A fire had recently torn through, affecting the fourth-grade classrooms. We met in portables—little trailers converted into classrooms.

I, again, was the new kid. Although I was starting to get used to it, I still didn't like it. I looked around to realize a complete lack of black kids. Coming from Martin Luther King Jr. Elementary School, where there were only a couple of white kids, this one ended up being a hard adjustment. I eventually found Tim, another kid of color besides my brother. We became friends and played together every recess.

A few weeks after my arrival, Tim and I were playing under the play structure as usual when a group of five classmates started making fun of us because we didn't know about the previous night's episode of *Beverly Hills 90210*.

"Shut the heck up. Stupid white show." Tim seemed to increase in size. I think he stood on his tiptoes.

"Yeah." I agreed. "Yeah." I wasn't sure what else to say. "Stupid white show." I'd never heard of it.

With five voices against two, he and I decided to relocate to the monkey bars. But the group followed, continuing to talk smack.

"That's enough crap." Tim walked over to the aide on duty and told the kids. The kids continued their mantra.

"Well, I've had enough," I whispered. Time to leave—much like I'd done before. Right as recess ended, I walked over to the side gate and left. I walked down Highway 30 until I reached Safeway. At Safeway, I remembered the school bus route. "I'll follow that." Many years of changes meant that I tried to memorize roads and routes wherever we went to exit as needed.

I headed to the house, following my memory of the bus route to school. I walked until I hit a fork in the road. "Wait. Is it right or left here?" I kicked a rock before choosing the right one because I was right-handed. Continuing my walk, I looked down a street as I crossed and saw the back of the school's field.

A complete circle. Why hadn't I chosen to leave?

Defeated, I walked back to the school. I slowly approached the portable my class was in. I didn't see anyone outside, so I tried to sneak in. I cracked the door and peeked in.

"Eddie! Come in, please. We were worried. Please never do that again." My teacher marched me to the principal's office.

There, I sat and crossed my arms against my chest. I lifted my chin. I refused to become nervous. Done with that. "What happened, Eddie?"

I frowned. "There were kids making fun of us at recess. The teacher wouldn't do anything about it. So, I left. Better than fighting, right?"

The principal sighed. He had to agree. "Better than fighting. But Eddie, you can't just walk out. Now, I've heard five different accounts of the story, and I will need to do more research. If you have any other issues, you need to come straight to me."

I shrugged and nodded at the familiar speech. It seemed that no matter what choices I made, they always brought trouble.

***

Once or twice a week, someone picked us up and took us to the CSD office. Our newest social worker was a lady—tall, skinny, and very white. She guided us into the office for a sit-down. During these visits, we'd either visit with her or see a counselor. Sometimes, we got to see Mom. The mom visits always felt weird. "All the bad things we've heard about Mom," I complained to Hector. "It pisses me off. What a bitch. But I miss her when I see her, so I forget about that part until she leaves."

Hector nodded. "Irks me too. I mean, either put us with her or take her away for good. Stupid."

I actually really liked our new worker. Nice and generous, she often stopped at one of two places on the way back to the Eatons' house after office visits. The first stop was a little Asian restaurant in a tiny town leaving Portland, where we enjoyed ice cream cones. Other times, she drove us to the Dairy Queen in Scappoose. At Dairy Queen, we loved the little dippers that came in strawberry, butterscotch, and chocolate.

Things soon changed yet again. The house after the Eatons was the Wards. They had two boys in the same grades as Lorenzo and me named Tyler and John. A Mexican family with two kids lived down the hill. A high school girl made all our hearts flutter, and a boy in Lorenzo's grade named Miguel played with us quite a bit. Miguel, Tyler, and John made up our friends while we were with the Wards.

All the neighbor kids usually played at our house, but our favorite thing to do was play at what we called the canyon—a wooded area located on the other side of the Wards' property. To get there, we'd cross the Wards' ten acres, scoot around somebody else's property, and walk down a hill. At the bottom of the hill, there was a creek. On the other side of the creek, another hill started. We spent our day playing in the creek, catching salamanders, exploring the woods, or doing whatever we wanted because we were all alone and could. Every time we went there, we'd stir up trouble.

We often came home after dark and sometimes caked with mud. "Look at you!" Sophia admonished. "Take those clothes and shoes right off. Up to the shower." She grumbled as she gathered the clothes up and opened the washer. "These kids! You aren't going back to the creek." Then, we'd be stuck at the house for a while until things blew over. And back to the canyon, we'd go.

On one occasion after our canyon adventure, we found another route home. We saw a house no one recognized, and our mouths watered at the sight of bunches of raspberries growing in the middle of the backyard. We snuck over and started eating them.

"So good." I munched another handful, and before we knew it, I saw none remaining. We hurried out and continued home.

Sophia met us at the door. "Got a call." She shook her head at our red-stained lips. "That's the last creek trip ever."

***

Around springtime, we signed up to play Little League baseball. Javel and I played in the same division because of how close our ages were. We played for different teams, though. I played for the Federal Credit Union. The team colors were baby blue and black. I wasn't very good at baseball and had never played on a team of any kind. I played right field, but I really wanted to pitch. I usually didn't do so well, but there was a week when I played really well. The coach noticed and set up a competition between me and the current left fielder for the left field position.

"Head out to the middle field," he instructed. He hit a pop fly to the outfield. "Get that, Eddie!"

He went back and forth between the two of us for a while. Then he called for me to grab one again. I took off after the ball. I ran until I got under the ball and waited for the drop.

But the sun was in my eyes. I lost track of the ball, and *bam!* The ball slammed into my mouth. "Ouch!" I dropped to the ground crying, blood gushing.

The coach ran out and helped me up. "Are you OK?"

A crowd quickly formed. I covered my mouth with my hand, and they walked me over to the dugout. Right before leaving, the coach found me again. "We're gonna keep positions as they are. You can stay in right field for the rest of the season." My shoulders slumped in disappointment, but I guess it's what I deserved. What kind of baby can't catch a ball in the sun?

I played Javel's team for the last game of the season. We had already played them once and lost. "Loser." Javel jeered at me for a few days after that last game. "Your whole team is chicken."

In this game, my team was up by a couple of runs, and it was my turn to bat. I hit the ball into center field and took off toward first base. As I approached first base, Coach waved me on. I touched first and sped off to second. At second, the third base coach told me to stay there. I never made it home, and in the next play, we got our third out, and the game ended. We won by two runs, beating Javel's team.

My victory was short lived. When I brought it up to Javel, he still teased me because we won by two runs, but when Javel won, they beat us by ten runs and implemented the Mercy Rule.

Chapter 12

Javel Loses Out

It was time to improvise. Without canyon visits, boredom reigned. We headed to the little wooded area in the Eatons' backyard instead. It consisted of about twenty trees and a bunch of bushes spread throughout.

One day, while playing near the woods, Javel, Lorenzo, and I started making tunnels through the sticker bushes and vines until we came to an opening. "That'd make a cool fort." Lorenzo stood near it, peering in.

"Big time," I agreed.

We started building with branches and anything else we found. Soon, Sarah and Jesse heard us in the bushes and wanted to play.

"Big kids only." Javel insisted. "You could get hurt real bad, so don't even try."

"Yeah. We're building booby traps, so stay away." I stuck my chin out. "Go back to the house."

Sarah and Jesse frowned and ran inside.

Soon, Sophia came near the fort. "You all have to play together. And there better not be any booby traps!"

We quickly undid the booby traps. After the first incident with the little kids, we all worked together. We spent all our time working on the fort. We each had our own little section. Soon, we invited friends to help. Later, Miguel, John, and Tyler had their section of the fort as well.

While playing in our fort one evening, someone found a porn magazine in the bushes. "Hey! Come look at this!"

Fortunately, only the older kids gathered. We ran over and crowded around the magazine in awe. After taking a few good looks, we decided not to tell any parents. "We better hide it." Javel grabbed it and headed into the woods.

The next few days, we showed it to several neighbors. We sometimes looked at a picture and ran off in shock or disgust. With all the commotion, the younger kids grew curious. But every time Sarah or Jesse came around, we made them leave.

Of course, that made them more curious. Somehow, they discovered the magazine. The younger kids told the adults about a book with pictures of naked women. Sophia and Simon called a family meeting. "Bring it here. Where did you find this?" Simon paced the floor and then threw the closed magazine on the table.

"Behind the bushes behind the house." I shuffled my feet, ever wary of Choker Simon.

"We tried to keep it away from them," Lorenzo piped up.

Simon grunted. Sophia looked from one of us to the other and then landed hard eyes on her husband.

The next day, we learned our consequences.

"Come into the kitchen!" Sophia made Javel, Lorenzo, and I sit at the table. "You can no longer play with Miguel, Tyler, or John." Later, I overheard Sophia and Simon talking about the Ward boys starting counseling because of the magazine.

Later, we received more bad news. Sophia called Lorenzo Jesse. And me to the living room. "Javel is going to a new home. He's older than the rest of you and old enough to know better."

We watched sadly later as Javel climbed into a car with his stuff. "You're going to live at an all-boys home in Portland," the caseworker told him before ushering him to the car. Javel's face hardened. I knew anger boiled just below the surface. I wondered if we'd ever be together again.

***

I didn't have issues with my younger foster siblings except for the occasional tattling by Sage or Sarah. However, that changed with the older ones.

"We hate you," Sam and Spenser often informed us. Sam pushed us around and made fun of us every chance he got. In his late teens, he towered over us. My knees knocked together when he was near, so I did my best to stay away. He maintained a busy schedule most of the time, so that helped.

Spenser, on the other hand, hung out at home much more. I think he disliked us even more than his brother. He talked badly about us. "I can't wait until you leave," he hissed, with emphasis on the "leave."

We couldn't do or say anything about it. If we told Sophia, Spenser would hit us later, and he wouldn't get in trouble anyway. If we talked back to Spenser while he was putting us down, he'd hit, too. His favorite move was to administer a short jab in the gut as he walked by. If we were talked to about anything we did wrong, Spenser would walk behind his talking parent, mouthing words, making faces, and laughing. My mission was to stay as far away from Spenser as I could. Some days, it worked better than others.

***

We continued to find trouble. In the beginning, our punishments included being sent to our room, grounding, or time-outs. Then, someone developed a bright idea. "Take this paper grocery bag, Eddie and Jesse. Fill it up with rocks from the backfield. Then you can think about what you did." We called it "pulling rocks."

We filled up the first few bags with rocks. It took about an hour and a half to fill one. By the third time we headed out to pull rocks, we wised up. We filled the lower half of the bag with dirt and rocks on the top half. This worked once or twice. Once Sophia realized we had finished in a third of the time, they started feeling the bottom of the bags to make sure they were all rocks and not dirt. Then we started putting dirt in the middle instead and hanging out to make up the time.

Pulling rocks was a punishment for foster kids only. Goody two-shoes, Sam never got in trouble. Spenser only received a talking-to. Sage and Sarah were usually sent to their rooms or time-outs. In the time I lived there, only one person other than us boys pulled rocks, and only once. Sage made her dad so mad one day that she headed to the field, too. But she only had to do half a bag.

One day, while I pulled rocks with Lorenzo, Sam and a few of his friends stopped by. "Look at the babies picking up rocks," they jeered. "What did you do now? Throw your bottles at someone?"

"Leave us alone." I picked up a rock and tossed it into the bag.

"Who do you think you're screeching at, baby?" Sam started throwing rocks at us. His friends joined in.

I ducked but got hit anyway. Tears rolled down my cheeks as I saw Lorenzo hit the ground and cover his head.

Sam and his friends laughed as they walked into the house.

***

While we lived with the Eatons, my half-sister, Maria Marie Bellmas, was born. CSD allowed Mom to visit us at the Eatons' home, and she brought baby Maria.

The first visit went well. After the visit with Maria, Mom visited more often. Once, we drove with her to a park. We visited and played on the play structures while she cared for the baby. Later, we played in the creek and caught crawfish. We played for a long time that day. Our eyes brightened with the chance to see Mom and to have fun, too.

A couple of weeks later, Sophia called us into the kitchen. "Pack up. The CSD office is releasing you back to your mom."

I jumped up and darted to my room. I packed my things faster than the Looney Tunes's Tasmanian devil eating a foot-long sandwich. "Let's do this!" I shouted as I piled all my things outside the front door.

But where was home now? A drop of sweat rolled down my spine. And who would be there? At least Javel and Jannet would be near, and that was good news. Javel had been returned to Mom a short time earlier after living on the road with Dad. And we'd actually be with a parent, not in a stupid foster home.

Our caseworker picked us up and drove us back to Portland. We pulled up in front of a big white house.

I was almost in fifth grade, and I was finally home for good.

CHAPTER 13

TROUBLE IN THE WHITE HOUSE

Mom and her boyfriend Miguel found a white house big enough for all of us kids—the final requirement for us to come home.

When we arrived, Mom and Jannet waited on the porch. I jumped out of the car. "Bye, Mike!" I yelled to our caseworker and ran up the porch stairs.

Jannet hugged me. "Come on." She pulled my arm. "I'll show you around." We walked into the living room. It ranged on the small side but held a fireplace. The dining room, open to my right, had a built-in hutch. What I learned was a chandelier dangling from the ceiling, tinkling a song when I reached up to touch it in wonder.

"Eddie, this is Miguel."

"Hi." He smiled at me. "Really, it's Manuel, but Miguel is cool."

"Hi, Miguel."

Jannet pulled me through the room and to the back door.

"Nice deck." I whistled. An imaginative space for games, for sure.

We drifted back into the house, cruised through the kitchen, and headed to the basement. Halfway down the stairs lay a side door leading to the driveway. The basement included both a large room and a laundry room.

"Big place." I stuffed my hands in my pockets as Jannet yanked on my arm to keep me moving. She dragged me back upstairs to show me the rest of the house. The main floor had two bedrooms with a bathroom between them. We headed upstairs and landed in a ginormous room. Once, the attic, I suspected, had been transformed into a bedroom for my brothers and me, complete with beds and other furniture.

By far, the hardest adjustment was the language barrier. Living in English-speaking homes for many years, I knew it well and was comfortable speaking it. I'd forgotten most of my Spanish. But Mom struggled with the English. When Miguel was around, he translated because he spoke both fluently. Other than that, we played guessing games. After getting in trouble a couple of times for not knowing what she wanted, I decided I'd better learn Spanish.

My technique, rough as it was, did enough to jog long-ago language memories. I heard a word and memorized it. Then, I made the rounds, asking what it meant. Once I figured out the definition, I used it every chance I got. After a few months of this, I stopped getting in trouble for not understanding.

My mom apparently met Miguel while we were all in foster care. Although Maria called Miguel "Dad," he wasn't her real father. Miguel was a light-skinned Cuban man of average height and build. He had served in the US Navy and now worked for Blue Cross Blue Shield in downtown Portland as a janitor. Every now and again, Miguel took one of us boys to work on his weekend shifts to help clean. Miguel was a good man—one of the best guys my mom ever chose.

***

Summer was over, and it was time to go back to school. I started my fifth-grade year at Laurelhurst Elementary. I had a tough time making new friends. There were always a couple of girls who liked the new guy in each place I enrolled, but we apparently were only shiny and new for a little while. Mrs. Kessler, my teacher, sported gray hair on top of her short and white body.

Lonely, I started picking on the other kids. One of those kids that I picked on was named Andrew, a heavyset white kid with glasses.

"Four eyes." I nudged him as I walked by one afternoon on my way into the classroom.

"Eddie. Come here, please." Mrs. Kessler stood up from her desk.

Oh, brother.

I followed her obediently to the corner of the room.

She looked serious. "Eddie." She frowned, then brightened. "Did you know that you have leadership qualities? Something I'm very pleased to see. If you became friends with Andrew instead of picking on him, others might do the same. Andrew!" She turned back to the rows of desks, and Andrew shuffled over. "You can exchange phone numbers. Get to know each other." She pulled out two pieces of paper from her desk and handed us both a pencil as we stared at her. I finally jotted down my number and shoved it at Andrew. He avoided my gaze as he handed his over.

I visited Andrew's house shortly after the exchange. He owned a lot of Nintendo and computer games. We played games, and he bragged all about his computer. I was more into the Nintendo than his computer. I stayed for about an hour before going home.

I visited a total of two times. The second time happened one evening as Javel and I walked home from the store around sundown. "I have a friend with a ton of video games," I bragged.

"Oh yeah? I bet you won't go this late and borrow one."

We detoured while I tried to conjure up a reason why I'd stop by this late. Then it hit me. Mrs. Kessler had just partnered with Andrew and me for a project. "I got it." We jogged towards Andrew's house and rang the doorbell. His whole family answered the door with puzzled looks.

"Uh . . . I was supposed to do a project with Andrew for school."

Looking confused still, his mom opened the door wide. Javel, Andrew, and I scooted to the basement and worked on the project for about half an hour, then Javel and I left. I am too embarrassed to ask, but I never borrowed a game and stopped hanging out with Andrew shortly after that.

Aiden, also in my class, started making fun of me around that time. I ignored him. "Stupid blackie. You must have a hole in your head the size of Mt. Saint Helen's volcano." He followed me in the bathroom, talking smack.

I turned around and started swinging. My fist connected with his jaw, and he grabbed it with his hand, eyes ablaze.

"Hey, what's going on?" A black kid named Adrian pushed the door open. I stopped the assault and ducked out of the bathroom. A couple of days later, Aiden asked how my day was as I rolled my eyes and walked away. He persisted, and after a couple of weeks, we became friends. I'd earned his respect with violence.

At fifth grade recess, we played Wall Ball. Most of us played every recess and it moved into a tournament—some kids waited all recess to attempt dethroning of the champ. The winner stayed in the game to play the next challenger. The loser slunk to the back of an extremely long line to wait another turn.

When my turn arrived to play the current champion, my palms grew sweaty as I waited. He hit the ball so far, and I took off after it. I got there, about to hit the ball back, when some kid playing foursquare nearby smacked the ball away. That made me lose the whole game. "Hey, you dumbass!" I pulled my arm back and punched him hard in the eye.

The aide on duty ran over, breathing hard. "Eddie, go to the office. Now."

"OK." I shoved my hand in my jeans pocket and walked away.

The lady principal pointed to a chair when I entered her office. "What happened in the gym?"

"I almost had the ball, and that kid smacked it away from me. He hit my hand." I puffed up. "I was just defending myself like Mom tells me to." Of course, I padded the story a bit. He'd never hit my hand.

"OK." She sighed. "Go back to class, Eddie. Stay out of trouble."

The next day, the kid was absent. I overheard the story. With a hairline fracture on his eye socket, he'd visited the hospital for treatment. He never returned to school.

At Laurelhurst, the fourth graders ate lunch first, then headed to recess, and the fifth graders ate second shift. I was walking to recess when some random kid ran up. "Hey, Eddie. Two kids beat Lorenzo up. One of them held him down! Oh there! There he is!" He pointed to the offender in the hallway.

I boiled inside as I marched across the hallway. Pulling my hand back as far as it would reach, I slapped that kid hard across the face. *Smack!* He cringed, and tears welled in his eyes.

"Hey there!" A teacher ran into view, waving an arm. "Stop it now. Go to the office."

We both landed there. While we waited to see the principal, the receptionist stepped out, leaving us alone with only a chair separating us.

I glared at him. "How'd it feel to get slapped?"

The kid glared back. "It felt good when I hit your brother."

I flew at him, knocking him off his chair. The kid fell on his back and started kicking. I got one decent shot back when I heard someone coming. I quickly returned to my seat. We both straightened up and sat, looking innocent.

"Why'd you hit him, Eddie? Didn't think I'd see you again." The principal leaned forward once she'd directed us to chairs.

I laughed. "It's my job to protect my younger siblings. Mom says so. Otherwise, I'd be in big trouble at home."

"That's probably a good idea to teach kids that." She mused, then sent me back to class.

Lorenzo looked a bit injured when I saw him at home that night. But he insisted that nothing happened.

The next day, Aiden ran up to me. "I got the other kid. I popped him one for holding Lorenzo." I nodded in satisfaction. Justice was sweet.

***

Hector didn't always live with us at the white house. He'd actually go between three places to live—Mom's, Dad's, and jail. When he lived with us at Mom's, he stayed in the big room in the basement, always bantering about girls. When Hector wasn't talking about girls, he chatted with one of his many girlfriends on the phone. He didn't really interact with us kids unless he was left in charge when Mom and Miguel went out.

When the grownups left, Hector let us do what we wanted if we didn't bother him or get him in trouble. If we did get in trouble, we quickly regretted it.

Hector created two ways to punish us. The first was the Quick Beat Down. I didn't mind that because it was over and done with. His second style was worse. "This is gonna be bad." Lorenzo breathed quickly as Hector lined us up along the wall of the basement.

"If you laugh, you're getting beat." He stood in front of us, doing whatever he could to elicit a chuckle. As soon as one of us laughed, Hector beat the offender and pushed them back to the wall for the next round.

***

One day, he showed up with a new trick. We learned how to make someone pass out. While we were up in the boys' room, Hector chose me. He told me to breathe in and out really fast, then touched my neck, and I was out. I woke up on the floor. He stayed a little longer than he left.

When Javel came home, I told him about the new trick.

"Show me."

"Breathe in and out fast." I touched his neck like Hector did with me. I let him go to see if it worked. Javel slowly tilted, and then SMACK! He hit the concrete basement floor with his face. He didn't move.

Fear immediately rose in my stomach and wrapped around my heart. I tasted bile. "Javel!" I pushed him with my foot.

No answer.

I took off upstairs. "Mommy! Javel fell, and he's not moving!"

Mom ran downstairs and tried to wake Javel up, but he was unresponsive. "Miguel!" She yelled toward the stairs. "Miguel! Come quick!"

Miguel thundered down the stairs. He picked Javel right up and carried him up into the living room. He dialed 911. Mom started crying, and my brother was rushed to the hospital.

The next day, we learned of his broken jaw. He had a lot of repair work and stayed in the hospital for a couple of days.

The whole time Javel was gone, I felt so bad. I wished I had never listened to him when he asked me to make him pass out.

"What happened?" Everyone at home wanted to know. It's all I heard for hours.

"He fell," I lied. "He was standing there and just fell. There one second and on the floor the next."

A couple of days later, Javel returned home.

"What happened, Javel?" Lorenzo, Jesse, and Jannet crowded around him as I snuck out of the bedroom in shame but listened just around the corner. What if he told?

"I had a piece of candy at a friend's house." Javel's hoarse voice hitched up a notch. "It had powdery stuff on it. Someone called the cops, and they searched the house. There were drugs. My mouth got hurt, but I'm fine."

He never told them the truth. I slumped against the hallway wall in relief.

***

My mom's best friend Ana, a short, white, heavyset Costa Rican woman, met Mom while we stayed in foster care. She lived with her daughter and two grandchildren. Ana always watched Keith, her grandson, because his mom treated him like crap. Keith called Ana "Mamma Ana," so we all started calling her that.

My mom and Mamma Ana partied heavily. They loved to drink Budweiser, smoke Marlboro cigarettes, and crank up Spanish music. They also loved to dance. Once they drank a few beers, they'd head to the living room and start dancing salsa or merengue. We learned to stay away. Whoever walked by the living room while they were dancing got snatched onto the dance floor. Whenever I got caught, I'd hear, "You need to learn how to dance. Because Latin women love to dance, so if you want a Latin woman, you need to learn how to dance."

We'd be stuck dancing until one of three things happened. The first? An empty beer. "Go get us a beer," I told a younger sibling to grab one, and it became enough distraction to slip out of the room. The second was a bathroom call. The third was when the cassette tape finished and had to be flipped over. This also gave me enough time to sneak off.

We loved it when Mamma Ana visited. She always stood up for us. If the trouble found us with Mamma Ana there, we knew that she wouldn't let my mom hit us or be too harsh. If Mamma Ana arrived in the middle of a punishment, she grew sneaky and helped us.

Our first Christmas at the white house, Mom and Miguel, strapped for cash, gave us an outfit each for Christmas. Disappointment filled me.

The next day, Mamma Ana breezed in. "How was your holiday, children?"

We clamored around her, still upset. Jannet sniffed loudly. "All we got was an outfit."

"Pair of pants and a shirt." I shifted my weight from one leg to the other, noting Mamma Ana's strange expression. She turned and left. About an hour later, she returned and called us to the living room. She held a huge black plastic garbage bag in her hand.

"Come over. Closer!" She motioned toward us until we all gathered. Then she dumped the bag on the floor. Toys tumbled all around—all kinds, from guns to dolls. They were used, but it didn't matter. That was the best Christmas I had as a child.

***

Mom and Miguel bumped along in their relationship. They fought quite a bit over a couple of things. If it wasn't Mom thinking Miguel was cheating, it was about Miguel's friends. Alcohol was often involved. They started drinking, then came the arguing, then screaming and yelling. The screaming and yelling really didn't bother me—it was when it got physical that I struggled. Sometimes, the fights grew violent, usually when Mom hit Miguel. Miguel always hit her back. If Mamma Ana was there, she backed up my mom and eventually calmed them down.

Once, Mom slapped Miguel in a drunken fight, and the neighbors called the cops. The police arrived and started talking to Miguel. Mom darted over to slap Miguel but caught the officer in the face instead. Furious, he corrected her and readied for her arrest, but for some reason, that didn't happen.

On another occasion, there was a party going on at the house when they started. I tended to hover close when they fought. I watched Mom slap Miguel. She'd surprised him, and he immediately smacked her back. I charged him. Miguel saw me coming. He grabbed me, caught me by my wrists, and held me back. Suddenly, Mamma Ana appeared and planted herself between Miguel and me. Miguel released me abruptly.

"What are you thinking, Estrella? Miguel, come on now. Keep your hands off them. Be a real man." Mamma Ana placed her hands on her hips, her face flushed. "Eddie, get out."

I ran out of the room.

Chapter 14

Girls & Gangs

In my sixth-grade year, I attended Fernwood Middle School.

"You're gonna get initiated," Javel teased me.

"What's that?" I kicked a rock as we walked to the front door of the white house. Javel thought he knew everything. Actually, he usually did. I decided I'd better listen.

He laughed. "The older kids have a go at the sixth graders. And they charge them for using the elevator."

I laughed along with him. I wasn't scared of any older kids.

We made some changes in my class. The popular sixth graders decided they were going to initiate the seventh and eighth graders instead. We walked around in big groups for protection, and whenever we saw eighth graders, we would jump on them. They tried to fight back at first—but that was useless. Eventually, the seventh and eighth graders had to roam in protective groups, as well. We had the numbers because as we walked down the hall, we literally recruited every sixth grader we found. The upperclassmen tended to roam around only in groups of friends.

It became quite fun to beat up the seventh and eighth graders with a huge group for backup. But danger arose when we walked around without our group. If we got caught, they'd beat us up. Once, we caught two eighth graders on the back stairway, and six of us jumped on them.

"Take that!" My face heated up as we punched all we could for at least twenty seconds. We then took off, running and laughing.

Once the dust settled from the "welcome to school" initiations, the sixth graders still stayed ahead. A new tradition, indeed.

A couple of friends came with me to middle school from Laurelhurst, but it was very different from elementary school—a lot more students, for one thing. And we had different class periods, instead of one class all day.

Popularity dodged me. It may have been that my clothes were out of style, mostly hand-me-downs—or perhaps I just had a hard time fitting in. "What's up, Booyah? Fly got your tongue?" I nodded at a pretty girl who stayed unusually quiet in my math class. I tried to fit in by trying to be funny or cool, but that usually resulted in just more notice of my clothes and shoes.

"Yo, Noob. Got some new hand-me-downs from dumpster diving?" They made fun of me all the time.

Yeah. For the most part, I was unpopular. Even so, I managed to entice a couple of girlfriends. Bada-bing. Rita, the first girl I dated in middle school, came from a different elementary school. She was so pretty, I started sweating every time I saw her. One day, on the walk home, I noted that she walked across the street from me.

"I'll just follow and see where she lives." I stayed back about a block so she wouldn't know. But I noticed that she kept looking back at me every time she crossed a street. I decided to abandon my plan.

About a month or so later, Rita and I started talking a lot. "Hey, Rita. Wanna hang out after school?" I started with the best opening line ever. We started dating shortly after.

"Man, she used to date Popeye," I started hearing from several people. Why did that matter?

"Whatever." I knew Popeye was popular, but who cared?

Rita and I dated for a couple of weeks—the usual amount of time for a middle school relationship. I visited her house after school and hung out with her and her little brother.

Once, she turned to me with her eyes flashing. "Eddie, did you follow me home once from school?"

"Oh, that? Chillax. I was trying to find a friend's house."

In sixth grade in Portland, Oregon, students attend outdoor school. Half of the sixth-grade class camped for a week to learn survival skills, bonding, whatever. Several schools and camps participated.

I attended Camp Howard and stayed in Bear Cabin. We received a little branch round necklace with our name and cabin animal. It looked like a little thin tree round. Throughout the week, one earned little stickers and beads to put on our necklaces.

Every day, our cabin hiked to different learning stations in the woods. "At this station, we'll learn about topsoil and the different types of dirt," a teacher announced while I elbowed the kid next to me and rolled my eyes. I was trying to get him to walk off with me, but he stubbornly shook his head. Suck-up.

At the next station, we learned about predators and prey, which was much more interesting. I pictured my class as the predators and the seventh and eighth graders as prey. That was about right.

Then came a stop to learn about plants and water.

At night, our reward came in the form of a huge bonfire. We sang songs and played little games before bed. On the last day, the camp held a huge competition with a bunch of events. The winners of each event received prizes and recognition at the bonfire.

I'd worked hard at the archery range and ended up pulling second place. My cheeks warmed at the same time I jumped up to get my prize.

The craziest thing about outdoor school was that while we were getting on the bus to go home, a lot of kids cried. The biggest surprise was that it was mostly the popular and tough kids.

***

Addison from Laurelhurst became my second girlfriend. We'd been in Mrs. Kessler's fifth-grade class together. We didn't talk much there, but in middle school, we started talking more.

"Gotta go." I pushed past my classmates to head to the hallway so I'd have time to find her and chat. Major crush.

"You wanna go out sometime? I finally asked. I crammed my hands into my hoodie pocket.

"Sure, Eddie."

I visited Addison's house after school and hung out. Addison lived in some apartments her mother managed. She and her mom struggled with their relationship, according to Addison. "My mom's always yelling about something. I can't do anything right." She figured if we stood by the dumpster, we'd remain unseen. We spent most of our time near the stinky trash dumpster, whether we were kissing or talking.

"Let's go to the movies." Addison flipped her hair over her shoulder. "I want to see *In the Army Now*. Pauly Shore is in it."

Dang. I crammed my hands in my empty pockets. Of course, girls wanted to do more than make out by a dumpster. And I needed a fast plan to get some change. "OK. Tonight. I gotta head home for a bit."

I decided to take some of the toys that Mamma Ana gave us for Christmas and return them to the store for money. I took several toys but returned only a toy gun for $5.35. "Lorenzo, you gotta help me out. Go return another of our guns." I hovered outside the store and sent him back in.

Now I had enough money. But the movie would soon start. Lorenzo and I ran to the bus right after the store and headed to the movie theater. He was going to hang out at the Tilt, an arcade next to the theater.

We rushed into the theater lobby. The movie had already started. I piled all my change from my ticket into Lorenzo's hand—only a couple of bucks remained for him to play.

I rushed in, finally seeing Addison toward the front with a friend. She stood and motioned me over. My knees felt weak as I slunk over to the chairs. I'd never been to the movies with a girl before. I sat down on Addison's right.

"Hi." She whispered and handed me the popcorn.

"That's OK." I pushed it back, too nervous to eat. I intently watched, not daring to look at Addison. As soon as it was over, I left to find Lorenzo.

In the back of the arcade, Lorenzo stood with his hands in his pocket, watching people play games. I hung out for a bit, and we caught the bus home.

Addison and I hung out a few more times at her house. We dated for about three weeks before I heard the inevitable, "Eddie, this isn't working out."

But we'd barely dated! I shuffled away without argument but felt miffed.

"Hey, Eddie, Addison's dating someone else," Javel informed me a few days later. He laughed. He headed into his room with his friends, but not before I saw him entertain his friends from the doorway. "Eddie got dropped like this." He pulled a pen out and dropped it to the floor.

Of course, they laughed and laughed.

***

Halfway through my sixth-grade year, the school went crazy. The popular kids began representing Eastside and the others, Westside. It started off with only the popular kids but soon spread. One of the groups started jumping anyone who claimed to be on the opposite side. Then, it evolved to kids walking down the hall in groups and asking other kids what side they were from. This went on for a couple of days.

Eastside started with a lot more people, so Westside started recruiting. And they found me. "Have you beat anyone up?"

I tried not to laugh. Had I? "My brother," I answered finally.

"OK, you're in."

I joined, and recruitment continued. We managed to get a lot of people in a short time.

The following Monday, a huge fight broke out in the parking lot of the grocery store across the street from the school. I arrived just as the crowd was dispersing.

The next day, on my way to school, I shoved my hands into my coat pockets. To my surprise, my fingers brushed three or four little pocketknives. Oh yeah, I remembered cramming them in there a couple of weeks ago. It was too late for me to return home—I'd have to keep them in my pocket for the day. At school, I showed them off to a couple of kids. "Can I hold it?" Jeremiah held his hand out as I plopped it in his palm.

In the next period, I showed some other kids. "Let me see." Another kid I didn't know asked as he grinned. I passed it over.

Next was the Basics class. Amy sat beside me and kept talking. "Shut up, already. Geez." I took out a knife and flashed it at her. Amy recoiled like she'd been bit.

Later that class period, after a break, my teacher called me out into the hall. "What's this I hear about a knife?"

"Knife? What knife?" My mind flashed back to a little book I'd once written and drawn in.

"You flashed a knife at Amy."

"I did?"

She glared at me, and I finally confessed. "OK, yeah, I got a knife." I pulled out a white-handled one and gave it to her.

Then she looked puzzled. "How many knives do you have, Eddie?

"Huh?"

"She said she saw you pull one out in the hallway that was red. Then she saw another one later in class. How many do you have?"

I shrugged, grinning. She glared at me again, and I sobered up. "Three? Four? I don't have the others on me."

"Where are they, Eddie?"

We visited class after class to recover the other knives. The people who originally held them passed them on elsewhere. After about an hour and a half, we located all of them. Then, the office sent me to visit the school counselor. "What's up, Eddie?" The counselor looked at me a bit sternly through his large glasses.

"I forgot I had knives in my pocket, Mr. Walters."

"I see. Well, why did you pass them out to other students when you found them?"

I huffed. "I didn't mean to. They kept asking to hold them. I showed one, and then the others wanted to see them, too. I wasn't the one passing them out all over the place."

"I believe you." Mr. Walters crossed his hands on his desk. "But we have to suspend you since the knives got out to others."

"Fine." He called Mom, and she told him I could walk home. Fine by me—now I'd be free for a few days.

After my suspension ended and I returned to school, I heard rumors and loud whispers. The kids thought I'd brought the knives to slash on the Eastside kids. I shrugged and puffed up in pride.

***

With seven kids, Mom struggled to keep us in line. She developed a wide range of punishments. First was "Old Reliable"—

when she hit with whatever was close. This included shoes, remote controllers, and her lighter—or anything else accessible. She also sent us to the corner of a room. We stood with our noses in the corner for a half hour with "The Corner Punishment."

If these punishments didn't work, she developed more tricks. One I particularly hated was "Using Hector." My mom sent Hector to beat our butts. Hector had little time in his schedule, so if he had to stop whatever he was doing because Mom said to beat one of us, his temper came right along with him. He'd continue until Mom called him off. Because he was four years older than me, the hitting seemed especially hard.

If Mom was really upset with us, she'd wake up at about seven in the morning on a Saturday. She quietly made coffee and smoked a cigarette. When ready, she walked over to the stereo system to start her "Spanish Music Punishment"—very loudly. She'd go around to each room. "Get up. Hurry up. Time to get up." We'd then get an assignment, and if anyone complained about getting up early or about cleaning, she found worse duties. The whole house shone afterward.

Her relentless tactics made me tired and frustrated.

"Dishes are done, Mom."

"About time. Now you can get a bucket of soapy water and wash the walls."

"Aw, come on . . ."

"Don't complain to me. Want a beating? Bathroom's next."

Once, she checked my work and made me do it all over again. When Jesse cleaned the floor, she poured Dawn liquid dish soap all over it and added water afterward. "It's not clean 'til the soap is gone." She pointed her cigarette at his face. This happened to each of us at one point. Anytime she chose the "Dawn Soap Treatment," it took a very long time to get all the soap out.

On very rare occasions, Mom reverted to some of Tony's methods – like making us kneel on raw rice. It took several minutes afterward to pick all the grains out of our knees.

The summer between my sixth and seventh grade, Aiden and I developed a great idea. We'd noticed that customers bought fireworks from the stand outside the grocery store and then entered the store with their bags. We decided to fill our bags with the fireworks from inside the store instead.

"Great idea." Javel gave some rarely heard praise.

It worked like a charm, and before we knew it, we'd stashed more fireworks than we knew what to do with—several bags, in fact. We rode our bikes behind our school to light some off. With the huge, paved parking lot, the risk of fire remained low.

We arrived at the middle school at about dusk. Some teenagers stood around, already setting off fireworks. We went to the opposite side of the lot. The teenagers lit flowers and threw them in the air. One lit one, and another tossed it in our direction, but it fell short. Another one lit a second flower—it got a lot closer. Javel grinned, and I smiled, too. We knew exactly what to do.

We returned fire. Those teenagers had no idea of the amount of fireworks we'd stolen. It soon became a war zone.

Javel launched one that landed on one of their heads. "Ouch!" The boy cried and started jumping up and down, his hands tearing at his own head. He got help, and they finally removed it. "Who did that?" He ran over, and the others followed, screaming and cursing. His hair stank. "What the heck!"

We pushed and shoved them back and eventually wore them down. They cursed at us and left.

With our fireworks supply at a low, Aiden and I decided to replenish it. We rode to the store with our empty bags. I pulled over, hopped off Miguel's bike, and leaned it against one of the pillars in front of the store. We ran in, filled our bags, and headed out.

But Miguel's bike no longer leaned on the pillar. It was gone! My heart fell to my feet as my knees started shaking. A weird taste rose in my throat as I frantically searched the parking lot to no avail. I walked home, trying not to think about what awaited me there.

Early the next morning, Miguel apparently noticed that his bike was missing. He told Mom.

"Eddie! Where the heck is Miguel's bike?"

I sat on the stairs. "Mom, it got stolen last night. I don't know how."

She stomped over and slapped me across the face. "Why the heck didn't you mention this last night?"

Tears rolled down my cheeks. "I don't know."

"Go get Miguel's bike, and don't come home without it!"

I left and walked toward Grant Park. I hung out at the park for about an hour, swinging on the swing and watching the joggers and dog owners go by. It was now about nine o'clock in the morning, and I figured Aiden might be up and willing to help me find the bike. I walked over to his house and knocked on his door. Jack, Aiden's older brother, answered the door. "Is Aiden home?"

"No, he went with Mom somewhere. What's the matter?"

"I got Miguel's bike stolen. I can't go home without finding it."

"Ah, man. OK, I'll help."

He and I walked all over the neighborhood, looking for the bike. We walked to two stores, the school, and anywhere else we thought of. After about an hour and a half of searching, John spotted a high school baseball game in progress and suggested we take a break and watch the game.

"I don't want to stop. I gotta find it." Oh well, I'd go on without him after we checked here. I followed Jack to the baseball diamond on the other side of the park from us. As we approached, I saw a lot of people watching the game.

"Eddie. Look over there." Jack pointed to a bike leaning against a fence. It looked just like Miguel's, only with the stickers stripped off. Jack grinned, walked over, grabbed it, and started wheeling it away.

I fist-bumped the air, relief pumping through my whole body. I followed Jack. As we walked, I realized that it was only about eleven in the morning. Since I wasn't allowed to come home without the bike, I'd gained all day to play. Mom would never know.

But what to do? I listed out several things in my head as I grinned.

"Hey, kids!" We turned around. Two men caught up with us, and one grabbed a handlebar.

"What the heck do you think you're doing?"

Jack grabbed the other handle. "Hey man, his bike got stolen, and this one looks just like it, except it had stickers."

"That bike belongs to my son," one man growled at us. "Come with us."

We walked back to the park with the bike, and someone called the police. They showed up and put us in the back of a patrol car while they talked to one of the men. The officer opened the door and slid his bulk into the driver's seat. "I'm taking you home now."

I turned my head toward the window. I knew a beating awaited me for sure.

We dropped Jack off, and I waited, locked in the car. Then we headed to my house while piles of dread collected in my stomach.

"Eddie took a bike that wasn't his." The officer nodded at Mom after she opened the door.

"Hery Acosta! Thank you, officer, for bringing him home."

As soon as he left, Mom beat me from the door all the way up into my room with her shoe. "Hector will beat your ass when he gets home!" She slammed the door, leaving me inside.

Great.

Chapter 15

The Refugees

Mom threw a party almost every month right after she received her welfare check, making a huge meal and inviting a bunch of friends over on a Friday night. Mom and Mamma Ana, the perfect hostesses, provided fun for all, even while dancing to salsa music and drinking Budweiser.

During these parties, we got away with murder. We watched bad movies. We stayed out as late as we wanted. We waited for Mom to get drunk, then asked for things, and she usually declined us. But because she was drunk, that changed. We'd ask for money, permission to stay at friends' houses, anything she would usually say no to.

Every now and again, a new group of Spanish refugees arrived in Portland. Every time Mom and Mamma Ana heard the news, they'd throw a party and invite the new arrivals over. When they came, Mom started showing off. She raved about the house, the country, and the way things were done compared to back home. "Do you know anything about my family in Cuba?" she often asked, explaining where they lived and what they looked like. Although the refugees always seemed impressed with Mom, few knew anything about her family.

On one occasion, a new group of Cubans arrived, and Mom and Mamma Ana took us to their apartment for a party. There wasn't much for us to do in the small apartment, especially when the adults were drinking beer and smoking cigarettes. We stayed outside in the dark and played Hide-and-Go-Seek in the parking lot. While playing, I ran from Jesse and straight into a rock, hurting the shin on my right leg. I hopped up and down, swearing.

A month later, I realized that my leg was getting redder and swelling more. "Every day, it's bigger," I complained to Jesse. "The bigger it gets, the more it hurts." I finally showed Mom, and she took me to the hospital the very next day.

"Your son's leg is very infected." The nurse made notes on a computer and reached over to adjust the blanket on the bed.

The doctor entered the room with a scalpel. I cringed. He numbed my leg and cut a little opening on it. As soon as the scalpel pierced the skin, a stream of puss shot out of my leg and landed on the bed. Mom visibly gagged as I now watched in fascination. The doctor took off his gloves and left, and the nurse squeezed out as much as she could before he returned with a pair of tweezers and a long roll of what looked like a shoestring. He started feeding the shoestring-looking dressing into the hole made by the scalpel. "We need to fill up the area where the puss was," he explained and patted me on the shoulder. He glanced over his shoulder at Mom. "Any longer, and we might have needed to amputate."

I stayed home for about three weeks with my leg elevated and taking medicine. I returned to get my leg cleaned, and the dressing replaced several times. To change the dressing, they tore off the old stuff and shoved a new dressing back underneath my skin with tweezers.

I figured I'd ask to stay home if any other parties happened at the refugees' apartments.

***

Hector stopped by for a couple of days, and he and Mom argued. She kicked him out of the house. "Don't open the door to him!" She stomped out of the room. A little while later, we saw Hector climbing in through a window. He rekindled the argument with Mom, and she kicked him out again.

"Who let him in?" She stood, hand on her hips, and surveyed us with a critical eye.

My feet were rooted to the floor as I looked around at the siblings.

"Me," Javel puffed up and shuffled his feet.

Mom smiled. "Well then, you're going with him. And if anyone else lets them in, you'll go to!" She stomped off.

About a week or so later, Hector returned. He stayed for a couple of days as if nothing had ever happened before leaving again. Then Javel showed up. When Javel also returned, Mom gritted her teeth. "*You* are not allowed here!" She pointed to the door, and he slunk out—only a few months" shy of his fourteenth birthday.

***

One day, Mom received a phone call about midday, and as soon as she got on the phone, she hopped up and down, smiling. After chatting for more than an hour, she hung up and hurried to me. "That was your father. He lives down in Florida. He's going to call back tomorrow to speak to all of us."

My mom always reminded Lorenzo, Jannet, Jesse, and me that we had a father different from Hector and Javel. "Their dad is Roberto, and yours is named José. José's a huge drug dealer who had to move away. The FBI is trying to find him. But there was a court case where he denied that he had you because he was married to someone else."

"I don't get it," I often mumbled. It seemed like just excuses as to why José never saw us. And how could our "real dad" do that to us anyway?

The next day, José called and talked to Mom again. "Hery! It's your turn."

I shuffled into the living room and took the corded phone she handed to me. She walked away as butterflies circled my stomach. Now what? "Hello," I finally said hesitantly.

"Hey, how are you doing?"

"Fine."

"How's school?"

"Fine."

"You having fun with your brothers and sisters?"

"Sure."

The silence grew thick. Mom hovered at the edge of the room.

"OK," José sighed. "Put your mom back on. I'll talk to you later."

She hurried over, and I handed her the phone. I practically ran out of the room.

This was only one conversation out of the few that happened over the next couple of months—all uncomfortable.

***

After Javel and Hector were kicked out, I became the oldest in the house, which meant that I oversaw my younger siblings. Many added responsibilities landed on my shoulders. I watched all the kids when the adults went out. Another responsibility was to make sure that my siblings did as they were told. I became an authority figure overnight. Shortly after my move into power, I also got my own room for the first time.

On the morning of my thirteenth birthday, Mom gently nudged me awake. "Hery, wake up. Hery." I opened my eyes. She knelt next to my bed, whispering. "Wake up, you're not going to school today."

I was half asleep until I heard that pronouncement. "Why?"

"You're going with me for the day. Get dressed." She left.

I dressed quickly and ran downstairs. I thought it was odd that I was the only one up and going. It must have something to do with my birthday. We headed out the door and walked down to the bus stop on the corner.

We rode the bus to 122nd in Portland, then walked up to some apartments. Mom headed up some stairs, and I followed quietly. She knocked on a door. What was happening? Where were we?

A man opened the door, and I recognized him. Jaime—one of the new Cubans who we visited at Mamma Anna's house a few weeks earlier.

"Hi. Come on in." He opened the door. Mom moved into the kitchen and started pulling food out of the refrigerator. She turned on the stove. I hovered by the kitchen doorway, very confused. My eyes about popped out of my head, and Jaime walked up behind Mom and put his arms around her waist. He kissed her on the side of the neck. Yuck. Mom was cheating on Miguel.

Later that day at home, I decided on a birthday present for myself. My heart stung each time I thought about Mom and Jaime. I grabbed the ice tray from the freezer, a sewing needle, and the bottle of rubbing alcohol and took everything to my room. I held two cubes of ice to my left ear, one on the front and one on the back. It didn't take long to completely numb my ear. I found a gold loop earring and swished it around in a cap of rubbing alcohol.

Methodically, I dug around for a lighter, flicked it on, and held it to the tip of the sewing needle until it turned red. After it cooled, I stood in front of my bedroom mirror and shoved the needle through my left earlobe. "Ouch! Gosh darn!" I hopped around my room with the needle still in my ear. So much for numbing first!

After calming down, I pulled the needle out and inserted the loop. I stood in the mirror with my new addition hanging from a beet-red earlobe.

***

A few weeks after I turned thirteen, Mom and Miguel fought. Miguel left for a couple of days. While he was gone, Mom moved Jaime into the house. We were OK with that because we'd learned that Jaime gravitated towards leniency—we could pretty much do whatever we wanted. The adults were too busy partying and didn't care. In fact, the house partied hard almost every night after the switch. During one of these parties, Miguel returned.

I walked out of the front door onto the front porch and found Mom and Jaime talking to Miguel, who was standing on the sidewalk.

"Are you taking responsibility for Estrella and the house?" Miguel's eyes narrowed at Jaime.

"Yes."

Miguel shuffled his feet. "I need my stuff," he mumbled. After he collected his belongings, he left. That was the last time I saw him.

Neither Jaime nor Mom worked, and they soon were scouring for a new home. One night, Mom had a visitor. Felipe, a friend from Cuba.

"Hey Estrella! I live in Kent, Washington now. A nice complex called Willow Brooks. How about I contact the manager? I know him well. Maybe they can get you in."

I saw her nodding. "See what you can do, Felipe. Thanks."

He left, and a couple of days later, he called Mom. When she hung up, she found us. "We have an apartment that will be ready in the next few weeks. We're supposed to be out of here before then, though, so gotta figure that out." She left the room and slammed her bedroom door.

Chapter 16

Kent

As we loaded our belongings into a U-Haul truck, I thought about all the good times in this neighborhood. After two years of living here, I realized that this was the longest I'd lived in one place ever. After we finished loading, I gave the house a final look.

"Get in the car!" Mom stood next to me. "Hurry it up. Time to go."

"You don't have to yell, Mom. Geez."

We piled into different cars. I wound up in the U-Haul with Jaime and one of his friends who came to help drive.

We pulled away from the house and drove to the corner. Mom got out of the car she was in and hurried up to the U-Haul. "We're stopping at the store to get something to eat." She ran back to her vehicle, and off we went.

Our caravan was parked on the outskirts of the store's parking lot. Mom and Jaime bought a bunch of jojos (potato wedges) and chicken strips from the deli. We ate in the parking lot. Once we finished, we piled back into the cars and hopped onto the highway that eventually landed us in Washington State.

It took forever. Jaime and his friend did not say more than twenty words the whole trip, making it a very quiet drive. I spent the time gazing out the passenger window. The scenery all looked all the same, but at least I had the window.

Finally, we pulled off the highway and into the town of Kent. We drove around for a few minutes before we pulled into a tan-colored apartment complex called "The Willow Brook Apartments." We drove to Felipe's unit.

"Hey." He greeted us with a big smile. "Good to see you. The apartment's not ready yet."

"Dang." The corner of Mom's mouth turned down.

Hadn't she said we had to be out of the house before the apartment would be ready? One would think the time to plan would have been before the day of arrival. I shrugged. Maybe we'd have to live on the streets. The adults set off to figure out what to do, and we kids took off to explore the apartment complex.

Felipe lived with his wife Tallulah, her daughter Raelynn from a previous marriage, and their three boys, Richardo, Fernando, and the baby Rafael. We kids ended up staying at Felipe's while Mom and Jaime stayed at Hector's apartment. Fortunately, he lived nearby in the apartments bordering the back of Willow Brooks, called The Courts. We loved this arrangement because Felipe allowed Richardo to get a little out of hand. We stayed up all night playing Hide-and-Go-Seek around the complex several nights that week.

Our three-bedroom apartment on the second floor was finally ready about a week later. It was very small compared to the big house. The boys shared the first room, the girls the second, and Mom and Jaime the third. But even with a smaller space, we found adventure.

Since I'd moved near the beginning of seventh grade, I started school as soon as we arrived. In Portland, I'd attended a middle school, but in Washington, the grade system differed. Their junior high schools served the seventh and eighth graders. I enrolled in Kent Junior High, but it was known to everyone as KJH. My first day of school there echoed all the other first days I'd experienced.

"Where are you from?" students asked.

"How do you like Kent?" the teachers wanted to know.

"Where do you live?" the boys lounging against the lockers in the hallway wanted to know. The school set me up with a guide to show me around the campus and to my classes. He was a light-skinned boy with very curly hair and green eyes.

They had special slang at the school. You referred to each other as "guy," and smack talk was "ranking on someone." The day went fast, and before I knew it, I was back in the new apartment with my family.

Because I was never very social, I still didn't make friends easily. I found other things to cover that up. I tried to sit at certain tables at lunch a couple of times and was rejected. So, instead, I walked around the campus while eating. I walked from the cafeteria to all the areas we were allowed in during lunch. It helped greatly with the embarrassment of not fitting in. I struggled to like this school but couldn't wait for the day to end so I could go home. I eventually made a couple of friends.

KJH was where I met one of the most awesome teachers ever—Mr. Aidens. This skinny, white man with short brown hair taught seventh-grade World Studies. Every lesson became fun. When we studied the countries of Africa, we had to memorize all the countries. He split the class into two teams. "Each team shoots a balled-up piece of paper in the wastebasket. If you make it, you get a chance to name the countries in the outline on the chalkboard. The team with the most points gets Tootsie rolls. Let's do it!" Of course, we all learned about the countries of Africa.

One day, while waiting in line for the gym doors to open so we could start PE, a group of students started ranking on each other. Not cool. I crept up behind a kid who was ranked a smaller kid and threw my arm around his neck from behind. He struggled. Onlookers started chanting, "Fight, fight!"

Five seconds later, the gym doors swung open, and the PE teacher stood there with a red face. "Let him go!"

I released him. The teacher pulled the two of us aside and asked what was going on.

"I have no idea." The kid held his hand up to his neck as he hacked. "He just came out of nowhere and started choking me!"

"Why did you do that?"

I shrugged and looked at the floor. "I dunno."

In the main office, they asked more questions. "Did you do that because he was picking on your friend?"

"Nah, I was just playing around. You don't gotta go there."

"Well, this is serious. You could have injured him badly. We are going to need to suspend you from school for two days."

The office staff spent the rest of the day trying to call Mom, but they were unable to get hold of her. I sat in the office the rest of the school day until it was time for me to catch the bus home.

Back at the new apartment home, I enjoyed friends and family. Not like it was at school. Besides Felipe and his kids, I found a new best friend, Jacob. Jacob lived in the complex across from the basketball court with his mom and her boyfriend. Sadly, he attended a different school, so we only hung out after school and on weekends. He loved finding new girls to talk to. We traveled all around our neighborhood trying to find new girls to chat up who were da bomb.

Each day, I'd wait until Jacob arrived home to hang out. I spent the time walking to Lorenzo's school to pick him up from the elementary school. On one of these trips, I saw Lorenzo and his friends talking to a group of cute girls. "Hey, give us your phone numbers." I saw Lorenzo sauntering around like a rooster.

Booyah. A very cute girl instantly stood out. I stopped in my tracks, my face hot. "S'up?" I looked right at her, ignoring my brother. I learned that Christina was a year younger than I was.

We started dating quickly. Because we went to different schools, I didn't really see her very much. We kept in contact through Lorenzo by sending messages and notes back and forth.

After a few weeks of living in Willow Brook, I'd collected a group of friends—Jacob, Lorenzo, and Lorenzo's friend, Tony. Tony, a tall, heavyset black kid, lived at the back of the apartments. Every now and again, Jesus, the neighbor kid, hung out with us as well. The little kids, my brother Jesse, Richardo, Fernando, and Rafael, followed us around.

About five apartment complexes bordered ours. A chain-link fence separated the buildings, which we jumped to get from complex to complex. We wandered around looking for girls to talk to or to find something to get into. There were always a few kids we didn't know who stared at us. We made it a point to talk a little crap when we walked by.

One of our favorite stops was McDonald's, where Hector and his fiancé, Maria, worked. We strolled to the counter and ordered one of the cheapest things on the menu. Hector or Maria gave us other people's meals along with it.

Another stop became Kmart, where we stole things. If it was Halloween, we stole candy and costumes. We took whatever we wanted or needed. Eventually, as we got comfortable, we stole larger and more expensive items. Our final stop on most days was the grocery store. We stole candy mostly, like boxes of Andes mints.

A routine developed as we headed home. We ate our candy on the steps of a certain apartment complex. We talked smack and ranked on people as we pigged out on stolen goods. Once done, we played a game that I've heard called Ding-Dong Ditch. The game included knocking loudly at someone's door and running off before the person opened the door. Way too easy—and hilarious.

This complex included two very long hallways—one on the first floor and another on the second. As soon as the last of us finished our candy, we booked down the hall, knocking on the doors. The first few times, the doors opened behind us, and people yelled. We eventually stopped this game because, after a few times of doing this with doors so close together, the doors started opening before we even knocked.

***

I'd managed a couple of girlfriends in middle school while I lived in Portland, but after moving to Kent, I went girl crazy. I didn't get a lot of time to see Christina—only after she got out of school for a few minutes. With her overprotective parents, we sneaked around on the way home from school. Christina's best friend, Rosa, lived on the other side of my building. Christina and I sent messages through Rosa so Christina's parents would not be aware. They felt she was too young to date.

At school, a heavyset girl in my class named Hillary crushed on me big time, but I dissed her as much as possible. One day, Hillary swayed over to me. "Hey, Eddie. You should meet my friend. She's super cute. You should get dibs."

After about a week of hearing about Hillary's friend, I decided to meet her. "OK. I'll come over."

When I reached Hillary's apartment, I met Ashley. We hit it off instantly. Ashley was a very attractive, blond-haired, white girl, also thirteen. We hung out for a few hours and, over the next few days, spent a lot of time conversing on the phone. At that time, we started dating—I now dated two girls at a time. Luckily, Christina and Ashley lived on opposite sides of Kent.

They'd never know. Right?

I spent a lot of time with Ashley. I caught the city bus as far as it took me toward her house, then walked uphill to her apartment. Ashley lived with her mom and her mom's boyfriend.

Lorenzo started joining me after a little while. Ashley, Lorenzo, Hillary, and I spent a lot of time hanging out at Ashley's house. Ashley smoked, the only one in our group who did. "Come outside with me, Eddie." She beckoned with her finger when she headed outside. I followed along.

"What's the deal with smoking?" I asked her one day after following her multiple times.

"I don't know; I just like it."

One day, while out with Ashley on one of her smoke breaks, I asked her for one. I didn't get why it was special, but I decided to join her.

***

I stood outside Rosa's window since she was restricted to her room for some shenanigan. "I'm thinking about getting Christina chocolates for Valentine's Day. What do ya think?"

I heard my name and jumped, turning around. Oh boy. Here came Hillary and Ashley! Walking right next to her! Hillary waved. My stomach churned. What the heck were they doing here? My breath hitched in my throat. "I gotta go," I hissed at Rosa and jogged toward Hillary and Ashley. When I got there, I breathed heavily. "Hey! Good to see you. Where are you headed?"

Hillary looked at me funny. I walked them to the bus stop and kissed Ashley goodbye before she boarded. I walked back to the apartment with a much lighter step, relief pouring over me. Rosa hadn't seen Ashley. Ashley didn't suspect anything. I was off the hook.

I started smoking regularly with Jacob. His mom smoked GPCs, and mine smoked Marlboro Reds. We stole cigarettes from both our moms—until they woke up.

"I know what you're doing, Hery," Mom sneered.

"My mom caught me too," Jacob informed me later.

Time for a new source. We started scouting out stores to steal from.

I really hated going to a school different from Jacob's. But a routine developed. I hopped off the bus and walked up to the elementary school to meet Lorenzo and to see Christina—always the longest walk ever. Each block equaled three Portland city blocks. I entered the school grounds just as school let out each time.

"S'up?" I punched Lorenzo and Tony on the shoulders or back, then kissed Christina quickly. She always needed to head home. After she left, Lorenzo, Tony, and I headed home and waited for Jacob.

One day, I walked to the elementary school like always. But when I got there, something seemed off. Lorenzo and Tony walked up to me. Tension crackled. "Hey man, Christina's gonna break up with you." Lorenzo shifted his backpack. "She likes someone else now."

"Who?"

He shrugged. "Dunno."

Later, I learned Christina's new love was Lorenzo. They'd kissed the day before we broke up. I didn't care much. Not that much, anyway.

***

One day, as I was hanging out at Hector's apartment, he noticed a rectangular lump in my pocket. "Come over here." He pulled the cigarette pack out of my pocket. "Where'd this come from?"

"My friend and I lift them from the store, man."

"If you steal me a couple packs of cigarettes, I won't tell Mommy."

"OK."

I walked to the closest convenience store. The Marlboro Reds, Hector's favorite, sat next to the cash register. When the clerk turned his back, I grabbed two packs and shoved them in my pocket. I walked around the store, bought a piece of candy, and left. I returned to Hector's with the goods, paying for his silence.

About a week later, Mom called me in from outside. "Empty your pockets, Hery."

"Nothing there," I murmured, pulling my pockets out.

"So, it's true what Hector said. You have tobacco pieces in your pocket. You're smoking! Shame on you!"

My heart jumped in my chest. I swallowed hard. A beating surely was next on her list. But she paused and stared at me for a few seconds. "Go back outside." She turned her back to me.

I walked out of the apartment, trying to figure out why I still lived. After mentally going over the details for about twenty minutes, I remembered Hector. "That SOB." He'd betrayed me.

I ran to Felipe's, looking for my brother. Hector was absent. I ran to his apartment, but he wasn't there either. Fine. I'd wait on his doorstep. When Hector finally returned, I confronted him. "Yeah, I told. But I made her promise not to punish you. Did you get in trouble?"

"No."

"OK then."

Dang. He was still a SOB.

***

Lorenzo, Jacob, Tim, and I entered stores and usually headed straight to the candy aisle. We got away with stealing so much that we decided to up the ante. We started to steal bigger things. We even started competing. We reserved different stores for different things. If we wanted candy, we'd hit the grocery store. If we had shoes or seasonal items, we'd walk or bike to Kmart. On Valentine's Day, I wandered in and stole two candy hearts for my girlfriends. Clothes also meant Kmart. I'd head to the dressing room and put a new outfit on under my street clothes. I even "returned" clothes that I'd never actually purchased. They didn't require a receipt like they do these days.

Whenever my shoes wore out, I'd hit Kmart. I'd place my old pair in the new shoebox, wear the new ones, and return the box to the shelf, making sure the coast was clear. I strolled out of the store with no one the wiser.

Now, it was time to change it up. I wanted a pellet gun. Lorenzo distracted the sales clerk while I walked behind the counter, slid the glass door open, and grabbed one. I found an empty aisle where I ripped open the plastic package. I pulled the gun out of the package and slid it into the waist of my jeans. I jammed the package to the back of the shelf, double-checked to make sure I didn't leave anything behind and ambled out of the store.

Our thefts got so bad that we couldn't go past a store without stealing something. We started boasting. "We can get whatever you need." Jacob bragged to Lisa and Lianna, two sisters who lived in our complex. The girls radiated skepticism, so to prove ourselves, we walked to the grocery store for candy. We wore backpacks, and I elbowed Jacob, puffing up like a peacock when we entered with the girls. I headed straight to the candy aisle, and they followed. We started shoving candy wherever we could fit it. I filled my backpack. We started for the door. But as we got close to the exit, a shadow loomed over my right shoulder, and someone grabbed my backpack. I screeched to a stop and turned to see two security officers.

They ushered us all to a little room in the back of the store. They searched everybody and placed all the candy on the table. They called the police.

Once the police came, they threatened to take us to jail. I shut up but seethed inside.

"Whatever." Jacob scoffed. "They trippin'."

The girls looked scared. Lisa started crying.

They took our pictures. "You aren't allowed on the property ever again." They questioned us about where we lived and who our parents were.

"I don't know the name of the apartments," I lied. Jacob nodded eagerly.

The police knew we were lying but couldn't break our resistance. "Your parents' phone numbers?" one asked. He looked bored and put his hands behind his head as he leaned back in a chair that squeaked like it was injured. He already seemed sick of this stupid game. I agreed.

"We don't get no phone," Jacob claimed.

"Yeah, we don't either." I stared at them defiantly.

Lisa and Lianna played along about the apartment complex, but they shared their parents' phone number for a ride home. Jacob and I stayed for another hour while they tried to figure out what to do with us. They finally just released us. Jacob and I walked the craziest route home, just in case the police decided to follow us to get to our parents.

***

One night, I hung out at Hector and Maria's apartment, talking to Maria in the kitchen while she washed dishes. Bored, I then went to find my brother. Hector lay on their bed with his pipe. "What are you doing?"

"I'm about to smoke some Chronic."

I didn't know anything about marijuana, but I did remember a classmate of mine back at Fernwood Middle School saying that Chronic was garbage. "Chronic is garbage."

"Oh yeah?" Hector puffed two tokes off the pipe and handed it to me. "Put this end to your mouth. I'll light it and then just inhale like a cigarette. Hold it in as long as you can." I followed his directions.

Maria walked into the room, took one look at me, and glared at Hector. "I know you aren't getting Eddie high."

"No." Hector yanked the pipe from me. Maria left the room.

About fifteen minutes later, I started feeling strange. I suddenly started laughing at everything. Hector laughed at me.

Maria marched back into the room. She stood there, looking at me for a while, and turned to Hector. "Why did you get Eddie high? I'm not taking the heat from your mom when she finds out."

"You OK, Eddie?" Hector grinned at me. I laughed at him. He was funny-looking.

"You better spend the night, bro."

***

I hung out with Ashley a lot after school at her apartment. Hillary, Lorenzo, and I all spent time at Ashley's apartment. Lorenzo and Hillary started dating, and he was done with Christina. We spent all our time either at Ashley's or at the little play structure, where we smoked and talked.

On the fifth visit to Ashley's, we hit the park and smoked when a black kid walked by and stared at our group. "OMG, that's him." Hillary looked frantically at Ashley.

"What's the deal?" I snubbed a cigarette out on the slide.

"Her ex. They broke up a week before you met her." Ashley scooted a little closer to me.

The kid walked back and forth a few more times before Ashley and Hillary started yelling at him. "Get away from us, you stalker! She doesn't like you." Ashley announced loudly.

He walked by again, looking sad.

He wouldn't go away. Maybe he wanted to talk? So Ashley and Hillary followed him through the hole in the fence. Lorenzo and I shrugged and followed, also climbing through the fence. As we popped out on the other side, I screeched to a stop. A whole lot of people walked toward us.

The kid swung around toward me. "What are you doing here?" he practically hissed.

I straightened my shoulders. "Here with my girl."

He leaned toward my face. "Any issues with my cousin, you gotta deal with me."

"Hey man, I'm just visiting my girlfriend. I don't even know who your cousin is, dude."

He reminded me not to mess with his cousin again before he left, and the crowd followed.

Weird.

We climbed back through the fence and toward Ashley's apartment. Once we got there, Ashley said to her mom. "See, Mom, Eddie's smart. He said that he wasn't going to get involved."

Ashley's mom gave me a weird look. "Smart, is he?"

After that day, we saw Ashley's ex every now and again, but we never talked about it.

Ashley and I often talked about intimacy. She bragged about being with two people. I bragged about four girls in my history. The facts? We were both virgins. As a thirteen-year-old boy, it was very important to keep up the lies. It seemed just as important for Ashley to do the same.

One day, Ashley's mom and boyfriend left, leaving Ashley and me alone at her place. We started making out. Before we knew it, our lies got us into a situation. We were to the point where a couple would usually start removing clothes and move forward. But we became very nervous. In fact, sweat dripped down my back as her eyes kept darting back and forth. We both stopped.

"Do you really want to do this?" I asked her, hoping she'd say no.

"Maybe next time would be better because I'm not sure when my mom and her boyfriend will come back."

I drew a big breath of relief and left shortly after. I ended up missing the bus to my apartment and walked home.

The next day, I called Ashley. It turned out that her mom and her boyfriend arrived home very late. I could hear Ashley's smile over the phone. "I wished you would have stayed."

Chapter 17

Gangsters Disciples

Ashley and I stopped talking shortly after that incident. We'd dated for about six weeks. Lorenzo and Hillary broke up about a week after we started hanging out.

I started spending more time with Jacob. We walked around the neighborhood looking for girls to talk to. Every now and again, we actually found some and tried to get their phone numbers. But with limited success, we'd then mostly just hang out, talking about the girls we wished we'd met.

Every now and again, Jacob spotted his cousin driving around. His cousin was a member of a gang called "GD." "GD" stands for Gangsters Disciples. Jacob's cousin stopped and gave us rides whenever he saw us. A couple of times, Jacob's cousin parked his nice purple Cadillac in the back of the school and rolled a joint to smoke with us. We flew so high we could barely walk home. Hanging out with Jacob's cousin was the best. We felt all grown up. If not full-grown, then at least almost-grown.

When Jacob and I weren't looking for girls or bugging his cousin, we'd hang out in the apartments with all the kids who lived there. We hung out with Lorenzo and Tim the most because they were closest to our age. Now, our group has become four.

Jacob had dated Lisa before I moved in. She was beautiful and had long red hair. They broke up before I arrived. After the stealing incident, Lisa and Lianna's dad said they were not allowed to spend time with us. After the girls were off restriction, they found us. Jacob was the one who suggested I mess with Lisa. After Lisa and I started dating, Lianna showed some interest in me. When Lisa was on restriction, Lianna flirted. "You should see it. It's ridiculous." I laughed with Jacob.

"You should mess with both of 'em." Jacob raised his eyebrows.

My brain started humming with ideas. This could get hilarious. Lianna, a couple of years older than us, made it seem extra cool. And, she was stacked. So, without much conscience, I spent my time with Lisa when she was not on restriction, but when she wasn't around, I hung out with Lianna. Lianna and I made out a couple of times while Lisa was on restriction. I saw that Lianna didn't treat Lisa well and wondered about it a few times. But I quickly pushed it to the back of my mind when I was busy making out with one of them.

Since the first time I smoked weed with Hector, I'd smoked it a few times with Jacob and his cousin. I was not a big smoker, but as a teenager trying to build a reputation for myself, I pretended otherwise. One day, while leaving school, I saw Lianna outside talking to some guy. I headed over.

"Hey, Eddie, do you want to smoke some weed?"

"Well, yeah. Who wouldn't?"

"OK, come on." Lianna, her friend, and I walked down the street away from the school. We stopped a few blocks away at a field that had a few abandoned railroad carts. We walked to one of them, and Lianna's friend pulled a metal pipe and a baggie out of his backpack. He loaded a bowl into the pipe and handed it to Lianna. She grabbed the pipe in one hand and a lighter in the other. I watched as she put flame to the pipe and inhaled. She immediately started coughing. She handed the pipe to me, and I repeated what she did. After that bowl was gone, Lianna glanced at her watch. "Oh shoot! I gotta get home! See you guys."

I headed back with her, but right before we turned toward our apartment complex, I decided to go to Kmart. "I need shoes." I headed to the door as she continued home. I walked straight to the shoe aisle. On the way there, a queasy feeling welled up. This was new. It's not like I was high at all, but different. The aisle of shoes wavered around me as I headed for the athletic shoes. What the heck?

I quickly switched my old shoes for a new pair. I put the box on the shelf and tried to leave, but dizziness swept over me. I fell, then pulled myself up and headed toward the door. I stumbled and fell again. I was lying in the gosh darn aisle of a stupid Kmart. I could hear everything around me—I just couldn't get up.

No one came to help. I listened to voices and spaced out for quite a while. Finally, I grabbed a shelf to haul myself off the floor and darted out of the store. What the heck was in that weed? I needed to find Lianna's friend and kick his butt.

I saw Lianna the following day. "Hey, the weirdest thing happened at Kmart. You OK? Anything happen to you?"

She shrugged. "I dunno. I went home and went straight to bed."

I never saw Lianna's friend again.

***

Lorenzo, Jacob, Tim, Lianna, and I walked back from the store after stealing cigarettes. We looked for a spot where we could smoke without being caught. "Hey, there's a blackberry bush." I nudged Lianna in the ribs.

I found a large piece of plastic and flattened an area of blackberry bushes to create a tunnel inside the massive bush. Once inside, I flattened out a large area. It became our fort. We brought things to sit on and made makeshift tables out of shopping carts. We had our own little areas in the fort—pretty much made an igloo of blackberry bushes. We hung out there with our stolen goods, sat around on our shopping carts, and fantasized about being gangsters. Jacob and I admired Jacob's cousin for being in a gang. One day, we talked about being gangsters when a light went off in my head. "Let's make our own gang."

"Cool." Tim nodded his head.

"Good idea, Eddie." Jacob stomped his cigarette on the hard dirt under the blackberry fort.

I knew some organization would be necessary. "What do we name it?"

"King Gangstas." A nod to the county we lived in.

"King City Crips."

The ideas flew around. We just had to chuckle about some of the names. "Nah. None of those really fit, guys. Come on. Wait, you know how Jacob's cousin is a gangster's Disciples, or a "GD" for short? That's what we should do. What about that movie *Scarface*? You know, the Tony Montana dude. We could be the Tony Montana Disciples. Or TMD."

"Perfect, man." Jacob nodded like he was all proud of me. And it was decided.

The next day, we started recruiting. In fact, we recruited all the kids in the Willow Brooks apartments. By the end of the day, Jacob, Lorenzo, Tim, and I had recruited 25 to 30 kids from ages six to thirteen. I took leadership, and Jacob was my second in command. Our main job as a gang was to go into stores in groups of ten people and steal as much as we could.

On a sunny afternoon, Lorenzo, Jacob, Tim, and I were smoking and burning ants with a magnifying glass when five or so of the little kids in our gang walked up to us. One cried, and I realized it was Rosa's baby brother. "What's up, buddy?"

"One of the twins punched him," a kid volunteered and shoved his hands in his pockets, his face flushed.

"The Twins" attended school with Lorenzo and Tim, and we were very familiar with them. Two white brothers who lived at the Courts apartments and thought they were gods or some crap like that.

"Well, we're gonna take care of that." I wiggled my shoulders to loosen them, and Lorenzo, Jacob, and I headed out. We jumped the fence to the apartment. I looked back and saw about 15 kids following us. We walked through the court's apartments like a mob. We turned a corner, and I saw the twins playing outside their apartment. I pulled Rosa's little brother near me. "Which one?" I shook his shoulder a bit.

Tears poured down his face as he lifted his arm, trembling. "That one."

"Beat his butt," I nodded at Lorenzo. 'Cuz you know that's what a leader does.

Lorenzo immediately rushed over to the twin on the left and punched him in the chest. The kid stumbled back. Lorenzo hit him two more times before he went down crying. I watched the other twin. Surely, he would jump in to defend his brother. But he never did. The twin on the right just watched while his brother got beat up.

After that, no problems arose with any of the kids from that complex.

"Eddie in the Rough, Forming a Diamond Book 1" by Eddie Acosta.

***

Jacob, Lorenzo, Tim, and I hung out at McDonald's, ordering a soda and getting much-bigger free meals, thanks to Hector and Maria. Then, we headed to play in the ball pit. The signs said we were too big, but we didn't care. And besides, we had relatives who were employees and would stick up for us.

"Hey, jerk-wad." I threw balls at Tim, and the game was on. Everyone was making fun of someone else and throwing balls as hard as we could. But then, Lorenzo and Tim started getting mad and saying hurtful things. Before long, the two wanted to fight. For real.

But as the leader, that decision was up to me. I hesitated. Tim was about my height, and he had about 40 pounds on Lorenzo, who was my brother, after all. After talking it over with Lorenzo and Jacob, I decided to let them go for it. I waved my hand at them, and they tackled each other with gusto.

They were evenly matched. Afterward, neither Lorenzo nor Tim is satisfied and wants to fight again. We went outside, and I let them go at it again. This time around, Lorenzo ended up on top of Tim and punched him hard. Jacob ripped Lorenzo off Tim. "He's the man."

Tim rose up. Somehow, he looked bigger than he had before. "Oh, heck no. He's not even close."

"I-I don't know." Lorenzo clearly hesitated and stood next to me.

"Ah, come on, dude. You got this." I slapped him on the shoulder. Lorenzo squared his shoulders and headed back over to Tim.

The third fight was like the first one. The fight was a tie. I stopped it.

"Hey. What the heck?" Tim yelled. "This is BS. I wasn't even done!"

Lorenzo turned away. When he did, Tim reached around and sucker-punched him in the face.

"Hey!" I jumped forward and punched Tim in the face three times and twice in the chest. "You want more?" I glared at him.

"I'm done." Tim covered his face. Tears leaked through his hands.

"Hey, Eddie. That's enough." Jacob stepped forward and pulled me back. I knew he was trying to calm me down. Did he even see what the guy had done to my brother?

After that, Jacob and I stopped hanging out, and the whole TMD crew kind of drifted apart.

***

About three weeks earlier, my brother Javel had arrived with little fanfare. He wasn't happy with his living arrangement elsewhere. We didn't really hang out at first this time because I had my friends, and he was older. But after the Tim fight, Jacob and I stopped hanging out. So, I followed Javel to Felipe's house. Javel tended to hang out with Hector and Felipe since they were older. Although I always wanted to hang out with them, I'd been told, "Go play with the kids." Javel was the missing link, and I needed to be seen more like an adult. Perfect. I noticed that Felipe and Hector stopped sending me out of the room so much when Javel was around.

Lorenzo made new friends and spent his time at their houses. So, when I wasn't out with Javel, I hung out with Felipe's kids. After a couple of weeks like this, I started hanging out with some Mexican kids from surrounding apartments.

***

One day, I walked into the apartment to see Mom packing up some boxes. "What's up?"

"Pack up your stuff, Eddie." She looked mad.

"What's going on?"

She went back to packing without answering my question. I wandered to my room.

I later found out that Javel had beat up my mom the night before and was arrested. We were headed to a battered women's shelter. But no male over the age of 12 could live there. Javel was fourteen, and his mom had arranged for him to stay with Felipe. Felipe couldn't take me in because he already had a full apartment. Mom talked to the directors of the house, and they made an exception for me to stay.

Chapter 18

Sheltering

The shelter was a big two-story house located out in the middle of nowhere, Seattle. Only the residents of the shelter knew the address. "Stop here, Felipe. Drop us off here." Mom's forehead wrinkled. She had dark circles under her eyes.

He braked. "There's nothing here, Es."

"I know," she hissed. "No one can know where it's at. We'll walk." She turned to him. "Thank you, Felipe." We packed all our stuff on our shoulders, and I was out of breath when we reached the large house three blocks later.

Each family had a bedroom upstairs. The room on the main floor was the staff's office. There was always a staff member on duty at the house.

Two other families lived there with us. A black woman and her son, and the other room was occupied by a white woman and her two kids. The moms talked during smoke breaks and at mealtimes. The kids played together when we could. Other than that, everyone stayed to themselves.

The shelter had a good-sized backyard and a big deck where the moms sat and smoked cigarettes. Down past the deck was a play structure with a couple of swings and a slide. In the backyard, there was also a big building, which could have been a garage at one point. I called it the playhouse. It held toys and games. The playhouse was where the younger kids played when it rained. But I didn't play in the playhouse. I was too old.

I spent most of my time around the staff members. I stood in the doorway of the office, talking to whoever would listen. I only asked about a hundred questions a day. "Tell me about your family. Where did you go to school? Why do you work here?" I scrambled for conversation. Living at a shelter was incredibly boring.

Eventually, one of the staff members would tire of me and send me on an errand to get me out of the office. "Hey Eddie, why don't you write me a short story?" one suggested.

I paused in my conversation as my brain screeched to a halt. A story? "Sure." I shrugged and set off to make it happen. I wrote a little booklet about two lions who were brothers, and one had to fight the other one to save the day—nothing like the little booklet I'd written before. I tacked the booklet to the corkboard that hung on the wall for the other staff members to read.

We weren't allowed to leave except for school. Our moms were only allowed to go to the store. Sometimes, Mom visited the local grocery store, sat in the deli, and watched people shop. She wouldn't buy anything—she was usually broke. We'd sit there for a couple of hours before heading back to the shelter.

It became harder to steal cigarettes from Mom. I decided to return to old habits and steal my own the next time we went to the store. About a week later, we headed out. I walked into the store and scanned the shelves for cigarettes. Next to the checkout, I grabbed a pack while Mom was checking out. I waited until she walked up to the checkout and scanned the area for any lookers.

As I reached out and grabbed a pack of Misty's cigarettes, I felt someone looking at me. I quickly turned away, leaving the pack. Before I could try again, Mom finished checking out.

The next time we went to the store, I recruited Jannet. This time, the plan was to look out for the employees while Jannet slipped the cigarettes into her pocket. It worked! The new plan worked many times.

When I was not bugging the shelter staff members, I tried to sneak a smoke. There was only one spot to do so—behind the playhouse. When the coast was clear, I'd head there for my hidden pleasure. I timed myself—it took me around six minutes to finish a cigarette. I always carried a travel-sized tube of toothpaste with me to cover up the smell afterward. The spot behind the playhouse only worked when it wasn't raining, though, and it had to be daytime as there were no lights back there. The rain put my cigarettes right out. What a waste.

One day, I discovered a second, drier and well-lit place. I completed my shower, and the bathroom was all steamy, so I opened the window. While I waited for the mirror to clear up, I looked out the window and realized that there was a lot of room on the roof. Sure enough, there was an area to sit completely out of sight of all the cars that passed by. I started going to the bathroom, locking the door, turning on the shower, and climbing out the window. I smoked many cigarettes in my new spot.

Again, I was the new kid at school. The questions started again. Where did I move from? Where did I live? But most students ignored me.

I did not like this new school very much. I didn't understand the work because we were doing other types of work at my former school. And, of course, as usual, I struggled to make friends. But I did enjoy PE. When the class completed their track and field segment, I discovered that I excelled at the high jump and the four-person relay. I held the second highest jump in class.

After school, I boarded the bus and rode 45 minutes to get the ten blocks back to the shelter. After about a week of this crap, I decided to start walking. Much better.

"Can you help me with my homework?" I asked staff members each day. Usually, one of them did what they could, so I did learn some, I guess. After I finished my homework, I turned on the shower and smoked on the roof. I was being pretty good these days, I figured, to only be stealing cigarettes and smoking.

Soon, the questions from other students started. "I went to KJH." I set my book down on my desk as I answered dumb questions from the nosy people. "Oh, Mamby is going to like him," some girl practically purred.

"Oh yeah." Someone else agreed with her. "For sure."

"Who's Mamby?" I wrinkled my forehead.

The students all started talking at once.

"She's like you, man," one kid claimed. "And she's loud."

Oh. A black girl. Well, OK.

"Gimme your schedule." A blond guy swooped it off my book. "She's in your next class, dude."

Sure enough, I met her the next period. I was sitting at my desk when I heard a person in the hall talking loudly. "Here comes Mamby." One girl grinned, and heads swiveled to the doorway, mine included.

A short, dark-skinned girl with long, curly hair walked into the room. A kid beside me stated the obvious. "Hey, that's Mamby." Mamby stared at me with a big smile on her face. Her very white teeth stood out next to her dark skin. She was very pretty. As she walked up to say hello, her large chest bounced. This made me like her even more.

Mamby and I hung out in class, and she gave me a hug every time she saw me in the halls. I liked her, but she didn't like me in the same way. I thought she was cute, and I wanted to date her. She wasn't interested. Mamby had many male friends with whom she hugged. I respected her, so I never made moves on her.

We prepared for a school dance. All the kids talked about it. "Are you going, man?" I kept hearing over and over.

"Nope." I didn't have anyone to go with, but they didn't need to know that. Plus, I couldn't dance.

"Going to the dance, Eddie?" Mamby hugged me, and I loved how warm she felt.

"Nah."

"Why not?" She pulled back, and her face fell.

"Don't feel like it."

She smiled, those white teeth flashing. "Would you go with me?"

I smiled back. "Yeah." I forgot I couldn't dance. Who cared?

That night, I ran and told the staff in the house. "Hey, I'm going to my first dance."

"That's great, Eddie." Andrea patted me on the shoulder. "What's your plan?"

"Plan for what?" I ran off before she answered to tell Mom about my good fortune. She didn't have much of a response.

The night of the dance came, and butterflies circled my stomach. With sweaty hands, I asked Andrea to give me a ride to the school. The gym had been converted into a dance floor. I couldn't find

Mamby. I walked across the dance floor and stood against the wall. I was too afraid to go out and dance, and no one stopped to talk. I stood against the wall for about 15 minutes before I saw Mamby. She danced with a group of her friends. But then she saw me and ran over. "Hi!" She grabbed my hand and pulled me out onto the dance floor. I danced with Mamby and her friends for two songs before she went to the bathroom with her friends. I returned to the wall. I stayed at the dance for another 10 minutes and decided to walk home.

A week after the dance, I walked into the staff office, and Andrea was waiting for me. "Eddie, your family will be moving at the end of the week, OK?"

I ran upstairs to find Mom. "Mom, they said we're moving."

"Did you think we were going to live here forever?" She laughed.

Silence descended. Then I took a deep breath. "Well, where are we going now?"

"Don't worry about it, Eddie."

I spun around and left. We spent the rest of that week packing up and getting ready to go to gosh knows where.

We landed in another shelter not far from downtown Seattle. This house was a huge two-story one with concrete stairs that went from the sidewalk to the front porch. Right inside the front door, a set of stairs waited. To the right, a somewhat inviting living room beckoned. And the dining room was on the left. Near the stairs sat a laundry room and bathroom. Past the bathroom was the back door that led to a backyard. There was a kitchen, of course, a bedroom used for the staff office, and then upstairs, there were bedrooms. Ours was a large room with a bathroom.

A Mexican woman named Candy (short for Candelaria) with two little kids lived in one of the rooms. A white woman who was a Jehovah's Witness occupied the second, and another was empty.

This bedroom, similar to our last room, held two bunk beds and a twin bed. Lorenzo and I shared one, while Jannet and Maria shared the other. My mom slept on the twin bed, and the staff member brought in a cot for Jesse.

The medium-sized backyard held a big deck where the moms and staff smoked. The deck had two benches and a little table with a large ashtray. A big ole play structure waited for us on the other side of the yard.

Candy's boys were six and two. Candy and Mom became friends over a cigarette and the commonality of the Spanish language. The other woman stayed to herself. All anyone knew about her was her religion.

Summer vacation started, and the kids started going nuts and running around, so the staff enrolled us in some kind of summer camp. I attended Eric Metcalf's football camp at Garfield High School. I'd never played football—just catch up with friends. Positions other than the quarterback one remained a mystery. They settled me in the tight end position.

"Eddie, when the ball is hiked, you need to run up and block that guy." The coaches encouraged me along.

"OK."

I was not a big fan of football, and the days seemed very long and hot, but it was something to do for two weeks.

***

One day, something seemed weird at the house. The staff huddled up, whispering while we kids watched TV. The director, a tall, skinny black woman with braids in her hair, wandered over to us. "Hey there, come to the dining room. We have a big surprise." She jogged ahead of us, and when we got there, she had her hands behind her back. When she pulled out her hands, there were a bunch of tickets spread out in them. "We're going to a baseball game. The Mariners and the Minnesota Twins. At the Kingdome!"

On game night, we jumped up and down, hyped up, and even more so when a white van pulled up to the front of the house. We piled in. When we arrived at the Kingdome, traffic was stacked. I groaned. "It's gonna take an hour to find parking."

"We're in luck." The driver steered his way into an area with other big vans. "See, just for us." We parked and spilled out into the parking lot. The staff steered us to the elevators, and we rode all the way to the top of the booths. Our booth had two rows of seats and a huge window in front.

"I got this one!" Lorenzo rushed to a seat, and Jesse quickly followed. The girls lingered behind, taking in the scene with a look of awe.

Food and drinks arrived shortly—nachos, hot dogs, and sodas. Later, a staff member left and returned with a Mariners goodie bag holding stickers, pencils, erasers, and things like that. None of the kids really watched the game—we were too excited. We left a little early to beat the rush of fans, piled back into the van, and eased into traffic. I leaned my forehead against the window, watching the buildings light up as we drove through Seattle and headed home.

***

Every once in a while, Mom called Felipe. "Hey, can you come get us this weekend?"

We'd start jumping up and down and got little sleep that night. When ready, we walked downtown and waited for Felipe, who drove from Kent. "Don't forget the rules, kids. No one can know where we live," Mom reminded us. That's partly why we loved going to Felipe's—visiting him felt normal, not like we were hiding. There weren't house rules; we could play in the old neighborhood and see all our people, including Javel and Felipe's kids. We hated when it was time to go back to the shelter. "Why can't we stay?" I whined.

"Felipe can't always be driving back and forth to Seattle, Eddie." Mom flipped her hair over her shoulder and walked away. I made a face at her back.

The drive back was the worst. After the drive, we walked back to the shelter. We hated going back because we were going back to boredom.

We went to Felipe's house on two occasions. The second trip to Felipe's house started as usual. My mom arranged things with Felipe the day before. On the day of the trip, we pulled ourselves out of bed early and dressed. "Hurry up, children." Mom rushed around, looking for her purse. "Shoes on. Jacob. Now. We're gonna be late."

As we walked very fast to meet Felipe, crowds of people started swarming. The mass of people grew thicker.

"Eddie, look!" Lorenzo stopped, his eyes wide. My head whipped around, but I'd missed it. "That lady just flashed everyone!"

I turned around. A naked dude was walking along the sidewalk. "Oh, dear," Mom murmured as another naked woman strolled by. "Children, come close, please. I don't know what's going on." Instead, I darted into a nearby store and asked the clerk.

"Oh," he said, looking bored. "It's just the Seattle Gay Parade." He snapped his gum.

We met Felipe half an hour later at the store where we planned to meet, with a story to tell.

***

Mom's friend Candy was 25. They often did favors for each other. Sometimes, Candy watched us when Mom felt overwhelmed. Mom also watched Candy's kids when needed.

I teased Candy about how she spoke. "That's not real English. You callin' me a 'jew' when you mean to say 'you.' I ain't no jew. I'm a Cuban."

"I'm going to bite you," she claimed several times. Strange comeback, but oh well.

One day, I searched the ashtray for a half cigarette and found one of Candy's half-smoked ones. I grabbed it, headed behind the play structure, and smoked it. On my way back into the house, I passed Candy on her way outside.

"What is that? I smell cigarettes on you, Eddie."

"Not me." I ran upstairs to brush my teeth.

Later that day, she pulled me into the living room. "I know you're smoking, Eddie. I'm not an idiot."

"I am not." I puffed up all big.

Hands on her hip, she got closer to my face. "I know you are. I put a half one out when I went to answer the phone. It was gone when I came back. You were the only one in there, Eddie. And then, you smelled like it."

I'd been caught. I froze. "Oh man, don't tell Mom. Please, Candy."

She sighed. "Fine. You quit, though. If you quit, I won't tell."

I agreed, but then I paid for it.

Candy's kids had a Nintendo in her room. One night, I asked if I could play it after her kids went to sleep. My mom and Candy agreed. I started Mario Brothers, and then Candy made a comment I couldn't hear. Then I died in the game. "Aw, man!" I shook the controller a bit.

Candy said something again that I still couldn't hear. "What?" I focused on the screen. No answer, so I paused the game. "I can't hear you."

"I said, what's the matter?" she huffed at me.

"I died in the game."

"Well, if you knew how to play, you wouldn't die."

"I bet I play better than you." I glared at her.

"I'm going to bite you."

I set the controller down and marched over to her. "Why are you always saying that? What a dumb thing to say."

Candy paused for a few seconds as she looked at me. "Come closer."

I did, and she kissed me. She stopped for a second, and then she kissed me again. We continued kissing for a while longer. Then she led me to the bed.

I remember trying to focus on what was happening so I could remember my first time. Candy got on top of me and, unfortunately, became my very first teacher. After it was over, I was hit with a flood of feelings. I felt happy, scared, wonder, and surprised all at once. We got dressed and smoked a cigarette on her deck.

While smoking, Candy became agitated, and her tears started. I was confused. "What's wrong? That was good. I had fun."

"I'll get in big trouble, Eddie. That shouldn't have happened. You're a kid."

Dumbfounded, I assured her that no one would find out from me. Other than that, I wasn't sure what to say. After the cigarette, we both went to her bed and slept.

The next morning, Mom stopped me on my way to our room. She grabbed my face as I walked by. She lifted my chin, looking at my neck. I had noticed hickeys on my neck when I looked in the mirror at Candy's. "What happened to you?"

"What? Oh, that? I'm not sure what happened." She turned and walked downstairs, and I overheard her talking to the staff.

As I tried to eavesdrop, Candy drifted out of her room, crying. "They're going to take my kids." Sheer fear sparked in her eyes.

"Aw, come on. They won't do that." I tried to reassure her.

My mom stomped upstairs. "Eddie, get in the bathroom."

"Golly, Mom." But I obediently followed her in. If I thought I was embarrassed before, now sheer mortification came as she made me drop my pants and told me I smelled like sex.

As we left the bathroom, I saw Candy escorted downstairs by the staff. As she walked down the stairs, she yelled at Mom. "Nothing bad happened to him!"

The police came and arrested Candy. Her kids were taken elsewhere.

"Let's chat, young man," a police officer said. "We can head outside." As we were walking out there, I overheard another officer say, "Him? I've never had a male victim before."

A victim? I looked at the ground. A horrible feeling twisted in my gut.

The officer pulled out his notebook as I shuffled my feet. "Have you had a shower, son?"

"No," I mumbled, looking up to see if all the neighbors were watching the most embarrassing incident in my life.

"I'm going to take you to the hospital." The cop put his notebook away, and I followed him to his patrol car.

At the hospital, the officer parked, and we walked in. A nurse walked me into a little room. "It'll be just a minute."

Another woman came in with a clipboard. "Hi, Eddie. Can you help me learn what happened?" Scared, I just nodded. "Can you tell me what happened? Can you tell me where you were last night?"

I shrugged, now terrified. I played dumb. She asked other, more personal questions, and I just told her I didn't know.

"Well, we're going to run some tests. We'll head to another room."

In the other room, the nurse asked me to change out of my clothes and into a gown. I obeyed and sat in a chair, waiting for the nurse. She returned with the doctor. More of the same embarrassing questions.

I shrugged. "I don't know."

At least the nurse was nice. The doctor, however, pulled out a black light and told me that with the black light, you could see any bodily fluids. Then the nurse shined the black light on his teeth, and his teeth lit up. I laughed. "I need to shine it on parts of your body you usually cover up," the doctor announced. "Please lay back on the bed." The nurse patted my shoulder as he lifted my gown, then informed her that he saw traces of bodily fluid. The nurse wrote something on her clipboard.

Later, they sent me away. I felt like a piece of trash.

Mom needed to move us but struggled to find a place. She called many shelters, but none of them had any openings. We had five days left to get another home when she received a call from one of the shelters saying that there was an opening. We started packing. The last few days there stayed weird. The staff members treated me differently. "Are you OK, Eddie? Need anything?" They paid close attention to me and made extra attempts to chat.

This made me feel uncomfortable, so I tried to avoid them.

***

As we approached our new shelter, the taxi driver announced that we were close to the University of Washington, where the Huskies played. As we drove, I saw houses with big shapes and letters on them. "What are those?"

"Frat houses." The driver adjusted his mirror.

"What's a frat house?" He didn't really answer, but the houses looked cool.

We pulled into a driveway on the same street as many of the frat houses. Now, it seemed very cool.

This shelter was like all the rest. A big house with many rooms. No front yard, but it did have a decent backyard—built on top of the garage. That was a first. It held a play structure and an area for the moms to smoke. A fence surrounded it, and a stairway led to the alley below.

This was the most boring shelter out of all of them due to the lack of other kids to play with. For the most part, everyone in this shelter stayed to themselves. Other than mealtimes, the other residents avoided us. In fact, they seemed irritated by the kids being there. They complained about everything. "Those kids are too loud. The kids are running around again."

I felt unwanted.

The room we stayed in was smaller than the others. The six of us shared a room with two bunk beds and a twin bed. The room barely fit the furniture. With all the residents complaining, we felt stuck, and we felt like we should stay in our room. But Mom was in our room—and Mom always seemed angry. I was starting to detest being around her. She snapped at all of us—all the time.

After a while, we all became edgy. Any previous patience flew out the window. We seldom played on the play structure because it always rained. We stayed cooped up in that room all day.

One day, Lorenzo messed with my baseball card collection. When I walked into the room, he was stuffing them back into my bag. I flipped. I ran at him and started punching him. Mom walked in. "Eddie! Stop! Hery! Stop right now!" She pulled me away. We stood a couple feet apart, and I saw Lorenzo's eyes sparking fire. He wanted to get me. "Why are you fighting? How many times have I told you if we get kicked out, we have nowhere to go? *Nowhere!*" She screeched and hopped around, then finally threw my whole baseball card collection in the trash. Lorenzo later retrieved them. A gesture of peace, I guess.

I gave Mom the silent treatment for three straight weeks. Inside, I seethed.

The only fun thing that happened there was visiting Felipe and hanging out in the old neighborhood. We loved going to Felipe's, but we hated leaving him. We always left early because Felipe didn't want to deal with the Seattle traffic.

One of those times when it was time to leave his house, I felt anger rising in my throat. It wasn't fair. I needed to stay. "Please!" I begged Mom and Felipe. "I want to stay. I don't want to go back there, Mom."

"No." Mom seemed firm and forced me into the car.

The whole ride back to the shelter, I clenched my teeth and my fists. I stayed silent—I was so pissed. If I truly had no voice, then that's what they'd get. Silent Eddie.

We reached our designated drop-off spot a couple blocks from the shelter. As we climbed out of the car, Felipe glanced at me. "Hey Es, maybe Eddie could stay the weekend with me?"

Mom gave me a withering glance and sighed. "Fine." She slammed the door closed after she stepped out.

Yes! I smiled all the way back to Felipe's house.

I spent the next day hanging out in the old neighborhood. While doing so, I caught a glance of Javel and his friend Duke talking. I strolled up to them, catching a bit of the conversation about the fair in town. "Hey, bro." Javel greeted me and held out his hand for a high five. I smacked it, grinning.

We walked to Felipe's house. As we walked up to the door, Tallulah, Felipe's wife, was already ushering their kids into the van. As they clamored in, I saw Felipe, Javel, and Duke slip into the bathroom. I quickly dashed in before the door closed.

"What the heck? Everyone gotta go to the bathroom at once?" Felipe frowned.

I grinned. "I'm with them." I motioned to my older brother.

Felipe looked at me for a second, a weird look on his face. He sighed. He then pulled out a pipe, loaded it with something, and passed it around. When it came to me, I shrugged. No one reached out to stop me. I hit the pipe a couple of times before it was time to leave.

We piled into Felipe's van and headed to the fair. I felt lightheaded and like I was flying at the same time. I felt chill, and that was sure nice. I followed Javel and Duke around the fair. Javel and Duke talked to girls and made fun of people passing by. I didn't ride any rides or play any games. I just walked around the fair looking around—spaced out, mostly. Before I knew it, it was time to go, and we were getting back into Felipe's van.

"Headin' to Seattle," someone announced.

But Felipe didn't like to drive to Seattle. Oh no. What if he was taking me back to the shelter? I started to freak out inside. Mom would know I was high—she seemed to know almost everything. I'd never get to go to Felipe's or see Javel again.

I watched the signs on the highway, and the closer we got to Seattle, the harder my heart raced. What would I say to Mom? For sure, I'd die once I got to the shelter.

Felipe pulled off the highway, turned into a Chinese restaurant parking lot, and stopped the van's engine. Turned out Felipe had driven from Kent to Seattle for Chinese food.

Chapter 19

The Motel

Mom arranged for us to move to a motel after our time was up at the shelter. The problem was that the motel was on the other side of town, and we had no car or money to get there with our belongings. Mom called around, trying to find anyone who would be willing to help in any way—with no luck. A couple of days before we had to leave, one of the women who lived at the shelter offered my mom a cab voucher. We'd never heard of a cab voucher, but the woman said that the hospital gave it to her. On our last day there, we packed up all our belongings. I called the number on the voucher, and a cab came and took us to the motel just like that.

The motel, a two-story building, might have been nice at one point but landed far from that now. Near the parking lot was a pool with green and brown sludge at the bottom. We stayed in a second-floor room that reminded me of a small apartment. A small living room held a pull-out couch, a coffee table, and a couple of chairs. We scored a full kitchen and bathroom. A bedroom with a queen-sized bed and a dresser rounded it out. Dirt reigned everywhere. I wrinkled my nose, but at least we had our own space without staff members around.

Lorenzo, Jesse, and I made friends with some of the kids who also lived in the motel. We also made friends with some of the local kids who lived nearby. A mobile home park bordered the motel. Most of the kids we played with lived there, and the majority needed to stay close to home.

After living there for a week, I met kids my own age. This made my day. The only problem was that the kids my age didn't hang out near the motel. They liked to hang out in another neighborhood. But I was supposed to stay around the motel to watch my siblings.

"Yo. You can watch the kids. I'll be back." I smacked Lorenzo on the shoulder and left with my new friends. We found another neighborhood and hung out with a couple of girls who went to the local school. We stayed about an hour and a half.

Then, my stomach growled. "Hey, I'll be back," I announced. Food—is always the priority.

But on my return to the motel, my siblings were nowhere to be found outside where I'd left them playing, so I trudged upstairs and opened the door.

Mom stood there with her hands on her hips, her hair awry. She turned to me. "Where in the heck have you been? Didn't I tell your butt to watch your brothers and sisters?" Before I could answer, she slapped me in the back of the head and sent me to the bedroom.

Mom grounded me there for a week.

Being grounded was the worst because there was absolutely nothing to do. No one to talk to but my siblings. I only smoked one cigarette a day. I could only sneak one in while I was faking a shower. I entertained myself by watching the world from my window. Occasionally, I saw the kids who lived in the motel playing beneath my window and talked to them. But most of the time, I pouted in the bedroom, not just bored but growing angry fast.

***

It was almost to move again. I could always tell when it was close because Mom paced the floor, muttered, and spent a long time on the phone calling any church, program, or anyone else who might help. For all her struggles and anger, she became very resourceful. She found a place yet again—a hotel that would accept us on a longer term basis. The problem was that the hotel was far from the current motel, and again, we had no money or transportation.

One day, Mom marched into the bedroom. "Get your stuff packed. We're goin' to a motel soon." She left and we scrambled to obey.

When done packing, I ventured to ask more. "How are we getting there, Mom?"

She gave me a dirty look. "Don't you worry about it? Eddie, call for a cab." But my stomach churned a bit. I knew we had no money.

"I'm using the cab voucher from the last move." She finally informed me. I think she saw my nervousness.

"That's not gonna work, Mom. We already used it."

"Shut up and don't worry about it. Just do what I told you and call the darn cab."

I groped for the hotel phone. Told them our address and where we were headed. The cab arrived, picked us up, and took us to the new place. As we drove up to it, my mind raced. The cab driver would ask for payment any second. I hopped out and quickly took all the biggest bags to the room. "Lorenzo, stay here with the kids." I briefly glanced at a black couple parked in the space next to us; their windows rolled down.

I ran back outside and rushed to Mom, who was handing the voucher to the cab driver. The driver took the voucher and read it with a puzzled look on his face. "I can't accept this. It is fifty dollars for the cab fare, please."

Mom shuffled around on the sidewalk. "I have no money. I was told this would work." Her voice took on a whiney tone.

The driver's face grew red, and he clenched the steering wheel. "Ma'am, come up with the fifty bucks, or I'll call the police."

Tears started rolling down Mom's face. My stomach gurgled as the adrenaline rushed. If Mom got arrested, we'd head back to foster care. I was only thirteen. Where would my siblings go? The driver opened his door, pulled himself out, slammed the door closed, and started walking to the hotel office to find a phone.

But suddenly, things changed.

"Hey there." The black woman in the car next to us stepped out. "Let us cover this for you."

The driver stopped and turned around. With tears rolling down her face, Mom thanked them profusely as she handed the money to the driver. I'm pretty sure they saw the amazement on my face as well.

We headed for our new tiny room that had a little dresser, a microwave oven, and a queen-sized bed in the middle of the floor. A TV awaited, mounted to the upper corner of the room with cable. The room was much smaller once all our bags were stacked up. They took up one whole side of the room. At bedtime, my mom and sisters shared the queen-sized bed, and we boys slept on the floor or in clothes bags.

One day, Mom entered the hotel room after being gone for a bit. "Kids, we're going to church."

I forced my head upright from the uncomfortable bag it rested on. "Huh?" Then I rolled my eyes. Yeah, we'd been to church before. However, it'd been a long time.

"Don't worry about it. Just get ready." Mom smiled.

We walked to the corner to wait for the bus. Once the bus arrived and we boarded, we rode for about half an hour. We walked from the bus stop, then up a hill to a white church. Growing up, we only went to churches to collect a food box on holidays.

The church was a medium-sized Spanish church. There were a few offices at the entrance and then a large worship room farther in. In the basement, they had a food serving area, a kitchen, and a class area.

I felt a sense of emptiness and out of place. Lately, I have often felt a bit removed, nervous, and shaky. I didn't know anyone there. But no matter how out of place I felt, I decided it beat being cooped up in that hotel. Shortly after arriving, the service started. They sent the kids down to the basement for Bible studies. Lorenzo, Jannet, Jesse, and Maria all followed the other kids. Mom walked up to the front row and sat down. I followed quietly and sat with her.

The choir sang. Then, the pastor preached. And then he looked around at all the congregants with kind eyes. "Does anyone need prayer? We are here for you. The elders will come to the front, and if you need prayer, please come forward today."

To my surprise, Mom jumped up and walked toward the front. Tears rolled down her cheeks. Once she reached the front, she knelt. I watched, fascinated. The elders placed their hands on her back and shoulders, bowed their heads, and prayed. She returned to her seat, her face radiant. I gave her hand a squeeze. I'm not sure what occurred, but I'm happy to see her filled with joy. After the service, everybody talked to my mom and shook her hand. A member of the congregation offered to give us a ride back to the hotel in the church van. My mom accepted.

After that, Mom decided we would attend church whenever possible. We started going to church four days a week. We went to church on Sundays, Mondays, Wednesdays, and even Fridays. Honestly, as much as I was happy to see Mom happy and treating us better, I started to hate the sight of that church van that drove us back and forth.

But I had to make the best of the situation. I tried to talk to the cute girls whenever I met them. I made fun of some of the other kids at church. Dread curled inside my stomach when we had to go, and I started hating that everyone asked a ton of questions. I started going to Bible studies downstairs because all the adults were upstairs, and that sucked to be there. Once, the church elders asked me to help with the younger kids. I intentionally did a bad job, so I wouldn't be asked to help again.

***

It was almost time for us to leave the hotel. "Where are we going now?"

"Well, I've kept in contact with José. In Florida. I think it's time to go there."

My father. My real father, that is. But my stomach rolled thinking about it. We hadn't heard from Roberto in a long time, so I guess he forgot about us. But everything inside me felt scared about connecting again with José, the infamous drug dealer and supposedly my true father.

The church, not knowing the real José or perhaps thinking family ties were of the utmost importance, took up a collection for our trip to Orlando. They bought us one-way Greyhound tickets. They connected us with a congregation there and seemed very excited for us.

On our last day at the hotel, we packed up our belongings into big black garbage bags. Would I ever see the end of big, stuffed garbage bags? We put all our bags on the curb and waited for the church van to arrive. Once it did, we filled the back row with our bags. We piled into the remaining seats. My mom rode in the passenger seat. Dread again settled deep inside of me. I suspected we were on a trip to nowhere but what could I do at the age of thirteen? Nothing.

We drove to the Greyhound station and said goodbyes. Before leaving, the driver reminded my mom about congregational members in Florida who wanted to connect. My mom agreed and expressed her thanks.

At the Greyhound station, I approached the ticket booth and got our tickets. I checked in our plastic bags. I noted that our bus was located at the far end of the station and let Mom know. I had become the man in the family—in more ways than one.

Lorenzo and I carried the heaviest bags, leaving the rest for Mom and younger siblings. We lined up at our bus, waiting to board. The driver walked out. "Time to load luggage!"

Mom and the siblings boarded while I made sure the luggage made it onto the bus. After the luggage landed underneath the bus and seemed secure, I ran up the bus stairs and was relieved to see that Lorenzo saved me a seat.

Our first stop on our trip to Orlando was Spokane, Washington. As we approached Spokane, the driver picked up the intercom. "I am sorry to announce that we are running late. Some of you might miss your connection." The microphone crackled. Mom sighed.

At about 10:45 p.m., we stopped in Spokane. I rushed off the bus and collected our belongings. Overloaded with bags, I asked a Greyhound worker what gate to go to. Of course, it was across the entire station. We rushed to our gate, hoping the bus was still there. It was! But it was already loading. "Leave your bags. Get on the bus," I told my siblings. They hopped on, and I stayed for my new job of making sure all our belongings made it onto the bus as well.

I boarded the bus to Montana.

Once in Montana, we switched buses again. The next one was headed from western Montana to the eastern part. It took about a day and a half. I spent most of my day looking out of the window. Montana boasted a lot of beautiful countryside. "What's that?" I asked Mom.

She smiled at me and shook her head. "Tumbleweed, Eddie." Another one scooted across the road, and I suddenly recognized them. Oh yeah, they had always shown up in the cowboy movies.

After eastern Montana, we changed buses once again. Now, we are headed to Chicago, Illinois. I could barely keep up with it all. I worried about the younger siblings, but they seemed to be OK.

We were late in arriving in Chicago and were sore and tired. As soon as I stepped off the bus, very thick, hot air blasted me in the face. We'd breezed in during a historic heat wave, and I later found out that the news reported many elderly people dying. "Lorenzo. To find the next gate." I sent him off and then waited for the luggage. It felt like my clothes were on fire. "Mom, take the little kids. Get into the station out of the heat." She did.

I gathered what I could of the luggage and left the rest for my older siblings. We rushed through the crowded bus station to our gate just in time to board. We headed off to Tallahassee, Florida!

The next night, while I tried to sleep in the uncomfortable bus seat, I overheard a voice. "We're almost in Florida, folks." I scooted up and whipped my head toward the window, just in time to see the "Welcome to Florida" sign. Within a few hours, the bus stopped in Tallahassee. Whew—only a few more towns before our final destination. At the station, I again gathered most of our luggage and walked to our next gate. The bags seemed heavier this time. After boarding, the driver picked up his microphone. "We have four and half hours ahead of us. Settle in and get comfortable."

We pulled into the Orlando Greyhound station. I grabbed our luggage once more, piled it on an available bench, and sat down. I expected Mom would have me call José now to come and get us. "I'm going to straighten up first." Mom grabbed her bags and found the bathroom while I waited with my siblings. She emerged from the bathroom, looking presentable. "OK, give José a call, Eddie." Uh-huh.

"Hey, José. We're at the station."

I moved our belongings from the bench and ground to the curb, and in thirty minutes, José approached us. Mom and the siblings smiled and jumped up and down. Only I held back.

"Hey, baby." José gave Mom a brief hug and rustled Jesse's hair, who grinned.

"Hi, Eddie." He turned to me and held out his hand.

I obediently shook his hand and mumbled. "Hi, José."

"What? You can't call me dad?" He tilted his head to the side and smirked. I stood rooted to the cement. José turned back to Mom. We then walked to his car.

"Put the luggage in the trunk, Eddie." Mom smiled at me.

We were off to José/Dad's apartment and a new life. As nice as it was to finally arrive, a funny feeling in my stomach swelled as we got closer and closer to our new home.

Chapter 20

Florida

We parked at the Lancaster Villas Apartments and walked to José's apartment on the second floor. Two lizards scuttled across the path, and Maria screeched. It scared me, too. "What was that?"

Mom laughed. "Lizards run wild here." I shuddered.

Right inside the front door was a tiny kitchen to the right and the living room to the left. Directly in front of me lay a hallway that led to the bedroom on the right and the bathroom to the left.

We sat our luggage against the wall in the living room. An older man walked out of the back room and greeted us. ChuCho, José's father. I stared at him, memories stirring.

"You all need showers. Go." Mom pointed to the bathroom, and we lined up.

While my siblings cleaned up, I got brave and faced ChuCho. "You remember me, boy? Our time in the Dominican Republic? We had a good time. *Buen Tiempo.*" He slapped me on the shoulder. It was vague—but there. That and the fact that because I looked like I was his dead son, he'd tried to steal me. I stepped away from him, and the hole in my stomach grew.

Soon, boredom came. "Can we go outside?" Jesse whined. Lorenzo chimed in, and I fully agreed, so we headed out and walked through the apartments, exploring. "Hey, it's a pool." Jesse pointed. Sure enough, blue water beckoned. A small diving board was at one end. We rushed back to the apartment.

"Can we go swimming? Can we, Mom?" Jesse begged.

"OK, but only if Eddie watches you." She rolled her eyes and started putting things away in the kitchen.

We quickly changed and ran back to the pool. We played in it until dinnertime. Maybe this new home wouldn't be so bad after all.

After dinner, we sat in the living room. ChuCho tried to make conversation. But we had a hard time understanding him, so Mom started translating. After half an hour, we warmed up a bit and started playing with ChuCho. "We should dress him up like a gangster." Lorenzo laughed. We found a baseball cap and put it on his head backwards. We found a pair of sunglasses and set them on his nose. Later, we found a plastic toy gun and had ChuCho cross his arms and pose with the gun in one hand. We rolled on the ground with laughter.

Mom smiled, too. "Hey José! Come here."

But when he came into the room, his whole face frowned. "What are you doing? It's not OK to disrespect my father like that."

"Not disrespectful, *mi hijo*." ChuCho grinned. "Just being kids."

José left the room. We continued playing with ChuCho until bedtime. He left and returned to the Dominican Republic two days later.

***

José had Dominican neighbors at the apartments and wanted to introduce us. They had two sons—one my age, Tim, and the other about seventeen. They owned a nearby restaurant. Their mom heard about how well Mom cooked and offered her a job.

She took the job at the restaurant. We visited occasionally to talk to Mom and eat the delicious Hispanic food. She worked long hours. Once, we walked in during an argument. "You expect me to do everything." She glared at them, hair awry. "You need to pay me more. It's the right thing."

She quit, of course.

We'd lived in Florida for close to a week when a group from the Washington church stopped by. They pulled in with an RV, stayed for dinner, and left the next day. Mom also made a friend in the complex named Carmen—a skinny Columbian woman with two kids.

Things went pretty good after that. Mom and José seemed to get along, and we started to feel a little more settled.

Until one night after dinner.

As we watched TV in the living room, José received a call and left shortly afterward. He stomped back in the door a little later. He grabbed a beer, slammed the refrigerator door, and headed outside. I caught Mom looking at him carefully, a funny look on her face. José returned again, but this time without his shirt on.

She stood. "What happened to your shirt?"

"It's outside. Don't worry about it."

"Outside; don't worry about it," she mimicked and scooted quickly to the door. I stood and followed her. Whatever was going down, Mom might need me. She grabbed his shirt, which had been tossed haphazardly near the door outside, and brought it in. She almost threw it in his face while I hovered behind her.

"Hey, it's my shirt. Who cares?" José swiped the shirt from where it landed on the floor. His phone rang again, and he pulled it out of his pocket. "Yeah? No prob. Hang on." He hung up and headed out the door, closing it firmly behind him.

I watched Mom. Her eyes sparked fire, and she took a deep breath. She marched to the door, ripped it open, and flew outside. "Mom." I followed, a little worried.

Outside, I saw a woman swing her fist at José and miss. Mom wound up and threw a looping left hook around José—connecting with the woman's head. I grinned. Until José spun around, grabbed my mom, picked her up, and started to carry her back to the apartment. I stepped forward with a frown. Mom started screaming and pounded him with her fists. "Nobody puts a hand on a man that I'm with!" Out of the corner of my eye, I saw a neighbor move a curtain and glance out.

I stood guard in front of the woman, who seemed dazed. She stood there for a couple of minutes, trying to collect herself before shaking her head, sending me a wobbly smile, and drifting off. I ran back into the apartment where Mom and José were now arguing in the back room. Oh, brother. I stayed with my siblings in the living room to distract them. From what I have heard, the woman is José's ex-girlfriend, who lives in the apartment. She hated that Mom was there.

Mom decided she could not or would not live with José anymore. She looked for a place for a couple of days and found an apartment that accepted us. Her new friend Carmen offered her home until our apartment was ready. We packed up our things again and moved down the street into a nice neighborhood.

The house mimicked the neighborhood. The couches still had plastic on them, as if Carmen had just bought them. I felt like I could not touch anything. It was weird. We stayed in the house, but the neighbors complained about us being too loud. We were bored and uncomfortable. Mom also felt weird because she didn't know Carmen very well. But we had no choice because we didn't know anyone else in Florida.

One evening, after living with Carmen for a week and a half, Mom grabbed a beer when Carmen wasn't home. One turned into a few, and before I knew it, Mom became a loud-talking drunk.

"You aren't living here anymore," Carmen declared loudly. "I won't have drunks in the house. The neighbors will complain, too. You're too loud!"

"Sorry!" Mom held up her hand. "But your house is like a museum. I gotta follow the kids around to make sure they aren't breaking anything, and your neighbors are a royal pain in the you-know-what. The kids are just bored. We don't have anywhere to go yet. I'll try and stay out of your way."

The two argued for a while. Fortunately, the following day, my mom received notice that the apartment would be finished and ready in two days. The two days scrolled by quickly, even in the "museum" and with the tension. We headed yet to another home.

The apartment we moved to was in the South Ridge Apartments. There were 150–200 units in about 20 buildings. And it was pink, like Pepto Bismol. But it had two swimming pools, one in the front by the entrance and another toward the back!

We moved into a unit at the back in the upper right. Mom had a room, Jannet and Maria shared the second room and we boys stayed in the larger master bedroom that had a bathroom with two doors.

In September, I started the eighth grade at Walker Middle School where mostly Hispanics attended—even ones who didn't speak English. It took a while to find friends. I returned to my usual habit—grabbed my lunch, ate quickly, and roamed around. I stood near the basketball courts and watched the kids play. If there were too many people around, I'd hit the library instead in an effort to make it look like I belonged somewhere.

In class, I frequently joined in on discussions. As usual, I didn't own all the cool name-brand clothes that my peers expected. Nor did I have the cool, expensive shoes. I wasn't outgoing. With all these facts stacked against me, finding friends was difficult, so I spent most of my time trying to stay out of everybody's way.

I started talking to some classmates and finally made some friends. Not friends I'd hang out with outside of school, but at least ones to sit with and talk to during lunch. We collected basketball cards and traded them.

In October, some new kids arrived from St. Croix. They sounded Jamaican. "Why do you sound Jamaican?" I asked as I wandered over to one of them.

He raised his eyebrows. "You ever hear a Jamaican speak?"

Huh. Nope.

"I'm Caribbean. And I'm Carlos."

I nodded at him. Carlos was lighter skinned than the others. Another boy was Manuel, a heavyset, dark-skinned boy. He was a bit shy. The third family had two girls—Olga and Maria. Maria was cuter than her older sister was, but both girls were very pretty and out of my league.

I hung out with Carlos a few times once I found out that he lived in the apartments behind South Ridge. I was near the Cypress Landing Apartments when I saw him. I ran over. "What are you doing here?"

"I live here, dingbat." We hung out for a couple of hours. As we were headed to Carlos' house, we saw his dad. He looked just like a chubby Fidel Castro. I had to grin and bite back a chuckle.

***

When the subject of moving to Florida came up, we immediately asked to go to Disney World. José worked there as a custodian and received discounted tickets. The dream day finally arrived, even though we weren't living with José anymore. We headed to Disney World on Jesse's birthday. We piled into José's Ford when he pulled up. Once there, José walked us to the ticket booth, paid, and told me to call when we were done. José and Mom left, and I took charge.

Once in Disney World, we had big decisions to make. Which ride first? They were free at the time, but all had big lines. "How about the Tower of Terror?" Jesse put his hands up like claws and chased Maria around a bench when she squealed.

After waiting in line for what seemed like forever, we piled into an elevator. As it started moving, a TV in the upper corner of the elevator blinked to life and started playing *The Twilight Zone* in black and white. When the doors slid open, we poured into a room with a bunch of chairs. Lorenzo saw a seat with a seat belt and rushed over to it. When the rest of us also found a seat, a metal bar came down over our waists. "Ha. Ha. I don't have a stupid bar. I got a seat belt," Lorenzo bragged. Jannet stuck her tongue out at him.

I kid you not—the room started moving upward. Suddenly, a large sliding door opened in front of us. "It's the whole park!" I looked for the entrance and then grabbed the bar as, without notice, we dropped. Screams echoed around the room. Jannet's hands practically turned white as she gripped the bar. Little flashes of light appeared, and then it was done. When we walked out, pictures waited on the counter, so we searched for ours.

I cracked up. There we were—every single one of us had an open mouth and fear in our eyes. We found Lorenzo's and saw that not only was his mouth wide open, but he also clung to the seat with both hands while the seat belt dangled above his head. "I got a seat belt; I got a seat belt," I teased Lorenzo in a sing-songy voice for about an hour. He punched me in the shoulder.

Next, the roller coaster beckoned. It threw neon lights out of the top of the building, so it caught our attention. We slid into a massive line, weaving our way through thick cords that dangled from poles. After about an hour of inching forward, we saw people getting on the roller coaster ahead of us.

Maria started shaking. "I don't want to go, Eddie."

"Aw, come on, Maria. It'll be fun." We only had two more groups ahead of us now.

"Maria, give me a break!" Jannet elbowed her. "You're such a baby."

But the closer we got, the more she cried. Everyone else was keen on the ride, but someone had to stay with Maria. "Jesse, take Maria back down the hill and stay with her," I said. He frowned and shook his head until I glared at him. He grabbed her arm and stomped away. Once off the roller coaster, we found them waiting at the exit.

"You're such a jerk, Eddie. It's *my* birthday trip." He refused to speak to me for a long time. But Maria was all smiles.

We discovered a train that connected the areas, so we took it to Epcot Center. Later, we saw a sign about the Muppets 3D movie. As we walked in, a person handed us glasses. We found seats and watched instructions on how to use them. "It'll look like things are coming right at you," they warned us. Once the movie started, and Animal looked like he was jumping out of the screen, we kept taking the glasses off and putting them back on to see the difference. It took a while before the glasses worked for me, but once they did, it freaked me out. An object shot out of the screen and over my head. "Dang!" I jumped out of my seat and turned around, trying to find the object. My siblings all said that they couldn't see anything. After the movie, we got back on the train and rode back to the main park.

Once we got back to the Magic Kingdom, we realized that the crowd had died down. There were still huge lines for the new or coolest rides, but the rest were still open with few waiting. We rode every ride that did not have a line.

Maria loved the kiddie rides and had a huge smile after each one.

Then, we found a go-kart ride without a line. We picked our cars and zoomed around the track. When we were done, there still was no line, so we went again. We rode the go-karts for about half an hour back-to-back. "Time to go home. It's getting dark.," I declared. "I'll call José."

The disappointed groans around me soared, but, hey, I was large and in charge.

Well, I was large and in charge until I realized that I didn't have José's new number since he'd recently moved. "Gosh darn. I don't know his number."

Lorenzo laughed at me. "Smart aleck. You got his number?"

"No, but you had better figure it out. I'm hungry, and the girls are cold."

"He does work here," I remembered. Yeah, that was it. I'd ask an employee for help. I found a man working on a light pole who reminded me that thousands of people worked at Disney World.

That was a problem.

Once the park closed, a security officer took us to an office. We sat in the tiny office for an hour, cold and hungry. Security was trying to find out who José was. Suddenly, I saw Mom and José walking up toward the security office, laughing.

"Don't laugh!" I busted out. "José, we didn't have your phone number. I knew you had moved houses and all. We're cold and hungry, and I'm pissed."

José's eyebrows wrinkled, and his fists clenched at his side. "You're stupid. I did move, but I kept the same phone number. Idiot." He reduced his tirade to a mumble while Mom squeezed his hand and smiled at us.

We didn't get home until about midnight.

***

Not long after starting school, Lorenzo and I met a pair of Panamanian brothers who lived in South Ridge. The older brother, José, was my age. The younger brother, Alex, was Lorenzo's age. José was a short, skinny light-skinned boy with glasses. Alex, a chubby dark-skinned boy. The two of them lived with their father in a building not far from ours. They gave us a tour of the apartments. "Here's another shortcut," Alex volunteered as he pointed toward a narrow area with a sidewalk. José showed us where all the cute girls lived.

Then we saw a pool. "No one uses that." José shoved his hands in his pocket. "The manager lives too close by. No fun 'cuz he comes out and yells all the time. We swim in the back pool instead. You can do whatever you want back there."

The maintenance workers enforced the rules at South Ridge while driving around in golf carts. We learned to avoid them at all costs because they always had something to say. If they told management, then management complained to our parents, and we received punishment. The maintenance workers left around five, so we just waited for them to go before we had most of our fun.

One day, Lorenzo, Alex, José, and I walked around South Ridge, and a cute girl wandered by. "Oh my gosh." Alex flushed, his hands literally shaking.

I grinned. "Go talk to her, man."

"Nah." He shook his head fast.

I decided to mess with him. "Hey! Come over here!"

She did, and we talked for a while before she needed to head home.

"Come on, dude; go get her number."

We elbowed Alex as she walked away. "I can't. One of you do it. I'll give you five bucks."

I jogged up to her and asked her for her phone number for Alex, which she provided. Alex ran around in circles when I gave it to him. "Thanks, Eddie. I'll pay you later."

José, Alex, Lorenzo, and I hung out every day after school until well after dark. We wandered around, looking for girls to talk to. One night, we sauntered around, trying to find something to do. We walked between some parked cars, and Alex saw a cup full of change in a car's cupholder. He grabbed the door handle. "Hey, it's unlocked."

We promptly ransacked the car, taking anything of value. We pored over our loot behind an empty apartment. We'd managed the cup of change, a pack of cigarettes, and a lighter. "Let's see if we can find more." José took the lead, and we checked out a couple of cars. But it was still light.

"This would be better in the dark." Lorenzo voiced what we all were thinking.

We walked back to our hiding spot to wait for the cover of night. We smoked cigarettes and talked about all the stuff we expected to find in the cars once darkness hit.

At dark, we set out, and I took command. "We should do teams of two. One person can search, and the other is the lookout. I'll go with José. Lorenzo, you go with Alex."

Whenever we found anything in the cars, we'd haul it to our hiding spot before going back out. After searching all the cars in South Ridge, we decided to go to Cypress Landing next door to check their parking lot.

We climbed the fence that separated the two apartment complexes. The parking lot in Cypress Landing was set up differently, so I decided to get back into a group of four with two lookouts and two searchers. After a couple of narrow escapes, we called it a night and headed back to South Ridge. Back in our hiding spot, we rifled through our spoils. We'd discovered a lot of change: about five lighters, a pocketknife, some cigarettes, some speakers, and a couple of random items. We split the change. José wanted the speakers. I got the knife, and Lorenzo and Alex shared the random items. It was time to go home. Stealing from cars was hard work.

The next morning, I awoke to a loud knock at the door. "Hey, José." I opened the door wider. "Coming in?"

"Eddie, I need that knife."

I rubbed my eyes. "What's going on?"

"After Dad left for work, I went to get the speakers out of the bushes. But some guy saw me and recognized them. They were from his car. So I gave them back, but now he wants the knife too. Or he's gonna call the police."

Shoot. I had given the knife to Lorenzo, and he wasn't home. "Ah, man, I gotta find Lorenzo." I pulled on my shoes, and we headed down the stairs.

"There. That's him." José nudged me.

A stocky man walked towards me, speaking Spanish. "You stealing my stuff too? Where are my things?"

I shrugged. "I don't have it."

"I think you do. I called the cops."

Crap. Why didn't we run? I guess the guy already knew where we both lived, so that was pointless. We sat on the curb. We'd just deny everything, we decided.

The police arrived shortly thereafter. As soon as they stopped, the man pointed at José and me. "There they are." The officer called us over and then separated us, questioning us both.

"We were walking around." I nodded, realizing that denying it all wouldn't work. I was sure he'd understand what we did when he heard the reason. "The door was partly open on the car. So yeah, we saw the speakers and took them." José and I landed in the back of the patrol car as the officer chatted with the Spanish man.

Looking out the back window, I saw Lorenzo walking by, staring at us. Lorenzo walked by two more times, staring at José and me in the back of the police car. Then, he strolled over to the officer. I saw his mouth move. The officer motioned for Lorenzo to sit on the curb, and he plopped down. The officer walked to my door, opened it, grabbed my arm, and pulled me over to Lorenzo. He took us both to the door of our apartment and knocked. You know—that well-known police knock that could vibrate pictures off the wall.

Mom opened the door. "What the heck?" Immediately, her hands landed on her hips.

"Ma'am, your sons have been stealing out of cars."

"You what?" Her eyes landed on mine, sparking the fire.

I suspect the officer knew that what awaited us was more punishment than he could ever give. She yanked us into the apartment as he headed out. As soon as the door closed, she grabbed the broom hung behind the door and beat us from the front door all the way to our bedroom. We each received at least two good hits.

We spent the rest of the day in our room talking about what happened. Lorenzo stretched out on the bed, rubbing his back. "I thought you'd get mad if I didn't get in trouble too."

"You should have stayed out of it. See, now you got beat."

"Too late, bro."

No duh.

***

Mom made friends easily—even in the checkout line. She'd start a conversation, which led to a home visit and dinner, and after that, the friendship badge was earned. She was the only one I knew who went to the store for cigarettes and gathered friends along the way.

One day, I walked into the apartment to find Mom getting ready to go out. "What's up, Mom?"

"I met a woman who lives near the entrance of the apartments with her husband. They invited me over for a few beers. She's Anna. He's José." She leaned toward the mirror, applying lipstick. "He's always working."

"Where'd you meet her?"

She looked offended. "At the store, of course. I heard a lady talking with a Spanish accent, so I asked her where in Cuba she was from? I'm taking Jannet and Maria. Stop by if you want."

Later that day, I walked toward the entrance of South Ridge and saw Maria running into an apartment. I walked over and knocked on the doorframe.

"You must be Estrella's son." Anna popped into my view.

"Yes. Is she here?"

"Come in." She motioned with her hand, and I followed.

Mom sat at the table near the kitchen, drinking coffee. "Hi, Eddie. This is José." She waved at the thin Mexican man cooking at the stove.

I nodded at him and sat at the table.

"We've got three boys," Anna told me. "My youngest lives in an apartment in the next building. His name is Roberto, and he lives with his girlfriend. My oldest is Luis. He lives across town. My middle is Javier, and he . . ." She sighed heavily. "He's in jail."

I started hanging out at Roberto's a little after we met the next week. He was eighteen and lived with Karen, who was Puerto Rican. There was always activity at their place. Luis, twenty-one, hung out with them regularly. We smoked blunts while we hung out. Blunts are a cigar cut down one side, but the tobacco is removed and replaced with weed. We only smoked blunts at Roberto's. I got so high that Roberto threatened not to let me smoke anymore. He figured his mom would have a fit.

"Roberto," Karen scolded. "Don't give Eddie more. My gosh!"

Then he'd hand me another.

At times, I messed with Roberto when I was high. He had quite a temper, and it was fun to get him going. When I talked crap, he would get upset and try to punch me, but his punches never hurt. When he got really mad, he'd bite his tongue when trying to punch me, and it looked hilarious. When I laughed, he got madder.

I tried to act as if I could keep up with my new, older friends.

When very high, I claimed hunger and left. Then I'd go behind a building, lie down, and close my eyes, trying to deal with the high. Unfortunately, the world always spun around me, and it became dizzying. But I laid there until the high wore off. Sometimes, it was hours before I was well enough to get up and head home.

Luis was more laid back than his younger brother. "How are you doing, Eddie?" He always asked. "Want to go to the store?" We'd hit the corner store, and he bought me things. I liked hanging out with him more than Roberto, but Roberto was more available. Luis lived across town and now only stopped by Roberto's apartment every now and again.

A few months after I started hanging out with Roberto and Luis, their brother was released from jail. Javier, nineteen, moved in with his mom. He treated me like one of the guys and not like a little kid. Javier told Roberto to leave me alone when Roberto was messing with me. After Javier came, I received invites to some of the parties they attended. I was like one of the gang.

***

We lived in South Ridge for a few months before we came home to an eviction notice on our door for nonpayment of rent. My mom frantically started looking for a new place. She talked to a friend who allowed us to move into a room in her house with her husband and two kids.

A few days before we had to leave, we moved in with Karen and Felix. Karen was a heavyset Mexican woman, and Felix was an older Cuban. "I've got a storage area. We'll fix it up for you boys." He led us back to the storage area and we helped him clean it out. Mom and the girls stayed in the spare bedroom.

Lorenzo and I attended the same school as before, Walker Middle School. But now we had to travel across town to get there. We had to get out of bed extra early and catch the city bus, then walk about fifteen city blocks to school. We hated getting up early, but we enjoyed the freedom on the way home when we hung out with friends and messed around in our old neighborhood. I hated being at Karen and Felix's house. I felt like a burden.

Mom and Karen worked at a hotel cleaning room. One day, my mom came home, and her face looked messed up. "What the heck, Mom? Did you run into a door?" I laughed.

She started crying and slammed the door of the bedroom.

It looked as if she was making a funny face and it stayed like that. Maybe she was trying to be funny all the time? But it didn't go away.

Mom headed to the doctor, who told her it was caused by extreme stress. They told her there was nothing they could do about it.

Mom's face was stuck like that for a week and a half. It was so bad that Maria started crying every time she saw her.

On the days I didn't have school, I helped Felix with projects around the house. One weekend, Felix and I changed the storage area we stayed in into a real bedroom. The following two weekends, we installed a pool in their backyard.

It was the least I could do, considering they were housing all of us.

On a couple of occasions, my siblings and I tried to befriend Karen and Felix's kids. They had two overweight kids, a boy and a girl. Both were around Jannet and Jesse's age. They loved to watch TV. They sat in front of the TV, each with a jar of peanut butter and a spoon, watching and eating. They watched American cartoons, but they had the audio in Spanish. It was the first time I had experienced that.

We stayed with Karen and Felix for about three months. Everything went well in those three months. On occasion, we boys argued, and Felix barreled into the room. "Knock it off, kids!" He was pretty good at yelling when he wanted to. But we weren't afraid of him, and he never raised a hand at us.

One time, on her day off, Mom decided to have a few beers. As was common, a few beers turned into a lot of beers. As always, her irritation escalated, and she made a scene.

The next day, they asked us to move out.

"Aw, come on, Karen. I'm sorry." Mom looked repentant. "I'll start looking, OK? Give us a break in the meantime?"

Karen conceded with a sigh. Felix nodded after what seemed like a long time. They let us stay until Mom found a new apartment in a complex named the Americans with the help of several local churches and organizations.

***

We moved into a nice three-bedroom apartment on the second floor at the beginning of summer. The apartment had a sliding glass door that led to a small balcony with a wobbly railing.

We'd lived at Americanas for a day when Mom told me about an old Puerto Rican she met. "They offered you a job, Eddie. Helping in their backyard." I frowned, remembering my job in a backyard long ago and what had later happened. But I nodded at her; making money motivated me.

The next day, we headed out. "I'll drop you off." Mom took me to the bus stop and we arrived near the couple's house. She knocked on the door and left after they opened it.

The couple was very nice. "Would you like something to drink?" The woman puttered around her kitchen.

"No. Thank you, ma'am."

In the backyard, a huge garden awaited. "I need you to move a few piles of wood and clean up this spot." The man smiled at me, and I found myself smiling back. It felt safe there.

After I was done with the piles, he had me help him gather buckets of water. "I'm collecting rainwater. We drink it. It's healthier and tastes better, too!"

Later, when I drank a glass, it tasted like plain water.

The woman had me pull weeds while she made lunch. We took a lunch break together. After lunch, the man showed me a couple of items he wanted me to help him move. After we moved them, he told me I was done. He entered his house, returned with twenty dollars, and handed it to me. "I like that you are working to help your family, son."

"Thank you." I took the twenty dollars and walked to the bus stop. On the way home, I saw a dollar store and stopped there. "The apartment is empty." I mused as I wandered the aisles. What would help us out the most? We didn't even have furniture. I found a broom and some cleaning supplies for the house. After I got what I could, I walked home with my bag full of house supplies. I felt like a grown-up providing for my family. But when I got home, Mom's eyebrows shot up when she saw my purchases. I believe she already had plans for the money.

During our first few days at Americanas, we explored. The complex had a pool, a laundromat, and a tennis court. To get to the tennis court, you had to walk around a mini-canal behind the apartments. We liked hanging out there because we were away from the adults' line of sight.

One day, while playing in the pool, we met a Dominican family who lived in the complex as well. Lorenzo's new friend was a skinny kid named Rudy. Rudy had a younger sister named Anna, who had a crush on Lorenzo. Rudy also had two little brothers, one named Luis, who was Jesse's age. The other was a toddler named Jesuslen. They lived with their mom, Selena, and an older friend. After the kids became friends, our moms followed suit. We kids played in the back room while the adults talked in the front room. Rudy, Luis and Ava showed us around to the hang-out spots, woods, and the shortcut to get to the store.

Lorenzo, Rudy, Luis, and I were sitting and talking on our stairs when a girl walked by. "Who's she?"

"That's Christina." Rudy leaned forward. "She's a Puerto Rican girl. About your age. She lives across from you with her mom."

I started hanging out with this new Christina regularly. We started dating shortly after we met. Christina's mom found out we were dating and slapped her in the face, leaving a mark. Christina's mom frequently treated her badly and grounded her for almost everything. I only saw her on the rare occasion she was allowed out.

***

After we'd lived in America for a couple of weeks, a black family moved in next door to us and immediately started problems. Jannet and Christina chatted out by the tennis courts when two of the neighbor girls started picking on Christina. Christina had had heart surgery when she was a baby, and it left a scar down the middle of her chest. The girls pointed and made fun of the part they could see. Christina cried, and Jannet tried to defend her. The girls started in on Jannet. Lorenzo, Rudy, and I happened to be walking by when Jannet waved vigorously. "Hey! Come here!"

After learning what was happening, I frowned at the new neighbors. "Leave them alone." I walked Jannet home. Christina followed while the girls kept yelling. Christina and I stopped talking shortly after.

I still stole cigarettes regularly and sometimes required my siblings to help.

"We want to help too!" Rudy and Luis both kept saying.

We headed to the store and enlisted a common but effective tactic. I had a couple of us act suspiciously or ask a lot of questions to keep the cashier busy while the others pocketed the cigarettes. It worked well, and we were never caught.

I never wanted any of Mom's friends to see me smoking. I decided to smoke on the other side of Americana since the complex was huge, with units on both sides of Americana Blvd. We walked to the far side of the section where we didn't live. There, a huge tree grew next to the fence. I called it the Oak Tree. I thought it was an oak tree. The tree became known as the Smoke Tree. We headed there to smoke daily.

One day, on the way there, I saw a cute, dark-skinned girl walking with a white girl. I elbowed Rudy. "Know who that is?"

"Never seen her." He blew smoke toward me.

"Luis, you go talk to her; then I'll come get you." I snuffed out my cigarette on the tree.

Luis did, and it worked. I came over to get him and joined in on the conversation. Her name was Bettina, and she was Spanish, which made me like her even more. She often visited her friend at the complex.

We were joking around when Bettina called me by name.

"Well, you're a mix between a wildebeest and a hippo." I grinned. Lorenzo, Rudy, and Luis busted out laughing.

"You're a jerk." Bettina stomped off with her friend.

Regret waved over me. "Hey, Bettina." I jogged over to her. "I'm sorry. I am."

She stopped while her friend rolled her eyes and kept walking. We talked for a while, and in a few days, Bettina and I started dating. We dated for about a week before she broke it off with me. I had no idea why she did, but we remained friends.

***

Lorenzo, Rudy, Luis, Jesse, and I spent our time roaming the neighborhoods, bored. We played in the pool and woods and tried to talk to any girl we thought was cute.

One day while we were exploring in the woods next to Americanas, Lorenzo wandered a bit. "Hey guys, I found something!" We rushed over and saw a pool with some nasty water at the bottom. A pink building nearby looked abandoned.

The coast was clear, so we started looking for a way in. We walked around the back of the building and found a gate that led to the street. The front of the building faced a busy street. "We'd better stick to the back," I declared. The other two followed me as we found a broken window and climbed in. "Be careful." I pushed a board back into its place. "Someone could be in here. Hey, there's some stairs." We climbed them to explore but only found empty rooms. Back on the main floor, we found some bedrooms, a kitchen, and two huge walk-in freezers.

Quietness enveloped us. We were definitely alone.

We headed into demo mode. I started by kicking a wall and making a huge dent. Soon, we ran around kicking off walls, climbing on counters, and jumping off.

"A fire extinguisher! Does it work?" Jesse grabbed it, pulled the pin, and started spraying it all over. We coughed and laughed. After the new toy ran out of powder, we practiced karate.

"Remember that movie where the dude missed it, and his leg went through the wall?" Rudy grinned.

We each tried—really hard. Two attempts later, my leg went through the drywall. I had to wiggle it hard to get it out.

Luis exited the kitchen with a pack of full salt and pepper shakers.

"Gimme one." Lorenzo snatched one out of Luis' hand, and the pepper flew. Some landed on me. I grabbed one of the saltshakers and tossed some salt at Lorenzo.

The war was on. Suddenly, a salt and pepper fight broke out. I don't recall who actually won because, by the time we got tired and quit, we wore an awful lot of salt and pepper. In our hair, clothes, and even in our pockets.

"Sheesh." I turned another pocket inside out, sprinkling salt on the ground. "I'm done. We can come back later."

We sauntered home—kings of our world.

***

Mom started out with a couple of beers with a neighbor. Whenever the neighbor finished, she bought more beer on the way home. When done with that, she always wanted more. In fact, she drank until there was no way of getting any more. Either the stores stopped selling it to her, money ran out, or she passed out. While drinking, she played loud Spanish music. And sometimes on repeat all night long. I was not a fan.

On several occasions, I walked into the apartment to see Mom drinking with a new friend she had just met. She'd go to the store, meet a guy, and flirt with him, so he bought beer. They drank it up, then disappeared to her bedroom. Some of these guys headed back to the store two and three times before she asked them to leave. In the morning, she awoke hung over with a headache and craving a Coke. She rarely remembered anything from the night before.

The only good thing about my mom drinking, which was often, was the fact that all the rules disappeared once she started. Within a short while, we started asking for all the things we knew she would normally decline. We stayed out late, refused to get up for school, had friends over, or whatever. No one was aware enough to enforce the rules. I even smoked in my bedroom while Mom drank. Sometimes, she gave me a cigarette, but only when she was very drunk. I usually stole them from her.

Since the time I started smoking, I hid it from Mom.

Sometimes, she saw evidence. She'd wave it in my face, whether it was a cigarette stump or a cup of ashes. "If I ever catch you smoking again, I'm going to slap the crap out of you!" And sometimes, "Eddie, you're grounded!"

One day at Ava's house, Mom gave me two cigarettes when she was drunk. Dazed, I walked off to my hiding spot and smoked them. The next day, she had no memory of doing that.

A few weeks later, we had a get-together at our house. "Here, son." She tossed two more at me. I smoked one that night and saved the other one for the morning.

When I woke up the next day, Mom was getting dressed and ready to go out. When she left, I lit up. But as soon as I put the cigarette out, I heard a noise at the bedroom door. I stood just as Mom opened the door. She stared at the smoke. "Now, what did I tell you about smoking?"

"Geez, Mom, you gave it to me."

She stood there for a moment, seeming to waver, then turned and left. Thirty minutes later, she called me into the kitchen. "I'm leaving now. These are for you." She set two of her Marlboro Reds on the table.

Finally, she saw me as an adult.

On some occasions, Mom walked to Selena's house for beers and talking. I saw her go one day when I was hanging out at the pool.

Not too long afterward, I heard voices. José and some of my siblings walked by. I ran over. Maybe he'd come to see us. "He's here to see Mom," Maria informed me primly.

That was BS, for sure. I walked off but shortly thereafter, I heard Mom getting loud and headed to Selena's. I automatically stood near Mom, whose hands rested on her hips as she yelled. *"Hijo de la gran puta!"*

A pit settled in my stomach. Yeah, she'd just uttered the one thing you never say to a Latino man.

José reached out, slapping Mom hard on the right side of her face. She stumbled back, holding her cheek. I lunged forward toward José, swinging my arms, trying to hit him. He grabbed my wrist and then shoved me. "Enough!" He released me and walked away as I bristled, wondering if I should jump on his back and take him down. I checked on Mom as Selena tended to her.

I started punching a wooden fence. The need for revenge rolled over me like a sneaker wave. Walking down the street to José's apartment, thoughts circled furiously in my brain. I could punch him, beat him down. Or perhaps push him against the wall, holding my arm against his throat. So many options—and he deserved them all.

About a half an hour later, I arrived at the main entrance to José's apartments. Fear slowly crept over me. I quickly shrugged it off by reminding myself of Mom's plight, thanks to him.

José wasn't home. I gained courage and kicked and punched the front door. Once I saw how little effect that had, I considered breaking a window. But people walked by, and they'd call the cops. My hands started sweating, and I jogged home instead to see how Mom had fared.

A few weeks later after Mom and José talked about their issues, José pulled me aside. "I'm impressed that you defended your mom. You should never let anyone hit your mother."

Chapter 21

Jasmine

After Javier was released from jail, I was allowed to hang out with him, Roberto, and Luis. Before his release, I was only allowed to hang out at Roberto's apartment. Javier smoked weed, but the drug he really enjoyed became cocaine. Roberto, a pothead, avoided it. Luis used both.

We headed to a friend's house for a party one night—a frequent activity. At the party, drinking started. After the drinks came the blunts. Finally, someone brought out the hard stuff. This was the norm for hanging out with my older Cuban friends and a hierarchy, which lowered our inhibitions as we continued.

"Hey Eddie, you gotta try coke," Luis drawled from his position on the couch with the coffee table and supplies spread out. "Bada-bing."

Everyone else was already smashed. I considered. "Alright."

They started me with a little bump on the end of a key. I felt relaxed and confident.

They laughed at me and taught me to snort it via table lines a few parties later. Whenever they cut up lines for themselves, they cut up a little one for me.

I finally felt like an adult.

***

One day, while hanging out at Ava's apartment, Javier took a phone call and started talking frantically in Spanish. He hung up. "Luis, we gotta go. Eddie, we'll be back in half an hour. If anyone needs anything, take care of them."

"Like how?" I frowned.

He pulled me over to his mom's china cabinet and reached up to the top. He pulled out two orange medicine bottles. "The little bag is ten, and the bigger one is twenty." They scooted out the door as Luis called back and said that he expected a couple of people very soon.

Shortly afterward, a man strolled up to the apartment. I stood outside, smoking a cigarette. "Is Javier or Luis here?"

"Nah. They'll be back later. What do you need?"

He frowned. "Just to talk."

"What do you need for real?" I turned my head to blow smoke away from him.

He threw a puzzled look at me and glanced around nervously. "Gimme two twenties." He pulled out money, which I grabbed, and walked outside. At the china cabinet, I pulled out the larger bottle and one baggie of coke.

I placed the two twenty-dollar bills in the bottle before closing it and putting it back on top of the china cabinet. I walked out, handed him the baggie, and continued smoking.

Later, Javier and Luis returned from their errand to find me smiling because I'd just made them forty bucks while they were gone. They high-fived me.

Yet, another step to being treated as a grown-up.

***

Javier dated an 18-year-old girl named Maria—a short, skinny, quiet Puerto Rican girl. Something had happened at home, and she needed a place to stay, so Javier talked to my mom and arranged for her to stay with us in our apartment.

Once Maria moved in, we met her older, more outgoing sister named Jasmine. Jasmine was a tall, heavyset 19-year-old with two kids—one a little boy about Jesse's age and a little girl a year younger.

Surprisingly, Mom and Jasmine became good friends. Mom took us to Jasmine's studio apartment regularly at the Lake View Point apartments. There, they partied hard with guys and drank. As they enjoyed themselves, my siblings and I roamed the new area to see what we could get into.

We quickly discovered a broken soda machine. We walked to the clubhouse to buy a soda and I pulled the coin return. It returned more than I had put in.

"Check it out," I told Maria and handed her a dime. She smiled and placed it in the slot.

Jannet bent down and checked the slot after pulling on the coin return. She stood up with an open hand. "Thirty-five cents!" She grinned.

That is a pretty good return.

We kept going until another person came to use the vending machine. We didn't want them to learn our trick.

At first, my mom and Jasmine would hang out at Jasmine's with friends. Later, they started going out.

This is when things changed forever. When the party started getting good, everybody wanted to leave. Mom and Jasmine offered me cigarettes to watch the other kids. At first, it thrilled me to both get free cigarettes and to be allowed to smoke around the adults. Perhaps they also were finally seeing me as a true adult? But after a couple of nights, when they were gone all night long and came back the next morning wanting nothing but sleep, I grew angry. "This isn't fair," I complained. "You keep saying you'll only be gone a few hours. And the next day, you're so plastered, I have to watch them all day." I couldn't very well go get plastered myself when I had to watch the kids.

They increased the bargain. Now, I received full and half packs of cigarettes for babysitting. This only worked for a few more all-nighters before I started complaining again. "Mom. I got a life. I can't be here all day and night." The all-nighters continued, but not as frequently.

On occasion, I spent the night at Jasmine's apartment to watch her kids or because I had even more freedom at her place. Jasmine smoked weed, and she let me smoke it with her and her friends. I wasn't even fifteen yet, but I was living as an adult in many ways.

On one of these nights, Jasmine and I started talking about relationships. We sat on the couch, and she laid her legs across my lap. "Are you a virgin?" Jasmine purred. I swear, she almost batted her eyelashes.

My eyebrows raised practically to my hairline. Was she coming to me? "Course not." I scoffed.

"Show me, Eddie. Or are you scared to do that?"

My cheeks heated. "Uh, I gotta use the bathroom." I shot off the couch and headed to the hallway, my heart pounding. There, I was questioning my ability and wondered if there was a way to get out of this situation. Besides, Mom might kill me—and Jasmine.

"Come on, Eddie. No taking care of things without me!"

I took a deep breath, left the bathroom, and found her in her bedroom, sitting on her bed. I sat with her, and we kissed.

In a short time, she got her wish.

Chapter 22

Independence

In August, I received a letter from Oakridge High inviting me to a ninthe-grade orientation at the school on a Monday morning. The night before, Mom and Jasmine threw one of their parties. They returned very late the night before to Jasmine's apartment with a car one of their guy friends loaned them. We stayed the night there.

I woke up around 7 a.m. I found Mom asleep and shook her shoulder. "Mom, can I have a couple of bucks for the bus? I have orientation today."

"Eddie, I got nothing," she mumbled and turned away to go back to sleep.

Dang. I ran out to the living room and found her purse, which had three bucks. I grabbed the cash and ran outside. I didn't want to be late. I needed a buck each way for the bus, so that left me with a dollar. I stopped by the store, bought a little pack of cookies, and walked to the bus stop.

The orientation consisted of a school tour and a few speeches from the principal and a couple of deans. After the tour and speeches, people hung around and talked to friends while I searched for a familiar face.

I found no one. Feeling a bit adrift, I headed back to Jasmine's apartment. I opened Jasmine's door. Mom was rushing around, getting ready. "What's up, Mom?"

"Oh, hi, Eddie. Where have you been? I have an appointment. I'm borrowing a car from a friend of Jasmine's. You can come."

But Mom couldn't drive, I thought. Interesting.

We got into the car and slammed the doors. "We gotta stop for gas. I've only got three bucks."

My heart jumped about three feet. Not anymore, she didn't.

She pulled into the gas station and parked at the pump. She started rummaging through her purse looking for the three dollars, as I shrunk in my seat. Maybe she'd think she spent it partying last night

"Eddie, I had three bucks. Do you know where they went?"

"I don't know anything about it, Mom."

She frowned and scrounged through her purse again. "Wait—I know you asked me for some money early this morning. Eddie, come on. Own up!"

"I don't know what happened!"

After sitting there for about ten minutes, Mom handed me a couple of food stamps, told me to buy the cheapest candy, and brought her back the change. They don't give food stamp change now, but they did back then. The change brought enough gas to get us to the appointment and back. After the appointment, I thought for sure I'd get beaten, but the stolen money was never brought up again.

Shortly after orientation, I come home to find Javier's girlfriend, Maria, crying and holding the left side of her face. "Oh, sweetie. I'm sorry. You'll be OK." My Mom patted her on the shoulder, trying to console her.

Something big was up. "What's going on?" No answer from Maria or Mom.

Jannet walked by, and I stopped her. "Javier stopped by and argued with her. Then he started beating Maria up. Mom tried to intervene and told Javier to stop or she'd call the cops. But he didn't, so she did. They arrested him."

"It was the neighbors who called, not me." Mom was in the kitchen wetting a washcloth for Maria with cold water. Jannet and I both rolled our eyes.

The next day, Maria moved out of our apartment and back to her family's house.

Shortly after the incident, we moved again. I'm not sure if it was because of the police coming, due to the rent not being paid, or both. Mom found a duplex not far away—a small, one-level building on West Lancaster Street. Back closer to our old neighborhood.

The duplex had two bedrooms. The girls shared one and the boys the other. A covered carport held storage at the back. I liked the fact that we moved back because I already knew everyone and everything to do in that area. A big tree grew in the middle of the buildings, and all the kids who lived there played in and around that tree. I became the leader, of course, and we decided to build a tree house.

We played with a group of Italian kids who claimed to be descendants of the Italian mob boss, John Gotti. "They're full of crap," I told my siblings. "If they were for real, they'd be rich." The Italian kids moved after a month and a half of us living there, and I will never know for sure.

We lived in the duplex for about three months. In those three months, Mom's friend Selena had moved into one of the vacant ones next to us. Things improved—at least for us kids. We had good friends to hang out with. We even started calling each other cousins. Mom and Selena helped each other out in any way they could.

Once, our power quit just like that. Selena sent one of her friends to turn it back on. He unscrewed the meter, removed it, and replaced it upside down. The power returned until the electric company came knocking. "Ma'am, I need to ask you about your electric meter." The man stood at the door, imposing and large.

"No—no English," Mom lied.

"Come with me." The man beckoned with his hand, and we followed him out to the meter on the side of the duplex. "It's illegal to tamper with a meter."

Following Mom's cue, I "translated" that to her.

"I don't know," she answered in Spanish. "All I know is it wasn't working, but now it is."

I turned to the worker and explained.

"I'm going to have to call the police and report it," the man threatened.

"Go ahead!" Mom's hands went to her hips, and she forgot to speak Spanish. "The fingerprints will prove our innocence!"

The worker sighed. He didn't call the police, but he did return the meter back to normal and placed a lock on it.

In those three months, Mom continued with her old ways. She held constant parties with all kinds of dudes coming in and out of the house. I spent most of my time out in the neighborhood. I hung out in Lancaster Villas apartments or South Ridge with my old friends.

But again, a move threatened. This time, it wasn't due to lack of rent, but the owners relocating us. We moved down and across the street.

***

One day, as Lorenzo and I explored our new area, I thought I saw Bettina. I walked over to the fence. Bettina, apparently at a friend's house, played in a pool. Lorenzo joined me at the fence. "Hey, Bettina!"

Bettina and her friend Rachel walked to the fence. "Hey Eddie, Lorenzo. This is Rachel. I live over there." She waved at a fence on the other side of the field from the duplexes.

Lorenzo, Rudy, Lennie, and I started going to the neighborhood and hanging out when Rachel's parents weren't home. One time, with just Lorenzo and me there, we almost got caught. "My parents are here!" Rachel called out as we hung out in her room, and the garage door started squealing. Lorenzo and I took off out the back door and jumped the fence back to our duplexes. Hanging out with Bettina and Rachel occurred in spurts.

One day, Lorenzo, Rudy, and I were at Rudy's house talking on the phone to Bettina and Rachel when Bettina said something odd. "Lorenzo, I got a secret. I need to tell you, but not with Eddie there." Lorenzo grabbed the receiver from me and put it at his ear, looking at me with apologetic eyes. I ran to the other room to pick up another extension. "I really like you, Lorenzo," I heard whispered into the phone—and it came across loud and clear.

Crushed, I hung up the receiver quietly.

"Sorry, man," Lorenzo called from the other room after he'd hung up. Whatever. I went for a walk, trying to convince myself that she wasn't a piece of crap.

***

After another party, Mom returned with a boyfriend, Sammy, who worked in construction with his older brother. A weird man. He had this little thing he would do. He mumbled or said some funny-sounding words, and as soon as you said "what" or asked what he'd said, he'd return with "Got you" and start laughing. I never did understand why he did this, but it soon became a thing we all did.

Resourceful Sammy climbed the electrical pole on Lancaster Street in front of our house and connected the cable. We had all the channels for about a week or so before the company shut it off.

I heard Sammy's big brother saw Mom as trouble, plus she brought along a boatload of kids. He made a big deal about Sammy being around us, so Sammy didn't see Mom very often.

One day, all of us hung out at Jasmine's apartment as Mom started flitting around and getting her lipstick out of her purse. "Sammy's coming over," she announced.

He arrived with a friend—a tall, black dude who worked in construction with Sammy. The party was like all the others. They announced that they wanted to go out and wanted me to watch the kids. A pack of cigarettes landed on my lap. A half hour after they left, I heard them come back and loud voices. I walked out into the living room to see Jasmine swaying on her feet and poking Sammy's friend in the chest. "You insulted me at the party!" She ripped her coat off, nostrils flared. She swiped away a bead of sweat that landed in her eye.

Mom walked in with Sammy, and they tried to calm Jasmine down.

"I'm sorry. I really am," Sammy's friend attempted.

"Get your black butt out of my house!"

"Oh, it's like that? Screw you." The friend turned to leave, and Jasmine jumped on his back.

He turned around, knocking her off, and blocked a few swings from Jasmine. "Enough of that," he roared and grabbed Jasmine. He took her to her bedroom, threw her on the bed, and ran out of the apartment. I went to the bedroom and leaned on the doorjamb.

"Oh, heck no." Jasmine popped off the bed and ran after him, slamming the door behind her. Mom and I looked at each other. She sighed.

"We better go." I opened the door and saw Jasmine in the parking lot. Sammy and his friend drove off as she screamed at the back of the car.

Mom hustled a drunk Jasmine into the house and tried to explain things to calm her, but I doubt her friend absorbed any of it. "You're just taking your boyfriend's side over mine!"

"I am not. You need to calm down. He wasn't being rude on purpose. You're drunk, Jasmine."

"And you're a bitch. Whose side are you on, anyway?"

I stepped forward, ready to stop Jasmine if she got physical. Mom grabbed the phone, and later that night, Sammy's friend returned and gave us a ride home from Jasmin's house. But he wouldn't come into the house.

It was a long while before Sammy came around again. One day, he was there having beers with Mom, and she sent him to get more. He looked at me. "Come with me, Eddie."

Having nothing else to do, I agreed, and we headed to Cypress Landing Apartments in his van to see one of his friends.

At his friend's house, the dude who lived there whispered in his ear.

"What? Really?" Sammy pushed his friend's arm, a wide grin on his face. "Let's go!"

The three of us climbed into Sammy's van and drove to the far end of the complex. We parked in front of a small building, and they got out. I watched them open the door, and then Sammy motioned to me. I got out, glancing around. No one seemed to be around. I headed to the door and leaned against the door frame, observing the maintenance supplies inside.

"Grab a box of tiles, Eddie." Sammy grinned and motioned to a stack. "These suckers will go for at least a hundred." They grabbed two at a time. I could only heft one since they were about fifty pounds each. We ran them out to the van for about ten minutes and then hopped in and took off.

Sammy pulled out his wallet and handed me a twenty-dollar bill. "Thanks for your help."

I started to do the math in my head. I'd carried about seven cases of tiles. By my calculation, that should have been a lot more than twenty dollars if they were worth one hundred each.

We dropped off his friend. On the way back to the house, Sammy tilted his head toward me. "You can't tell your mom about this."

"I know, dude."

Once at the house, Mom's eyebrows raised. I saw her hands almost go to her hips, but she stopped herself. "Where's the beer?"

Sammy shuffled his feet. "Let's go. We'll get some on the way. I got a place."

Sammy took all of us out to a house he was working on in a rich neighborhood—way outside the city. We pulled into the driveway of a nice house with construction all around. The house was empty of furniture inside. Sammy brought in some construction blankets.

"Sit on these, kids. Where's the beer?" Mom turned to Sammy.

"Ah gee. I'll go to the store. Come on, Eddie."

I shrugged but felt weird. What were we going to do now?

On the way to the store, I found out. "I need your twenty, Eddie. A man has to provide for his family. I'll pay you back." He'd seen my frown.

With my money, Sammy bought the beer, cigarettes, and some snacks before returning to the house. That night, Mom and Sammy hung out and drank beer in the new house while my siblings and I played Hide-and-Go-Seek.

The next morning, we discovered a pool in the backyard. "Mom! Sammy? Can we swim?" We rushed back into the house.

"Sure." Sammy shrugged his shoulders. We stripped down to our underwear and jumped in.

Later, Sammy's brother showed up and started yelling at Sammy. "They can't be here, idiot! This is a client's house. Do you want to get us fired? Darn, you!" They argued for a little while. We heard Sammy's brother drive away in his big truck.

Sammy popped into the backyard, slamming the gate. "Time to go."

After Sammy dropped us off that day, I never saw him again.

***

Since we now lived closer to South Ridge, I often headed to Roberto's apartment or hung out with kids around my age. I saw José and Alex every now and again, but we didn't talk anymore after the car burglaries. Plus, he never did pay me that five bucks. They started hanging out with one of the older kids in the apartments named, Macho, who also lived in South Ridge.

I hung out with Attlee, who also lived in South Ridge. We walked by a stairway where José and Alex sat on the steps. I glanced over, and they glared at me as we walked by.

"What's that all about?" Attlee flicked a fly off his arm.

"Screw them. I should beat Alex's butt for that money he still owes me."

Attlee paused his stride. "Wait a minute, Alex owes you money and won't pay? Then he sits there and stares you down like that and you're not going to do anything about it?"

"It's only five bucks."

"I'd screw someone up for a dollar."

"Fine then. Let's go."

We reversed our route. They still sat there like dummies. I walked up to Alex and pointed in his face. "Where's that five dollars you owe me for getting that girl's number for you?"

"I don't owe you anything." He lifted his chin.

"Man, he's not giving you nothing." Attlee elbowed me.

"He's not giving you anything." José echoed.

Alex heaved up the stairs and started to walk off.

I pushed at him. "Where's my money?" José stepped between us, so I pushed him, too. José grabbed my wrist, and I yanked it away. I started to punch José in the back of the head.

"Ow, man!" he yelled.

Alex started swinging wildly at me over his brother's back. I swung back. Alex moved back when he got hit, and I prepared to punch José again. Attlee grabbed my arms from behind. While Attlee was holding me, José hit me, and Attlee finally let me go. I landed a solid punch on José. As I was winding up again, their dad appeared suddenly and grabbed me by my wrist. "What do you think you are doing?" He started flapping my own wrist against my face. He finally let us walk away.

"Why the heck would he grab me in the middle of a fight?" I fumed on the way home.

"I thought you were going to kill him, so that's why I grabbed you."

"Never grab me while I am in a fight, Attlee. That was stupid."

I was the most mortified that his dad had grabbed me and hit me with my own hands, of course. Boy, must I have looked like a dumbass?

After leaving Attlee at his house, I walked over to Roberto's apartment and told him about what had just gone down. I also told him about the dad grabbing me. An hour or so later, Roberto and a couple of his friends decided to take a walk and smoke a blunt with me. As we walked, we saw José, Alex, and their dad walking up to their apartment. I pointed the dad out to Roberto and his friends. Their dad looked worried, but nothing ever came out of it.

***

I started attending Oak Ridge High School shortly after moving to the duplexes. Oak Ridge, one of the biggest high schools I had ever seen, owned their own baseball field, soccer field, football field, and tennis court.

As usual, making friends became challenging. I again found myself trying to come up with things to do that didn't tell everyone that I was alone. The worst time to not have friends was lunchtime, of course, and the most noticeable time to others. I again ate while walking around. Sometimes, I grabbed my lunch and tried to stand near a group in hopes others would think I was a part of them. Sometimes, after finishing my food, I walked around the crowded areas, hoping to find something going on that I could watch.

The students smoked in the bathrooms all day long. They lit up in the stalls and I never understood why the school put up with it. Once, when I was in the bathroom waiting for a urinal to open, one of the deans walked in and stood next to me. I thought for sure he was going to address the massive cloud of cigarette smoke that we stood in. But he just waited his turn and walked out.

I eventually made a friend when a new kid came to the school. Jacob was a heavyset, white, blond kid who had moved to Orlando from out of state. The school paired us up because we both were new. But Jacob and I only had Art class together and not even the same lunch. For the most part, we only hung out in class. On a couple of occasions, we crossed paths, either going to or coming from lunch. "Hey." He stopped me in the hall one day. "Let's go swim at my house. My folks aren't home."

Oak Ridge, as a closed campus, did not allow students to leave the school except to go home. This rule made it difficult to go swimming. We escaped by climbing the fences that separated the different fields. We ran across the field to a Bryan wall that separated the field and the woods. There were truancy officers who patrolled certain areas, but we knew once we were in the woods, we'd be safe. Jacob's house was close to the school. Swimming was quite fun—much more fun than school anyway.

The third time Jacob suggested going to his house for a swim, I agreed again. We cleared the first fence. We waited for one of the deans to pass by our hiding spot. Once he walked by, we ran across the baseball field. We reached the Bryan wall and started to climb. Once on top of the fence, I saw a group of kids smoking on the other side. Jake and I jumped off the fence, and they formed a semicircle around us. "What are you doing?"

"Skipping. Duh." I recognized one of the kids named Saloon from Walker. "Hey, what's up with you these days?"

"Not much." He kicked a rock that bounced against the wall.

"Let's go, Eddie." Jake smacked my shoulder blade.

"You go ahead. I want to hang out with them."

"Ah, man. OK." Jake walked away, his shoulders slumped.

***

My mom kept in touch with José, so I kept up with José sometimes. José stopped by the house occasionally. Sometimes, he drove me to one of his friends' houses or to his girlfriend's house. We mostly landed at his girlfriend Margarita's house.

José drank his Miller High Life beer as I hung out with Wilson, Margarita's son. Her daughter, Josefina, was a year older than I was, and Margarita's other daughter, Sofia, was a few years older. We became friends.

While José was busy with Margarita, Wilson and I stole José's car keys and took turns driving around the apartment parking lot.

For the most part, José stayed uninformed. One time, he came out to find us parking his car, but we never got in trouble. That is probably why we kept doing it.

On occasions at Margarita's place, I met guests, and it always felt weird. As soon as they found out José was my dad, they'd come up with all kinds of crap.

"Hey, tell José to get me a car."

"Ask José if take us all to the new nightclub, will ya?"

I don't know why they thought I had any sway with José—much less why they seemed to think he had a ton of money—but I never asked.

We went to Margarita's a couple of times a week. Once, Wilson and I were chatting in the back room.

"Hey, boys, come out here."

We wandered out to the dining room, where José grinned. "Time to get jobs. 'Bout time you earned your keep. It's dishwashing at Bill Wong's Famous Buffet. I'm taking you to apply."

We both got a job at the rate of $4.75 per hour, minimum wage back then. About a week into the new job, Wilson quit. He moved to another restaurant in the same shopping mall as Bill Wong's Famous Buffet.

The work wasn't bad and kept me busy. The worst part was dealing with the scalding hot water and taking out the trash. My job included spreading the tub of dirty dishes on a plastic rack and spraying them off with a hot, high-powered sprayer. The rack then slid into the dishwasher. The process left me soaked with water and spattered food. This was still better than the trash, which stank like ten garbage dumps and stuck to your hands and clothes if it was aimed a bit awry. We took a gray Rubbermaid trash can half-full of half-eaten foods and tried to twist the trash can onto a roller designed to fit the bottom of the cans without making a nasty mess. Once the can was in place, we pushed it to the compactor. It took two of us to lift the trash can up and into the compactor. Although we attempted to do it without getting sprayed by garbage, it seldom worked that way.

About two weeks into working at Bill Wong's Famous Buffet, Wong, one of the owners, called me into the office. "I looked at your ID from school. It says you are only fourteen?"

I suddenly realized that José had pulled strings. I wasn't legal to work yet. But I really wanted to keep my job. "Uh . . . that's the old ID."

Wong gave me a puzzled look, shrugged his shoulders, and walked out of the room.

After a month and a half of working as a dishwasher, they offered me a promotion from dishwasher to a greeter. I bought a white button-up shirt and a black tie, per the rules. I added black slacks with black shoes, and they gave me a black apron to wear. Spiffy.

As a greeter, my duties included keeping all the soups filled and answering questions. I did well at both.

"The egg drop soup is low," I'd overhear and run back to the chef to get it refilled. Other than that, I stood there and smiled at people. The best part of being a greeter was getting to split the busboy's tips every night.

The best thing about working at Bill Wong's Famous Buffet as a growing boy who had little to eat at home was the food. Each night, employees ate leftover food. We ate BBQ pork, shrimp, and all the good stuff. Once everyone was finished, we wrapped up the rest to take home. I brought home Chinese food every night. Eventually, neighbors asked me to bring them food. After a while, I stopped eating Chinese food for a long time.

Work became more important than school. I soon was too tired to get up for school in the mornings. I wanted money more than school. I received my first paycheck and didn't know what to do with it. I cashed the check and gave the whole thing to Mom. After all, hadn't José said I needed to earn my keep? "Here, this is for you and my brothers and sisters."

"Thanks, Eddie." She actually got tears in her eyes.

I did that with my first few paychecks. After two months of giving Mom my whole paycheck and seeing her blow it on parties and having fun, I decided to keep the next one.

The next payday, I went shopping for new clothes and shoes. I took Lorenzo out to International Drive, where all the outlet malls were. "I need shoes." He watched me try most of them on while I strutted back and forth in front of the mirror.

I bought myself a new pair of Reeboks. It felt good to pay for them instead of stealing. I later went to a couple of clothing stores and bought two outfits. The last thing I bought myself was a Dickie brand jacket. After shopping, I took Lorenzo to lunch at Bill Wong's Famous Buffet.

He stuffed himself, and I enjoyed spoiling him. "Hey, don't blow up or anything." I elbowed him as we forced ourselves out the door.

"Let's go see a movie." Lorenzo's eyes brightened.

"Yeah, OK. We can go to the mall."

We hopped on a bus and rode across town. At the mall, I disembarked with three big bags. "What do you want to see?"

"What about that new fight one?"

"Nah. Let's go for some laughs."

"OK. You're paying."

Before we entered the theater, I decided to put on my new shoes. I put my old shoes in the new box. As I walked in, I handed Lorenzo my bags. I walked up to the register and paid for the tickets. I also bought popcorn and candy. Guess I wasn't as stuffed as I thought. I carried all the food into the movie.

I got to my seat and got comfortable. The previews started, and I was startled when I glanced at the floor. "Lorenzo, where are my bags?"

Lorenzo's eyebrows raised, and so did the palms of his hands. I jumped up quickly and rushed past him and into the lobby. He followed.

We searched to no avail. I asked the person at the register. "I didn't see anything, dude."

I ran outside the theater, hoping to see someone walking with my bags, but no one was around. We walked by the dumpster and saw one of my bags. I opened the bag and saw my shoebox. Inside, my old pair of shoes. I took my old shoes and stomped off. We never went back to the movie. I wouldn't even speak to Lorenzo. He hung his head and looked sad.

We walked home, and I made him carry my old shoes the whole way. After we dropped my shoes off at the house, I decided to go to

South Ridge. On the way to South Ridge, we found a shopping cart. "Lorenzo, push the darn cart."

"What? Why?"

"Do it," I practically growled, and he pushed it for a bit. "Keep going." It was the least he could do to make up for it, I thought. It didn't dawn on me that I was being a bully or just flat out abusive, and emulating others in our lives. I made Lorenzo push that shopping cart for about five city blocks.

"It's heavy. And I'm too hot," Lorenzo complained a few times.

"Well, you're the one who forgot my bags in the lobby when I was busy buying you what you wanted."

"Whatever, dude."

***

To get to work, I usually took two buses since it was nine miles from the house. When I didn't have bus fare, I walked. I was no wimp. It took me about three hours to walk one way. Other times, if I got off too late and the buses had stopped running, I also had to walk home.

One time, I got off work late and headed home on foot. Exhausted, I crashed into bed as soon as I got to it. I woke up late for my next shift. I glanced outside. Why was it still dark? Weird. I rushed to get dressed and ran out the door, walking as fast as I could. It'd be my first time late, so they'd surely understand. Three hours later, I finally walked into an empty parking lot. Confused, I approached the window of the restaurant. Inside the window, the clock blinked. I was about twelve hours early to work.

***

Not long after I started working at Bill Wong's, Mom started working at Kmart. For the first time I could remember, we were off welfare. With my mom and I both working, bills got paid, and groceries filled the refrigerator. We didn't need to find churches for food boxes or go to the food banks anymore. I was so proud to help out with the bills—just like a man providing for his family.

Then I noticed Mom started missing her work shifts. Shortly after I noticed a decline in Mom work, she quit. A couple of days after she quit Kmart, she called me into the kitchen. "I want you to quit your job."

"Huh?"

"Eddie, we need benefits from the state. We don't qualify with you working."

Dang. She wanted back on welfare. I was really upset with my mom's choice, but I complied and quit my first job.

***

I took charge of my siblings, as always, when Mom left. I didn't particularly want to stay home and babysit, but I had to. I developed a different approach to childcare. With complete power over my siblings, I made up competitions to serve me. When we were hungry, the person who made me the best sandwich could go out and play. If I wanted something that we didn't have, I created a contest to go out and obtain whatever I requested.

One time, Jesse wanted to go play outside.

"Fine. Go steal me some candy from the dollar store."

He was gone for a while, and when he came back, he looked mad. "I tried. I got caught."

"You got caught?" My fists clenched, and I stared him down. "What the heck, Jesse? You aren't going out to play at all."

Jesse threw a huge fit, and I issued more consequences.

***

On my fifteenth birthday, I woke up excited and ready for a fun day. I walked through the house.

"Happy birthday, Eddie!" Jannet smiled at me, and Maria echoed her words. Lorenzo slapped me on the back.

I found Mom in the kitchen. She didn't say anything. "Is there anything planned for my birthday, Mom?"

"Eddie, you know I don't have any money for any birthdays."

I thought she was trying to outsmart me.

Later in the day, one of Mom's friends stopped by. I overheard them talking. "I'm so upset I couldn't get Eddie anything for his birthday," Mom sniffed.

Mom wasn't playing with me at all. Didn't I deserve something? I worked hard to take care of this family, too. Disappointment and anger rolled over me in waves, and I left, slamming the door behind me.

I walked up to Winn-Dixie and looked at the cakes. I bought myself a personal-sized cake, about 4 x 6 inches. I walked back home and gave each one of my siblings a little piece of cake. I ate the rest myself. About an hour later, Mom's friend returned with another little cake for my birthday.

***

Shortly after I fought José and Alex, a rumor circled that their friend Macho, wanted to fight me. Macho, a year older than I, also lived in South Ridge. The reason for fighting me wasn't clear, but his intentions were. After we argued a few times, we arranged to fight. I was going to fight Macho, and Lorenzo was going to fight José.

The day of the fight arrived. It was scheduled at the field in front of my duplex. Lorenzo ran into the house to tell me that Macho, José, Alex, and a bunch of people were walking up Lancaster toward our house. By the time they reached the driveway, Lorenzo and I were already strutting out to the field.

Lorenzo and José fought first. José first charged Lorenzo with his head down, then grabbed him by the waist. Lorenzo wrestled José to the ground, landing on top of him. He punched like a madman and dropped knees into José's chest. "I give up. I give up!" José squirmed around as Lorenzo rose. Alex helped his brother up.

Then, it was time for Macho and me. We squared off, and I took a couple of swings at him without making contact. He did the same. The fight ended quickly when a police cruiser pulled into the entrance of the duplexes. A female officer got out of the cruiser and separated Macho and me. "What's this fight all about?"

"What fight?" We both claimed innocence.

She patted us both down, also checking our midsections. All the bystanders had a heyday with that.

***

Mom used her usual method when there was no money: flirt with someone to get a beer. She brought many new men home, and they always held a 12-pack of beer. She'd introduce her new friend and start drinking at the table.

One day, I arrived home to find Mom and another new man at the table, drinking beer. After introductions, I recognized him. He was the stepdad to a teenager I knew who lived in the duplexes across the street with his mom. They were halfway into an 18-pack of beer already. Feeling protective, I decided to stick around until he left.

About an hour later, with the beer finished, Mom wanted to go to bed. "Time for you to go home. I'm heading to bed."

"Come on, Estrella. Let's have some more."

"Thanks." She yawned. "I'm kind of wasted."

"I think we should hang out a little longer."

"Suit yourself. See you later." She went to bed, and he left.

After he left, Lorenzo and I decided to find some friends. We walked around the neighborhood, but it was too late, so no one was out and about. As we headed back to the house, we saw a girl running across the street. "Who is that?" Lorenzo stared at her.

"It's Jannet!" She'd gotten closer, and I recognized her.

"Eddie, Lorenzo." Our sister sounded frantic.

"What's going on?"

She pulled in a deep breath. "That guy got in the house and is in the room with mommy."

I took off running toward the house, leaving Jannet and Lorenzo behind. Jesse and Maria waited in the living room. I rushed over to the bedroom door, but it was locked. I ran to the kitchen to get a butter knife. I picked up the lock and opened the door. When the door opened, I saw the man on top of Mom. Her pants and underwear bunched up at one of her ankles. He jumped up and landed against the door, closing it on me. He relocked it.

I unlocked the door again and started pushing against it to get it open. I pushed it open just enough to see him holding the door with one hand and trying to pull up his pants with his other. "Lorenzo, come help me!" Lorenzo and I managed to push the door open.

"*Que estás hacienda!*" I barged into the room. What was he doing there?

"Hey, dude. No issues here. Your mom said it was OK."

I didn't pause. "Get the heck out. Now."

He slowly walked to the door, trying to explain himself. "I spent all that money on beer. Your mom was fine with this. She knew when I bought the beer how it'd all end, son."

"She can't be OK when she's passed out. Leave!" Lorenzo seemingly grew taller next to me and stepped forward. The other kids huddled in the corner of the living room.

He stepped outside, and I locked the door behind him. He started beating on the front door, trying to get in. Then he started beating on the window. This scared me because he could break the window and get in. I decided to go out the back door and get him out of the carport. "Stay with the kids, Lorenzo. Don't open the door for anything." I grabbed the broom and stalked outside to the carport. "Hey!"

The man turned toward the carport and faced me in the little field. "Leave now! Go far away."

"What if I don't?" he sneered.

I shook the broom at him. I'm sure I looked very threatening.

He seemed undeterred. "Your mom was fine with all of that. She invited me."

I realized that the man was not leaving, and my threats weren't doing anything. Hearing a noise behind me, I spun around. Lorenzo joined me. I turned to face the man and threatened him again with the broom. Zero reaction.

Out of ideas, I looked down and saw an empty beer bottle in the grass. I picked it up. "I'll hit you with this if you don't leave."

He started walking toward us. "Really, boys, isn't this a little out of hand? Your mom invited me here tonight. She's not going to be happy when she hears how this went."

I chucked the bottle at him but missed. He stumbled over to the bottle and picked it up. He launched it back at me. I dove to the ground as the bottle flew past. Lorenzo dodged it, as well. The man started to stumble away. We followed him at a distance.

Suddenly, he stopped and came back toward the house. Once back at the carport, the man banged on the door and the window again.

"Hey, knock it off! You gotta leave!" My heart about pounded out of my chest now. I took a deep breath. Low on ideas, I handed Lorenzo the broom and told him to stay put. I walked to the back of the carport and picked up a bike frame with missing tires. I held it over my head, facing the back of the man. "Hey!" When he turned around to face me, I again told him to leave. He again pled his case. After one more round of this, I moved the bike frame toward him and shook it. Would he get the point?

He didn't budge.

I sighed. "I'm counting backward from three. Got that? Three . . . two . . ." With every second, my fear increased to ten. By "two," sweat dripped off my forehead. The bike frame almost slipped out of my hands. I paused. The man just stood looking at me calmly. I hesitated, then raised the bike frame a little higher and bonked him in the middle of the forehead. He stumbled back. I heaved the bike frame back over my head, ready.

The dude stood there for a second, and blood started running from his hairline. "Ah, come on, man. You know she invited me."

I looked at Lorenzo, who just shook his head. Unbelievable.

I turned back to the intruder. "I will hit you again."

He stumbled once more, then wandered off. I followed to ensure he didn't return.

The next morning when Mom woke up, I was so pissed that I started yelling. "Do you have any idea what happened? He was in your bedroom, in your bed, on top of you. Had your freakin' pants down, and you were passed out. Passed out, Mom. We had to get in the room, and get him out of the house, and he still didn't leave. I had to hit him with the bike frame! And you didn't even wake up!"

"Why didn't you call the police?"

I kicked the wall, quite sure my eyes bulged two times their size at this point. What a bitch. "Oh, OK, sure! That's a great way to let the cops know you were completely drunk and have them send all the kids back to foster care." I jerked my head toward my wide-eyed siblings sitting in the living room. A dead silence descended. Mom rolled her eyes, turned, and walked to her bedroom. She closed the door without saying a word.

Two days later, I walked down Lancaster when the man's stepson saw me. "Hey Eddie, what's up?" My insides started shaking, but I headed over. "Was my dad over at your house the other day?"

"No, man, I don't know what you mean."

The kid looked at me with obvious disbelief and started to describe what his dad looked like. I was well aware of what the man looked like, and I hoped he still bled from his head. But I lied and told the kid I wasn't aware of his dad's activities. I was too scared of repercussions.

I never saw that man again. And that's probably a good thing.

Chapter 23

Friends

For the most part, I spent most of my time in South Ridge apartments because I knew so many people. After the Macho fight, I avoided the area a bit and hung out instead at Lancaster Village.

One day, some friends and I were talking about boxing. This led to a few of us slap-boxing. Out of nowhere, an older Puerto Rican kid popped up. "Who's winning?"

Eyebrows raised. The one kid pointed to me. "Eddie."

Oh, sure, throw me under the bus.

"Oh yeah?" He snapped his gum. "I bet you twenty bucks I can beat you."

I sized up my competition. Smaller than me but oozing confidence. That threw me off a bit. "Nah, dude. Thanks, but I gotta get going."

The following week, I returned to Lancaster Village. This time, one of the residents, Marvin, held boxing gloves. He loaned them to me. I was boxing a kid in a little field next to a building when, out of nowhere, the same Puerto Rican kid appeared. He walked over to my opponent and took his gloves off. Putting them on his own hands, he grinned at me. "Now we're going to see how good you are."

Trying to hide the tremble in my voice, I agreed due to the pressure of the crowd forming around us.

We started. Nervous, I tried to keep my distance. He kept trying to take my head off with one punch. Each time he tried, I scooted out of the way or used my reach to block him. We continued for about ten minutes. He never hit me. In fact, he ended up having an asthma attack and quitting. One of the kids who was watching ran and got his grandmother to help. She brought out an asthma machine and hooked him up to it.

At school, buzz hit the halls fast as word flew from one student to another.

"Eddie." Marvin wandered over to me in the hallway a couple of days later. "Come over and box after school."

I puffed up. "Sure. Why not?"

I showed up at Marvin's house to find a group of kids from school waiting. Marvin pulled me into the circle. "Why don't you start with someone else? This is Todd."

I nodded at Todd. He was about my size but stockier.

The match started with the two of us circling each other a couple of times. A couple of jabs came next. Then, Todd smacked me hard. My head flew back and when I got it leveled out, the crowd around me spun. Still woozy, I managed to catch the kid with a right hook and backed him off. The fight was an even match.

Marvin was next. We squared off. Marvin hit me with a right that snapped my head back. I stepped in and hit Marvin with a couple of quick jabs to the body. He got me with a big shot—I was done. Enough of that crap. I took a lesson from the Puerto Rican kid and faked a breathing problem to stop the fight.

I later fought a black kid. This match, more of a back and forth, started with circling. We traded a few punches. I hit Andre with a little combo and backed him off. When I stepped in and hit him with another combo, he fell to one knee and announced a slip. The bystanders backed me up, and we restarted. Andre came at me with his own move that backed me up. We traded combinations again. This time, when I was hit, I stumbled back, and the bystanders reacted.

A burn started in my stomach. Now he was pissing me off. I frowned and decided to turn it up a notch. I hit Andre with a long combo and backed him up into a little garden that was nearby. He went down. "Slip!" But we boxed for a few more minutes before the fight was considered a draw.

I ripped off the gloves and threw them to the ground. None of the knockdowns counted, or I would have won the stupid fight.

***

I spent all my free time at either South Ridge or Lancaster Village. As it became hotter outside, my brother and I started looking for pools. Both the complexes had pools but only for residents. Although we were past residents of both, we weren't at that time, and people knew it. When we jumped into the pools, adults threatened to call management. We started looking for other places to cool off.

One day, at the back pool of South Ridge with no one the wiser, Lorenzo and I swam happily, then noticed a couple of girls we didn't know heading over. They slid in at the other end. One of them, heavyset and dark-skinned with a big chest, caught my attention. Lorenzo elbowed me and I realized my mouth hung open. I snapped it shut. The other gal, thin and light-skinned, started a backstroke. "Hey, go ask around about them, Lorenzo." He swam over to them.

Eventually, we talked, and I learned they were sisters. "I'm Gloria," the dark one said. "My sister here is Sarah. We just moved here with our mom."

"Eddie," I mumbled, for some reason feeling out of my element.

These two spoke three languages. I easily interpreted the Spanish and the English. When they wanted privacy, they busted out in French, making my jaw clench.

I started hanging out at Gloria's house regularly. A local kid named José started hanging out there as well. The four of us often hung out on the stairs next to the girls' apartment. Eventually, I started dating Gloria, and José started dating Sarah.

Gloria was inexperienced with boys—she didn't even want to kiss. We spent most of our time talking. I stopped by the house during parties and the girls sneaked me and Lorenzo a beer or two. Gloria and I only dated for about two weeks, but I still stopped by occasionally afterward.

One day, I sauntered through South Ridge when I saw evidence of a party going on at Gloria's house. I stopped by and spotted Sarah out front. "Hi, Sarah."

"Hey, Eddie. How are things?"

"Good." As we talked, I realized I had more in common with Sarah than Gloria. And she was a year older than me. Sarah sneaked me a beer, and we kept chatting.

After a few beers and a good conversation. I mustered up some courage. "I'm kinda into you."

I swear her smile almost wrapped around her whole head. A pretty pink mounted her cheeks. "I kinda like you too, Eddie."

When I woke up the next day I, Gloria and Sarah waited in the living room. "Who do you think you are?" Gloria stood, glowering, when I arrived at the entry. "Why'd you tell Sarah you liked her?"

"I dunno. Well, I knew she wouldn't keep a secret from you."

"Oh. Well, that was smart. She told me right away."

Sarah just stood there, smiling sweetly.

Although I still liked Sarah, I never tried to talk to her like that again. I didn't need the wrath of Gloria. I stopped hanging out there as often after that. I just talked to them at school and occasionally around South Ridge.

***

Lorenzo and I stumbled upon a small apartment complex with a pool. We made friends with a short kid named Carlos, who lived there. Carlos became our tool for pool time since residents could host up to two guests at a time. We spent a couple of days in a row there, enjoying the cool-off. We swam, splashed, and tackled each other all day when I suddenly froze. A beautiful girl appeared at the edge of the pool. "Hey Carlos, come here."

"Who is that? Does she live here? What's her name?"

"Geez, man." He splashed me, laughing, so I grinned back. "That's Jessica. She lives about a block away in the duplexes. We dated for a bit."

"Is she free now?"

"Sure. I don't care." He swam over to talk to her.

I made my way to the edge of the pool where she sat, dangling her beautiful legs. "Hi, I'm Eddie. I don't think I've met you."

"No, you haven't, and no, you don't need to."

Well then.

My luck later changed, though, and she slowly warmed up to me. One day, as she and I walked to Winn-Dixie, I heard my name and turned around. Sloane. I hadn't seen him since I last skipped school and climbed the Bryan wall to go swimming. After we chatted, I walked Jessica home because he'd been checking her out.

A few days later, I saw Sloane and one of his friends, Bruno. Close friends. The fact that I'd seen Sloane without Bruno a few days before was rare. They were known for not just their friendship but their constant pot smoking. "What's up, Eddie?"

"Nothing. Just hanging out."

"Who was that girl you were with the other day? She's a beaut."

Turned out that Sloane was just looking for information about Jessica. I got out of the conversation as soon as possible.

***

One time, I was riding my bike when I saw Sloane, Bruno, and a couple of their friends walking in South Ridge. I braked. "What's up, guys?"

"We're heading to a friend's house. Come with."

I followed them because I was bored. Turns out, their friend was an older black man with a New York accent. He apparently lived alone and used Sloane to get weed. At his house, Sloane picked up his phone and arranged for a deal. I decided to head outside. About ten minutes later, Sloane and Bruno left his house but came back. I pedaled around on my bike, waiting to see what this was all about. "Hey, Eddie," Sloane called me over. "Can you go out to the entrance? You know where the sign is? Wait for a green car, and let me know when it comes."

I shrugged and pedaled off. At the entrance, I circled for about ten minutes. Looks like we had a no-show. I headed back to the apartment and knocked on the door. Sloane cracked it open. "No one came."

"OK then." He closed the door. I heard laughter from behind the door. Oh brother. I hopped on my bike and rode home.

Two weeks later, I saw Bruno at Winn-Dixie. Bruno was heading to the high school, so I tagged along. We walked up to the front of the school, where a group of students stood talking. As I approached, I realized they were the popular kids. Bruno walked up to the group, and they greeted him. Several threw me a weird look but then greeted me as well. Hispanic girls greeted people uniquely—a half hug and a kiss on the cheek. Some of them made me sweat just looking at them—extra hot.

After seeing Bruno at Winn-Dixie and walking with him to the school, he started talking to me whenever he saw me. I learned eventually that his older brothers were a part of local gangs with other well-known people in Orlando. "It's all about who you know," he often reminded me.

After I started hanging out with Bruno, Sloane joined in. I could tell that Sloane didn't care for me as much. He poked fun and put me down every chance he got. I gave it back. It seemed like Sloane just talked to me to get to know Jessica. But Bruno became a genuine friend. It was a little weird because Bruno and Sloane had known each other for years, and I'd known Sloane for a long time. But Bruno and I became the closest out of the three of us.

Sloane lived in a duplex with his mom, her boyfriend, and his little brother, Jamel. The three of us spent most of our time at Sloane's. His mom allowed him to smoke outside, so it became a popular place to hang out.

Sloane had a gray broken-down Honda sitting in their carport. We sat in the Honda for hours, smoking. Sloane claimed the driver's seat each time, and Bruno usually sat in the passenger seat. Every now and again, I sat in the passenger seat when Bruno wasn't there. But my typical spot became the back seat.

Shortly after I started hanging out with them, I noticed people treating me differently. "Hey, Eddie," I'd hear. The guys nodded at me, and the girls flocked to give me a kiss on the cheek and their half hug. Once I passed a whole group of kids at the high school and overheard someone asking who I was. "He's Bruno and Sloane's friend," someone answered. I puffed up like a peacock.

Everywhere I went, I was now known as Bruno and Sloane's friend, and I enjoyed the respect. Nobody messed with Bruno because of his older brothers. Nobody messed with Sloane and me because we were friends with Bruno. For the first time in my life, my peers accepted me. I was finally popular.

***

Bruno, Sloane, and I spent much time trying to get cigarettes and weed and having smoke fests. Bruno developed a system. "First, we need to scrounge up two bucks to buy a pack of Newports. Then, we'll stand out by the store and ask people to buy them."

It worked, and once we obtained our cigarettes, we hung out and smoked them. If it was school hours, we'd skip and smoke in the woods behind Winn-Dixie.

One day Sloane and I found some local kids from Sloane's neighborhood. I really only knew one—Hector. Sloane, Hector, two of his friends, and I decided to walk around the neighborhood. We walked by a small apartment complex with a basketball hoop and decided to shoot for a bit since a ball sat right on a nearby bench. I started dribbling. A woman leaned out of a parked car, "Hey, you guys don't live here!"

"So?" Sloane lined up a shot and swished the ball through the hoop.

"So you can't play. Get out of here."

We turned to leave. I grabbed the ball and took a parting shot. The ball hit the rim and skipped off, bounced on the ground twice, and hit the woman's car. "Gosh darn you! You jerk!" She was still yelling as we exited the apartment complex.

We started walking back towards Sloane's house when a brown hatchback pulled into the apartment complex. We watched the person in the car talk to the woman. They spoke loudly, pointing to us. Dang. The car backed out quickly and sped past us, getting close to one of Hector's friends ahead. It stopped and turned around three blocks ahead of us. The car sped back to the apartments and pulled in again. We kept watching—even though my heart started a funny, fast beat. The car quickly backed out again. Out of the corner of my eye, I saw Sloane watching the car intently. As it backed out again, he picked up an empty beer bottle from the ground and held it ready. The car sped toward us again, and as it passed us, he threw the bottle. It landed in the car. Brakes squealed as the car stopped in the middle of the street.

We took off. Sloane and I headed in the same direction. We ran like crazy and ducked into someone's backyard. We ran through another five backyards, jumping fences. Once we got to the street, I pulled up short. "Where's Hector?" I gasped.

Equally winded, Sloane wiped sweat off his face. "Did they run the other way? I hope they didn't get caught. I'm the one who threw it." We took off again and ran about six blocks, finally stopping behind a dental office. After catching our breath, we contemplated going back to our friends.

"Real friends would go back," I mused.

"Yeah, they would," Sloane huffed but agreed.

We started jogging back to the apartment complex with the basketball court. As we neared, we saw the cops. "Oh crap, I've got weed," Sloane grunted. He stashed it under a tree in a corner. When we got closer, we saw Hector and his friends talking to the police. "Oh man, I got cigarettes too!" I chuckled as he dropped them. As we approached Hector, it appeared that they were releasing them. The cop found some teenagers nearby to chat with, then left and drove by Sloane and myself. Hector and his friends walked off ahead of us. As we tried to catch up, we walked by the group of teenagers. "Oh, you're in trouble." They said as they recognized us.

"Shut up." Sloane glared at them. "This ain't none of your bizness."

"We saw you," one claimed. "We might tell the cops."

"Go ahead," I dared them.

"See ya, losers. Trust me, you have no idea who you're messing with." Sloane flipped them off as he and I sauntered by the group. We continued toward Hector and company.

As the cop car reached the corner, an older man waved at it to stop. He'd apparently seen Sloane drop his cigarettes as we turned the corner because the cop got out, picked them up, and hopped back in the car. The car came flying at us in reverse. He pulled in front of us and jumped out. "Get on the ground!"

Sloane sat quickly with his legs crossed. The cop grabbed him by his collar and slammed him to the ground on his belly. My stomach rolled. I quickly hit the pavement, belly down.

"I can give you an MIP charge for that," the cop bellowed at us both. "Do you know what that means?"

I shook my head miserably. I didn't dare turn my head to look at Sloane.

"It's a 'minor in possession' charge. You want to be in trouble, boys? Sure, they'd love you in juvy."

OK. He got me there. My legs started trembling, even though I wanted to get up and punch someone out.

After a few more stern sentences, the cop released us.

Sloane and I shook it off and caught up to Hector and his friends, who were a couple of blocks away.

"Those idiot teenagers saw us. They jumped out and grabbed me." Hector shook his head as he pulled out a cigarette he'd apparently hid from the officer. Yeah, I needed one too. "We were right behind you till they did that. They held us until the cop came."

The five of us walked back to Sloane's house. Bruno and his big cousin Frado waited for us. "Man, you won't believe what happened." Sloane and I told the whole story and complained about the teenagers who'd dared hold them captive. We told them where they lived and watched with satisfaction as Frado grabbed a pocketknife and started toward the teenagers' houses, along with Bruno. We waited for their return, and they came back shortly thereafter. The teenagers were nowhere to be found now.

"Who'll help us?" Sloane shuffled his feet in the gravel.

"I have two older cousins, Luis and Roberto." I raised my eyebrows.

"Let's go."

Bruno and I ground out our cigarettes and headed to South Ridge.

We found Roberto at his mom's house with Luis. I called them outside and told them what happened.

"Nothing is going to happen, Eddie. They're all talk." Luis had the audacity to grin.

I shook my head vigorously. "No, man. I think they might be out to kill me."

"Roberto! Luis!" Their mom poked her head out the door. "I heard that. Get your butts in here now. I don't want you involved."

"Let us know if anything happens." Roberto stuck his head back out the front door once they entered the apartment.

Later that night, Bruno, Sloane, and I walked down South Ridge Road. A dark van pulled into a driveway about ten feet ahead of us. Two people got out and approached us. It took me a few seconds to realize they were the teenagers from earlier. "Hey, Bruno."

This froze me in my tracks.

"And Sloane. What are you doing throwing a stupid bottle? You could have been shot." One of the guys kept his hand in his pocket, and my eyes kept going there, even though I didn't want them to.

"You know me, Bruno. You know me," this guy repeated a few times.

Bruno excused our actions and calmed them down enough for them to finally leave.

I later found out that those people were Bruno's older brother's friends from New York—and not ones you wanted to mess with. The person was on edge and, with his hand in his pocket, carried a gun. Because we were with Bruno at the time, nothing had happened. I've always wondered what would have happened if Bruno had not been there. It was not the first or last time that it appeared someone was looking out for me.

After learning who they were, Sloane and I decided to develop a peace offering. We found a bag of weed and walked over to the house where the teenagers lived. We knocked on the door, not knowing what to expect, but figured we were trying to do the right thing.

The door opened, and one of the teenagers peeked out, looking puzzled. Sloane held up the bag. "A peace offering?"

"Hey Joe!" the teenager called over his shoulder.

Joe appeared, and I recognized him from the night before. "Come on in, boys."

Once in a back room, I quickly apologized for the happenings the night before.

"That was my mom at the court." Joe straddled a chair. "You hit her car."

I nodded. Now, it made a lot more sense. "That was my ball. I'm sorry. It wasn't on purpose, I swear."

We smoked and talked. He seemed impressed that we came back after getting away.

"They're our friends," Sloane explained.

"Your one friend? Hector?" We nodded at Joe. "He gave up all kinds of information about you after being caught. Hector told us your names and described where Sloane lived." He calmly blew a stream of smoke our way.

My stomach burned. Sloane stood quickly, knocking his chair over.

We left, vowing to get Hector back for snitching. About a week later, Sloane informed me that Hector had been beaten up by one of our friends.

***

One day, while we were at Sloane's house, Bruno's brother, Raul, stopped by. Sloane was readying to smoke, as usual. "Let's go for a ride." Raul reached over and grabbed a cigarette out of Sloane's pack.

We climbed into Raul's girlfriend's car and headed out, smoking on our trip across town. Raul stopped by the house of one of his friends for about ten minutes before we started. On the way back to Sloane's house, Raul turned off Orange Blossom Trail Road. We drove down a side street because the main one was packed, and I noted Raul looking into his rearview mirror several times.

The brakes squealed as he slammed his foot down. My forehead almost hit the dash. What the heck? He'd stopped in the middle of the street.

Raul shoved the stick into reverse and hit the gas. From the back seat, Sloane tapped my shoulder. I turned to see a puzzled look on his face. Right behind us, out the back window, was a car full of guys. Sure enough, we slammed right into them. I grabbed the handle above the door on impact. Raul pulled forward, parked, and jumped out of the car. We hopped right out after him. He went to the car we hit. "Get out."

We stood outside the car, waiting for people in the car to do something. Something was going on, but we knew nothing. The people in the other car looked shocked. "Follow me over to Americana Boulevard," the driver requested when he finally looked undazed.

"Get out now!" Raul rattled the door handle. It was stuck.

"No. Follow us! Come on."

Traffic started moving again, and the driver hit the gas. The other people in the car waved at us to follow them. Instead, we got back in the car, and Raul sped to Sloane's house. "Thanks for having my back, guys. But you didn't have to get out of the car."

We nodded. I felt a little numb. This whole thing was just weird.

At Sloane's house, Raul looked over the car. Of course, the dent showed prominently on the back passenger side, and Raul scrambled for an excuse to his girlfriend. We weren't much help there. He stayed at Sloane's for about fifteen minutes before taking off.

Once Raul left, Sloane and I reviewed the day's events. "What was that all about?" I plopped myself on the grass in front of the house.

"I dunno. Weird."

We never did figure out why it happened. Raul never mentioned it again. Obviously, he'd been getting back at them for something, so they deserved the damage. We told everybody we saw about the incident. The best and scariest part remained the fact that Sloane and I stepped out of the car to back Raul up. Going up against the car full of eighteen- and nineteen-year-olds seemed terrifying, but we refused to let Raul go against them alone.

***

Bruno, Sloane, and I hung out almost every day. Bruno and Sloane often argued. "We're at my house," Sloane often reminded him. "Time for you to leave."

"Don't be stupid, man."

"I mean it. Get out."

"Fine, but I'm not coming back again."

Sloane's mom entered the room. "Both of you should go." She nodded briskly with a certain amount of happy cheer. "It'll go better if you all talk about it tomorrow."

Bruno and I left and walked toward my house. I lived a lot closer to Sloane's than Bruno did. As we walked, Bruno fumed. "He's so selfish. He only cares about weed, cigarettes, girls, and himself!"

"Maybe we shouldn't hang out with him anymore." The reasonable side of me was sure a solution hovered nearby.

But Sloane always had weed. If he didn't have weed, he could always buy it. Didn't matter. We decided to stop hanging out with him and give up the weed. We'd grown tired of his attitude. We started hanging out at each other's houses instead. Bruno lived in one of the worst apartment complexes in Orlando, Sand Lake Apartments. Most of the weed buys happened there, and police raids were frequent in the area.

As we hung out at my house one day, Mom paused on the couch where we zoned out on a movie. "I'm going to get a beer."

"Hey, why don't you get us some too?" Bruno grinned at her. "Just a quart."

"OK." Mom swept out of the room, and Bruno laughed at me when my jaw dropped. She later returned from Winn-Dixie with two quarts of Miller High life. Bruno and I climbed up on my roof and drank.

One afternoon, as Bruno and I headed to my house, I saw a ten bag of weed on the ground. I hurriedly glanced around, then snatched it up and ran over to Bruno. "What should we do with it?"

"Someone must have ditched it in a raid."

We smoked it, of course, so we'd apparently decided to start smoking again.

After about two weeks of us not hanging out with Sloane, his mom stopped by Bruno's house.

"Bruno, you two have been friends too long to let an argument end it. I know Sloane can seem selfish at times, but he's a good person and so are you."

We felt chastised. Bruno blushed as he looked at the ground and agreed to put the argument behind him. We started hanging out with Sloane again.

Chapter 24

Business

Since the sudden ending of my first job, my wallet stayed empty. So when Sloane came to me with a proposition for making money, I listened. "I met Trina. She just moved here from New York with her nephew. She sells weed, and I'm helping. Money's good. You and Bruno want in?"

Yes! I was gung-ho. Bruno, on the other hand, refused the offer.

Sloane and I sold 1-gram bags of weed for five dollars. Out of the five, we took home two for ourselves. Trina started us off with ten to fifteen bags at a time. She asked us to add more and took us to her apartment. As we pulled in, I realized that she lived in the same apartment as my dad's girlfriend. We filled baggies there. It didn't take long for her to decide to have us bag and fill all the orders.

At first, Sloane and I only sold to people we or Trina knew. Her nephew also sent some buyers. We set up shop in South Ridge. I sold it to Roberto, Luis, and their friends. The first time I stopped by their house to sell them a bag, Roberto cornered me. "Gimme a freebie, Eddie."

"I can't, man. I'd have to pay for it." As much as Trina seemed to trust us, she stayed on top of the inventory.

"Let me look at what you've got."

I handed him the bags. He removed a little piece out of each one. "See, now you still have the same number of bags."

"I can't sell them short, Roberto." I grabbed the bags and left—my fists clenched. At home, I made the bags look good, but I was still one bag short. "Mom, I need five bucks for school."

Somehow, Mom produced five dollars the next day. I replaced the stock by buying one from Sloane and vowed never to let anyone hold my bags again.

Once we started selling to anybody and everybody, we really started making money. At first, my hands shook a bit with each transaction. I knew any one of them could be a cop. We tried to make certain stash spots, but that quickly became inconvenient for the customers. I started keeping my bags with me.

I remember once, on a very hot day, when I tried to get rid of some bags in South Ridge. Business slowed with the heat, and I grew tired of sweat rolling down my back. The next day, I planned ahead and had two pairs of shorts – one pair in my bag and the other on me. I snuck around the back of the complex and dove into the pool.

After a while, Gloria and Sarah joined me. I started messing with them, calling them names and splashing them. They grabbed my shorts and took off running out of the pool area.

I slapped my hand on the water. They now held all my weed bags. I hauled myself out of the pool and took off after them. I ran around a building and saw them walking back toward the pool area with strange looks on their faces. I quickly grabbed my shorts back and glanced at Sarah. She especially looked very disappointed, like she might even cry. I slumped back to the pool.

They never really talked to me much after that. I figured they saw what was in my shorts. They were good girls who'd never even tried a cigarette and wouldn't sleep with boys, even while dating.

The first problem that came from selling to anybody was that everyone learned what we were doing. Not just customers—but eventually the cops and other sellers, too. I started hearing rumors about the Sand Lake residents losing weed customers and wanting to do something about it. Even some of the local gang members approached us to sell for them. I turned them down, even though I trusted them the most. Fear of messing up with them held me at bay. But I did like the fact that they saw us differently and trusted us.

Everything was going well until I got behind five dollars. Trina stomped into Sloane's house, looking for me. I wasn't there. When I found out that they were looking for me, I biked over there quickly, but she'd left by then.

I zipped over to Sloane's. Bruno was there too, and Sloane picked up the phone when he heard my concerns. "He's here." He hung up.

When Trina arrived, she seemed agitated. "Do you want me to have my nephew pay you a visit?" She turned and left.

"Huh? Why doesn't she want the five bucks?" I held up the bill. I'd scrambled to find it for nothing.

"Screw it." Bruno grabbed the five from me, followed Trina, and bought a bag with the money.

I stopped working with Trina that day. Turns out, Sloane owed her money as well. He owed her about fifty bucks. Trina returned to Sloane's house, demanding the money.

"What is it you want?" Sloane's mom stood there frowning at the return of this woman.

"Your son owes me a hundred and fifty dollars," Trina sneered at her.

"Oh, for gosh sake. I'll pay you, then you need to leave these boys alone."

"Mom, you don't have to do that," Sloane protested as she glared at him too.

After Trina received three times more than she was owed, I never saw her or her nephew again.

***

After I became popular, people from my past took notice—one being Bettina. I still liked her and we started talking again. Shortly after, we resumed dating.

We'd dated for about a week when Bruno jogged up to me at school, grinning like a fool. "I hear you're doing the you-know-what with Bettina."

I lifted my chin and shrugged nonchalantly. I didn't mind if he thought he knew it all. Turns out, Bettina said that our friend Jannet was sleeping around. Mad, Bruno had lashed back.

When I told Bettina, she apologized. "I didn't mean it like that."

Bettina and I dated for a few more weeks. Things headed downhill when she asked Sloane to get her a bag of weed one day after school. While looking for me, she found him. "Hey, can you get me a ten bag? Here's the money."

He took it and arranged to see her later.

Later, she stomped over to me. "I gave Sloane money for a bag and I haven't heard from him."

"I'll take care of it."

I searched for Sloane for a little bit and didn't find him. Later that evening, Bruno and I walked to Sloane's house. He walked out, laughing. He handed me a bag of weed. "This is for your girl." I looked at it and realized it was missing some weed.

Sloane slipped back into his house as I showed Bruno the bag. "Dude, that's messed up."

I resisted pounding on the door, even though I wanted to. I'd tell Bettina not to buy from Sloane again. I went to find her with no success, so I headed home. Once home, Mom and I argued, so I smoked the bag. No biggie—I'd just replace it with a full one.

But I never came up with the ten bucks I needed for that.

After a week of me not having Bettina's bag or money, she became very upset. We stopped talking shortly after that.

***

My relationship with Mom had tilted into a rocky one ever since she'd asked me to quit my job at Bill Wong's Famous Buffet. She always put us kids into bad situations that could have been avoided, like having to move every few months for nonpayment of rent. I hated her choice of men—they all wanted to come in and take over without providing anything. Mom seemed content living off the government and excuses. So, I started doing whatever I wanted and came home very little.

One time, with Bruno and Sloane, I drank and smoked weed all night. We drank a couple twenty-two ounces of St. Ides and smoked two blunts before I walked home. I stumbled the whole way, arriving about five in the morning. The front door resisted my pushing—it was locked. I knocked softly, hoping to wake up one of my siblings, but no one woke up. I started knocking louder and louder until Mom woke up. I literally heard her stomping to the door. But I wasn't afraid of her anymore. A deep, bitter feeling crept in instead.

"Where in the heck have you been?" she screamed right in my face.

I pushed past her. "I'm tired and going to bed." I walked straight to my room and closed the door behind me. I collapsed on the bed.

Around eight in the morning, Mom kicked open my bedroom door, swinging the broomstick. She hit me twice before I shot up out of bed, scrambling away. Mom blocked the doorway, but the window was partially open. Worth a shot. I started to climb out the window, and she grabbed my legs. My torso was already out the window, so I fell to the ground. Once outside, I ran.

I roamed the neighborhood for a few hours before I returned. I walked up to the house and saw Jannet out front. As soon as she saw me, Jannet turned her head to check if Mom was around. "What happened, Eddie? You aren't allowed here. She said if we let you in, she'll kick us out too."

Yeah, we'd heard that before. But this was the first time it was all about me.

While we talked, Mom opened the front door. "Since you think you're grown, you can stay out there. Don't come back! Remember, you're grown. You are in charge of you. Goodbye." She motioned at Jannet, and my sister scurried into the house. The door slammed.

Now what? I walked away and tried to go to Sloane's house, but they had other stuff going on. I walked back home and hung out in the field where I knew Mom could see me if she looked. I went to the bedroom window and talked to Lorenzo a couple of times. Jesse hovered worriedly in the background.

Later in the evening, the sun started sinking. One of the neighbors walked over to me. "Eddie, come here. What's going on? You've been out here all day. Aren't you hungry?"

Of course, I was hungry. And getting cold. I knew I wasn't supposed to talk about what happened at the house, especially to strangers. Not that she was a complete stranger—Mom and she talked sometimes. But she was not a person to tell family business. Then, my stomach growled. "Mom kicked me out and told me not to come home."

The woman paused for a second. "You can stay at my house for a bit. Come along."

"That's OK, ma'am. But I appreciate it."

"I'm not taking a no for an answer." She guided me into her house. "You can sleep on the couch. How about a sandwich?" Strangely, that brought back foster home memories. I was well-versed in evening sandwiches at strangers' houses. The lady fed me and fixed me a bed on the couch for the night.

When I woke up the next day, she informed me she was taking me home.

Numbly, I wondered what Mom would say. I followed her slowly as we walked to my house. Once there, she knocked.

Mom opened the front door, looking surprised to see the neighbor. Her eyebrows crinkled when she saw me behind her. Shoot—she was mad.

"Eddie stayed over last night. I couldn't bear to see him outside anymore."

"Thank you." Mom smiled and motioned for me to come inside. I walked past Mom while she continued chatting. I went to my room and slammed the door. I might as well have been in prison.

The door opened and hit the wall behind it hard as Mom burst into the bedroom. "Why in the heck would you go over to that lady's house? You don't know her or who she might talk to."

I decided quiet was the best answer. I let Mom yell at me until she was done. I tried very hard not to roll my eyes. I think I succeeded. Once she left, I relaxed and talked to my siblings to see what I had missed.

***

Our relationship got worse, continuing a steady, downhill slide. Each week, it seemed more awkward. One evening, I was home for about fifteen minutes before Mom started arguing with me about my behavior. "You think you're all grown, Eddie. Smoking, drinking, and staying out all hours of the night."

"What about your behavior?" I leaned towards her. "All the drinking. Men here, just so you can have your stupid beer."

"I don't have to answer to you! Who do you think you are? Go to your room!"

In the room, I sat and fumed. Lorenzo listened to my complaints. "Normal kids don't have to fight grown men because their mother wants to drink. No one else moves every couple of months because their mom would rather have a party than pay rent."

"Yeah. Other kids actually have food in their kitchen. That's why I'm here as little as possible." Lorenzo stood and started pacing in our small room.

"Life would be a lot easier if we didn't have to deal with her. Let's run away."

"Yeah, let's."

We packed a bag, discussing what we needed to survive. We got warm clothes and, of course, needed food, but we found there wasn't much in the kitchen to take. Lorenzo managed to grab some crackers. Mom had beans and rice on the stove, but we had no way to pack it up. Jesse had a bag of potato chips he was taking to a class party the next day. Lorenzo took the bag of chips into the bedroom, unnoticed. With our clothes and now with food, we decided to jump out the bedroom window and to freedom.

The first place we headed was South Ridge Apartments. We walked to the pool closest to the front entrance, sat down on a couple of lawn chairs, and started eating Jesse's potato chips. Suddenly, we heard Mom. "There they are, right there."

What? Sure enough, I looked over to see Mom in her friend's van. Lorenzo and I grabbed our bag and took off. As we ran, I heard Mom's friend said in her New York accent, "Youz guyz shouldn't be doing this to your mother!"

Screw that.

That night, we stayed in an abandoned apartment in South Ridge. It was two units down from Gloria's. We stopped by there to hang out for a while until they had to go in for the night. We told them that we had run away, and they sneaked us some food for the night.

The next morning, Lorenzo and I woke up early and hungry. We didn't have any money to buy anything, so we walked to the closest and easiest place to heist— a Shell gas station. But they only had candy. We needed more than just candy to live on. "Let's go to school, Lorenzo. There, we get breakfast and lunch."

While I was outside in PE class, I noticed one of the school deans driving one of their white golf carts onto the track. I watched the golf cart as it meandered my way. The dean pulled up right in front of me and stopped. "Hop on, Eddie. Let's go talk in the office."

I considered running, but I was just in my PE clothes, and besides, he had a vehicle.

The dean took me into the office, and we sat. "I know you ran away. A truancy officer already picked up Lorenzo and took him home. I want you to go home, too."

I felt resigned. "Fine."

The dean grimaced. "They got Lorenzo because he decided to walk through a mobile home park on his way to his school to steal some socks from a clothesline." He shook his head.

Boy, he just didn't get it. Of course, Lorenzo would need socks. I felt guilty that I hadn't packed any. And if the dean understood what he was truly sending us back to, maybe things would change.

Shortly after Lorenzo and I returned home, Mom brightened up. "I'm sending you both back to Portland. Your brothers are there. And I'm fed up with your behavior. When I get my money this month, I'm getting you tickets. And that's final. No arguing!"

We didn't argue. We were so excited that we started calling Javel almost every day collect.

He now lived in Portland with a friend named Darrel King. Darrel, a churchgoing man, met Hector one day around the neighborhood. Somehow, Hector wound up living with Darrel for a little while. Javel later found his way there, as well. Darrel King has continued to help our family ever since. Somehow, he saw the best in us. Somehow, he knew that we were destined for greater things.

Lorenzo and I told everyone we saw that we were moving back to Oregon. It was the answer to all my problems. I no longer had to deal with Mom and all her crap. I could live my life without having to put up with her drunken episodes. I did not need the responsibility of an adult at fifteen. I couldn't wait for Mom's tax return money to come in.

About three days before Mom was to receive her money, she pulled me aside. "How about instead of sending you boys to Portland, I give you money for school clothes instead? You can have five hundred and Lorenzo three hundred. Talk it over and let me know."

I started trembling. Surely, she couldn't pull this. But I found Lorenzo soon after and shared the offer.

"No way. Bad idea. I want to go back to Portland." He seemed adamant. Me? Relieved.

I went to find Mom. But before I could speak, she did. "I don't want you to leave, Eddie. I really want you both to stay here, but it's up to you." She looked incredibly sad as she stood there, waiting for our answer.

Although Lorenzo and I had discussed doing otherwise, I couldn't do it. "We—We"ll stay."

Mom's face lit up. It made me feel good that she was happy, but now I had to tell Lorenzo. He was busy bouncing around the bedroom. He was so excited to move back to Portland. As I mumbled the news, he clenched his fists at me. "What the heck, Eddie? I can't believe you did that."

"She was sad—"

"I don't give a crap. She doesn't give a crap about us."

When the tax money finally came, I received two hundred, and Lorenzo received one fifty. Maybe Lorenzo was right after all.

***

One evening, as Lorenzo and I walked through South Ridge, we saw the maintenance workers putting away their golf carts into a building that looked like a small airplane hangar. As soon as they locked up and left, we found a hole in the door and peered through it.

Golf carts lined the wall, full of supplies. I also saw that the side of the building had an opening. "Go see if you can fit through there, Lorenzo."

Lorenzo jogged around to the opening. After a little maneuvering, he tumbled in as I followed. I stood guard at the opening while he searched. Soon, he found a pocket knife and rushed over to show me.

"Nice. Keep looking."

"Eddie! Hey Eddie!" Sheesh. He was like a kid in a toy store. I peeked in the hole and saw him running to me again. He held a handful of apartment keys with numbers on them. He handed them over. I shoved them into my pocket and sent him back for more. Lorenzo ran back, grabbed another handful, and climbed out. We now had about thirty keys.

We didn't know what the keys were for. But maybe to the actual apartments? I went to the apartment number on one of the keys and watched to see if there were any signs of occupancy. After watching for a while, I sent Lorenzo to peer through a window. He didn't see much, so I knocked on the door. No answer, so I slid the key in and turned it. I peeked inside and saw a bunch of sheetrock and building supplies. Lorenzo and I quickly walked in and closed the door behind us. Inside, we searched for anything of value. There were toilets in one room, sheetrock in another, and a bunch of paint cans. Nothing we wanted. "Let's try a different apartment, Eddie."

We picked another key and went through the same process. This time, I saw a fully furnished apartment when I peeked in. I quickly closed the door and took off running. Lorenzo, startled by my reaction, followed without explanation. Once we were clear, I explained. "Someone lives in that one. We gotta start watching longer before we go in."

But after a while, we lost interest in the keys.

Chapter 25

Home

Mom started a new job at the Sealy mattress company. Shortly after she started, she met a short white man named Pedro. They dated, and shortly thereafter, he moved in.

I didn't mind Pedro. He helped with the bills and gave Mom something to do. The two of them often took Jannet and Maria out for food and things of that nature. Pedro did not involve himself with us boys very much. The only time I really talked to him was when he went to trade in his old Ford for a Firebird. At the dealership, I translated part of the sale. Afterward, Pedro took me on a drive to test it out.

After a while, things with Mom normalized yet again. We fought at almost every opportunity. I started calling Javel every day from a pay phone, again complaining. "All she wants to do is drink and have a good time. I'm more of a parent than she is."

Finally, one day, his usual sigh resonated over the phone line. "I'm going to send you a bus ticket, Eddie. OK? Things will be alright."

I started jumping up and down. I ran over to the house. "Lorenzo! Javel is sending me a bus ticket to Portland!"

"What about me?"

"I'll ask him the next time we talk," I promised. Then I started telling everyone again that I was leaving. No one believed me this time.

I talked to Javel soon after. "What about Lorenzo?"

"Dad and I can only afford one ticket. It'll be at the Greyhound station on Friday. In two days, OK? You get there, and I'll see you soon."

I took off running, happiness bubbling. I jumped in the air a few times. I even belted out a couple "woo-hoos." I ran home and told Mom. She acted as if she didn't care. She just looked at me, turned, and walked to the bedroom.

The next day, I wandered the neighborhood, saying goodbye and telling people it was for real this time. Thursday night, I hung out at Sloane's for the last time.

On Friday, I woke up at Sloane's house and hung out until 4:00 p.m. or so. My bus was leaving at 8:00 p.m., and José was picking me up. I went home to gather my things. Mom and Pedro were gone. Jannet, Jesse, and Maria waited at home alone. I sighed and told my siblings the news. They seemed happy for me, but sad too. Jannet and Maria started crying. Jesse didn't seem to care so much. I already knew Lorenzo was completely pissed. Here I was the one who decided we needed to stay a few months prior, and now I was leaving alone.

As I packed, I realized that my smaller siblings were watching carefully. The girls started crying again. I paused. "I love you. I will see you again." I remembered that I was once in their place. And here I was, following my older brother's footsteps. When I finished packing, I waited around. Surely, Mom would return for a goodbye. As the clock crept forward, the ball in my stomach grew as I realized she had no intention of seeing me off. I said goodbye to my siblings and walked back to Sloane's house to wait for José.

At his house, a group of friends gathered. Bruno, his older brother, cousins, and even one of Brain's big brother's friends waited—about 10 to 15 people ready to see me off.

José showed up around seven. Everyone decided to come along to the Greyhound station. When I left Sloane's house, two cars full of friends followed.

At the station, José pulled me aside and told me that if I ever wanted to return to Orlando, I should let him know, and he'd buy a ticket. "Thanks, José. Do you have any money for food?" He pulled out his wallet and gave me twenty dollars. "Thanks again."

My friends waited for me to finish with José. After José left, all my friends said goodbye. Bruno was the last. He gave me a hug and a half of a pack of Newport cigarettes. "Don't forget about us in Florida." He slapped me on the shoulder.

My friends left about five minutes after José did.

I still had about 30 minutes. I went to the counter, collected my ticket, and sat on a bench. It felt surreal. Was this really happening?

I heard the call for my bus to board over the intercom. I grabbed my bags and walked to my bus. I placed my bags underneath and climbed in to find a seat. I wanted one by the window and found one toward the middle on the driver's side. I sat down, hoping a strange person didn't sit next to me. The driver gave his final boarding call, and the bus pulled out of the station. I was on my way home, scheduled to arrive on Wednesday morning.

I spent my first night on the bus, looking out of the window, thinking. I thought about how Mom might be feeling about me leaving and perhaps that she struggled with saying goodbye. I considered my siblings. I realized I'd left them alone with Mom, basically abandoning them. After the whirls of thoughts and stress of the day, I finally slept.

I woke up to people rushing off the stopped bus. We had stopped at a restaurant for food and a bathroom break. I climbed off and smoked a cigarette. I climbed back on, curled up in my jacket, and tried to fall asleep again.

Turns out, long bus rides are very boring. I opened a book that I bought. I hate reading, but I read most of the book. It was about a black young man living in Detroit. With a tough temper, he remained a good student and grew up to become a doctor.

I spent the first two and a half days reading the book and staring out the window. The only other entertainment was the drunks at the back of the bus. They were caught several times trying to sneak alcohol on board. One got so sloshed he peed himself, and when the driver confronted him, he decided to fight. The driver backed off and called the police. The police came and arrested the drunk person. We all cheered when he was removed from the bus.

Everywhere we stopped for food was expensive. I ran out of money and cigarettes after three days. I was able to get a couple of cigarettes from people I asked at stops. But I was getting very hungry. I finally called Javel. "Bro, can you get me money for food? I'm broke."

"What's your next stop?"

"Boise."

"I'll send it to Western Union."

"What's that?"

"Don't worry. I just need to give you a password. You gotta fill out some paperwork and give them the password." He gave it to me, and I repeated it in my head a dozen times, just in case.

When I arrived in Boise, I saw a Western Union stand and rushed over. I completed the paperwork from the holder and waited in line for my turn. When it came, I gave the clerk the paperwork and told him the password.

"How much money are you expecting, sir?"

I had no idea. "Fifty?"

The clerk checked the computer and asked for the password again. He typed a few things into the computer. He finally opened the cash register and counted out twenty dollars. Oh man, I'd have to stretch it for sure. I rushed over to a food stand at the station and bought a sandwich, some chips, and a drink. I was so hungry that I crammed the food. Then I called Javel. "Got the money. Thanks. I'm arriving tomorrow about 3:00 a.m."

"OK. We'll be there."

I couldn't afford cigarettes, so I bummed one from someone outside. I smoked it as fast as I could before the bus pulled off. We had one more stop and about nine hours before we arrived in Portland. I stared out the window for a while to pass the time.

"We should be there early if we don't stop much," I overheard a man say. After hearing this, I felt lightheaded with excitement. But even my sheer joy didn't prevent me from sleeping. I was a teenage boy, after all.

"Portland arrival." Someone called, and I woke up quickly. I jumped up and looked out the window to see if I recognized anything. I saw a huge, dome-looking thing off to the left of the highway.

"That's the Rose Garden," a lady explained. Oh yeah, I'd heard of it. It was still under construction when I moved to Kent, Washington, years before, but people talked a lot about it.

Butterflies tackled my stomach all at once. I gathered my belongings, getting ready for our imminent arrival. After what seemed like an eternity, the bus pulled into the station. I quickly rushed off and waited impatiently for the storage compartment under the bus to open. Once opened, I grabbed my bags and hurried into the station, looking for Javel. I was tall enough to see over most people and I caught at first a glimpse. Then, his smiling face came into full view as the crowd surged forward with me. Dad stood next to him. I quickly walked over and gave them each a big hug.

Finally home, I'd come full circle at the age of fifteen. I had no idea that my true journey was just now beginning.

Made in the USA
Middletown, DE
01 April 2025

73554187R00154